Missing in Paradise

Ian Stout

Mafe Media Ltd.
Toronto, Ontario, Canada

Published by Mafe Media Ltd.

524 Palmerston Boulevard
Toronto, Ontario, Canada. M6G-2P5
Copyright: Ian Stout 2011.

Cover and text design: Rajai Sawalha of Print Xpress

Editor: Peter W. Taylor

A CIP catalogue record for this book is available from Library and Archives Canada

ISBN 978-0-9866903-3-4

Printed and bound in Canada by Transcontinental
10 9 8 7 6 5 4 3 2 1
First Edition

Any resemblance characters in this book have to any person living or dead is a coincidence. This work is fiction, the people products of the author's imagination.

The author used as a background for his story events that occurred in the 1980's and has made every effort to present them accurately.

Acknowledgments

Writing a book involves more than banging out brilliant prose making readers swoon in admiration. It requires many people who assist the author in diverse ways and if not for these unseen worthies, few books would get finished. These supporters cheer the author on, like punters at the rail near the finish of a horse race.

Like my brother Bill Stout who flew to Cuba with my wife and I for research before reading the first draft. Mrs. Nancy A. Provan-Jones also read the first draft and surprised me by showing what new eyes can see. Her suggestions, written by hand, are kept with the treasures one accumulates while writing a book.

Michael Sinelnikoff scrutinized my book, generously pointing out things that might make it better. His long career as a director, writer, actor, and adjudicator provided a wealth of experience for me to draw upon.

I thank Major Mark Adkin, retired British infantry officer who wrote an excellent book **'Urgent Fury, The Battle For Grenada'** which I carried when I visited the island. He took my calls to his home in Bedford England, graciously offering help and encouragement. In 1983 Major Adkin was the staff officer with the Barbados Defense Force Caribbean Operations and was deeply involved in the Grenada invasion.

Thanks to the staff at the National Museum of the Marine Corps in Quantico, Virginia. The people at this spectacular facility were patient and helpful. The U. S. Marines have a right to be proud of their museum.

Others include Grenadian Yolanda Cornwall of Air Canada, Jennifer West of Calgary, whom I should hire as my press agent, Sandy Philpot of Oshawa, who wore out her eyes checking my spelling, and Kevin Price,

Toronto artist extraordinaire who drew the maps of Grenada.

Peter Taylor, Bill Hushion, and Rajai Sawalha all showed great patience with me that helped make this effort possible.

The best, of course, I save for the last. Sharon, my wife of many years read the original draft, and then listened to me for hours bouncing ideas and scenarios off her. I consider myself lucky.

To her, and all who helped, a heartfelt 'thank you'.

A Special Note from the Author

At the launch party for my first novel, Necessary Larceny, a draw was held giving attendees the chance to win a unique prize; a role in my next book.

The rules were simple. The winner had to agree to be in the book and would have to sign a release. They could read a first draft, make suggestions. and could opt out any time before printing.

Over a hundred people entered and the winner was Anne Vanderhyden, of Grimsby Ontario. She and her husband Peter have been dear friends and constant supporters over the years.

Sharon and I spent a week in Grenada with them on my second research trip and Anne's good natured co-operation and insightful input helped.

The draw was a fun idea, a suggestion of my wife Sharon, and I think I'll do it again.

About the Author

Ian Stout has a varied and colorful past. From his early days working in Elliot Lake, Ontario, then a bustling frontier town filled with hard drinking uranium miners, to his year and a half walk-about through Europe, to his eleven years on Hamilton's city council, he could be found at the centre of the action.

Ian loves to travel and has visited over 35 different countries on five continents and finds most people are pretty much the same everywhere. He finds if you treat them decently, no matter if it's in Brazil, China, Israel or Costa Rica, they will treat you well.

Although he calls Mississauga his hometown, he and wife Sharon are often away in some far-off place looking for adventure. Recently their five week visit to Australia found them in the Outback looking for opals as well as on the shores of the Tasman Sea looking at penguins.

Ian's next book will hit the shelves in the spring of 2012. A 'who-done-it' set in the city where he was born and raised. The story, populated with literary types, is certainly something he knows about. Keep your eyes open for the new 'Will Deas mystery titled **Murder Unedited.**

Chapter One

Day One: Late Afternoon, Toronto

The voice sent chills down Nick's spine, shaking him, almost making him drop the phone. The first words were "Nick, my granddaughter's missing, more than enough to scare the hell out of anyone.

"They can't find her Nick, please, you gotta help me," the voice went on, desperately begging for help in the frightening late afternoon call.

No 'hello'. No 'how are you' and no 'is Mr. Archer in?' No niceties gushed from the phone, just a story of disaster poured out by a grown man overflowing with fear. The anxiety and panic in his voice could be tasted as his words flooded from the receiver into Nick's ear.

For several long minutes the panicked grandfather poured out his problem without seeming to stop for air. His name was Fred Lusinski and he said he had just found out an hour ago. A friend in Bradenton suggested he get hold of Nick Archer up in Canada. He was terrified and needed help. His only grandchild was missing.

Fred and his wife were expatriates from the snows of London, Ontario, Canada, a city of several hundred thousand which actually had a Thames River running through it 'when it wasn't frozen' Fred would always say. They owned a nice home in a gated community on University Drive near the Bradenton airport.

Tired of London's ability to attract every snowflake within a hundred miles, they had moved to Florida fifteen years earlier when homes were cheap and taxes low. His family: brothers, sisters, one son and assorted cousins, were still spread throughout southern Ontario, shivering seven months of the year, or so Fred claimed, usually with a big grin.

One of those northerners was Fred's pretty twenty-one year old granddaughter Rachel, a post graduate student of Marine biology at the University of Guelph in Ontario. Lately, she had been studying in Grenada, a tiny island in the Caribbean near Barbados. Her studies had something to do with the difference in death rates of salt water plant life in warm waters as compared to those in colder northern regions off the coasts of Maine and New Brunswick.

Rachel Lusinski was the only child of Fred's only child Anthony and Anthony's ex wife, Irene. This probably made her the only grandchild he would ever have. There could be no wonder he was in such a panic.

The distraught voice on the other end of the line explained that the girl was bright, pretty, and an 'A' student up in Ontario. She was working on her Master's degree and could become one of the youngest in her school's history to achieve that lofty position. The whole family was proud of her but now she was missing, and no one seemed able to help.

Fred filled Nick in on those details he knew.

Rachel had vanished early the day before. She hadn't kept a luncheon date with her fellow student and room-mate Sylvia, which was unusual. By five in the afternoon Sylvia was concerned, called a few friends, a dive shop Rachel sometimes used, and the hospital. Drawing a blank, she walked to the local police station to let them know of her worries. They took Sylvia's concern seriously, grilling her for almost an hour with questions about Rachel, her habits and her appearance.

Fred told Nick the police prepared a search plan during last night and early that morning mounted a well organized and spirited search across the southwest part of the island, even though the proscribed twenty-

7

four hours hadn't passed on the missing person complaint. So far, twenty-four hours since the initial report, they had no hint of her whereabouts or what could have happened to her.

Nick learned the officers from Grenada's main police station had carefully gone through Rachel's personal effects at her lodgings and that all had seemed in order. They meticulously scrutinized each item in her room, collecting several for dispatch by air to an off-island forensic lab for further study. Sylvia was questioned extensively about drugs, booze and boy friends, but Rachel was a worker, not a party girl. Nothing indicated her running with a bad crowd or ever engaging in unruly behavior. For the moment, the police were stumped.

Once done with this preliminary part of their investigation, the officers politely helped Sylvia gather her belongings and moved her to another room in the guest house. This done, they sealed off Rachel's room with yellow tape, apologized to the manager for the trouble and inconvenience, and headed out to join those other officers assigned to the search.

Systematically, and in an ever increasing circle around Rachel's residence, dozens of people were interviewed. Within two hours, the police had constructed a detailed itinerary of Rachel's activities leading up to her disappearance.

Sylvia, the first to be interviewed, had been Rachel's room-mate for the past three months and could reasonably be called the party girl Rachel wasn't. Sylvia's South American heritage gave her an exciting and vibrant air and this, combined with a wonderful smile, long dark hair and a spectacular body, made her a natural target in any bar or club she entered. Sylvia was pretty, well shaped, and didn't wear clothes designed to hide her many attributes. She loved the attention of men who found her attractive and sexy; a group which included every straight male capable of breathing, and was much sought after when parties were being planned at the medical school at True Blue Bay or in town at one of the clubs.

She had come in late as usual the night before Rachel disappeared, and slept in, which also was her norm. Sylvia recalled rolling over at about six a.m. as her room-mate pulled shorts up over her bathing suit. She remembered mumbling something about what the hell she was doing up at such an ungodly hour. Rachel claimed she had some early work to do and told Sylvia to go back to sleep. She also told Sylvia not to forget their luncheon date at noon before heading out the door.

The guest-house cook prepared a light breakfast minutes later. It was her usual, some fruit, a couple slices of toast and strong black coffee. The cook was busy setting up for the day so they spoke little and the cook had no idea what Rachel was up to. She did say Rachel was in good spirits, which was normal, and when she picked up the small bag she always carried, she waved cheerily and left. That was about six-thirty a.m.

The police started walking all possible routes away from the guest-house and finally found an elderly local who had seen her striding down a road to the shoreline outside of town. He was sure it was Rachel because of the time. He described her: blue and white skin-tight top, her white shorts, and the red and black knapsack slung over her shoulder. During the officer's questioning he asked the oldster what made him notice her. The senior threw back his head of curly silver hair laughing.

"Are you kidding?" he said. "Man, have you seen her? She must be the prettiest girl to visit this island in years. Hell sonny, I'm old, not dead."

The man was the last to see her but wasn't quite sure of the time "cause he had no watch" he said.

The police drove him to the road and he was able to point out the exact spot where they had passed and exchanged smiles and a polite 'good morning'. He remembered the location on the road, he told police, because as soon as she passed, he stopped and turned, watching her long legs and cute backside in her tight white shorts as she strode away from him along the road.

Laughing, he said he remembered because she had turned and caught him watching. He smiled, saying she had laughed, and waved a finger at him, as though she knew exactly what he had been looking at. Then with a wink she turned and moved out of sight around a curve in the road. He recalled this all happening just as she passed a large old truck tire abandoned in the ditch not three feet from where she had turned.

They found the tire, did some measuring and then instructed a female officer to walk back to the guest house to work out an approximate time Rachel had passed the tire. When done, they knew where she was at seven fifteen that morning. It was between then and noon, when she didn't show for lunch, that she disappeared; less than four and a half hours. Fred thought the local police had acted quickly and had conducted an excellent investigation but were no closer to finding her now than when they had started. It was thirty-four hours since Rachel was last seen and Fred was frantic, wanting Nick's help. Nick promised he would do what he could.

Fred was one of a group of Florida seniors who had needed Nick's help a year before. This one, along with close to forty other retirees, had been cheated out of a pile of money by a gang of very slick con artists. The bad guys ran an elaborate offshore confidence scheme targeting retired people around Sarasota-Bradenton. By the time they were done, almost two million dollars had been extracted from bank accounts throughout the community.

After all avenues of recovering their money came up as dead- ends, Nick got involved and helped organize the victims into a cohesive group. He taught them how to track down the bad guys using internet search engines, and helped them set up a scam of their own to steal back their cash. The project had been a resounding success and this frantic caller, Fred Lusinski, a bald, retired, schoolteacher in his mid seventies, who weighed no more than a hundred pounds soaking wet, had played a major role in the endeavor.

Nick finally hung up and sat quietly for several minutes thinking about Fred's problem before reaching again for the phone. He dialed Harry Stanton, an old buddy and confidante living in semi-retirement in Bradenton, Florida.

Harry, the main sparkplug in retrieving the money that had been stolen from him and the other seniors over a year before, knew Fred and Alice and didn't live far from their home.

Nick led that bunch, and ever since, whenever one of them had a problem, or needed some advice, he got a call. All of them trusted, respected and liked Nick, knowing he would always be ready with a good suggestion or two. This was different though. This was not just a problem, this was a catastrophe.

"Hi Harry, how's Kitty?" Nick asked about Harry's wife, exactly as he did every time he called.

"Compared to what?" came the same old answer. It was as though they were talking in code.

"Have you heard about Fred Lusinski's granddaughter?"

"Just a little, I told him to call you. Obviously he did. What's up?" Harry was his usual loquacious self.

"She's missing on the Caribbean island of Grenada," and he filled Harry in on all of Fred's details. When done, Nick suggested a call to another of the 'originals', their logistics man LJ Livingston for a meeting at their favorite seafood restaurant the next day. Somewhere floating in the back of Nick's mind was a faint memory tying LJ and Grenada together.

He also asked Harry to call Ed Fisher, the restaurateur at the seafood place, and yet another of the old gang, to give him a heads up so he could sit in with them. Harry agreed, saying it was an ill wind that blew no good and how nice it would be to see some of the old Phoenix gang in action again. Thirty minutes after Nick hung up, Harry called back with details of their meeting the next day.

Nick called Fred, told him a meeting was set for one o'clock the next day at Ed's and to bring some things with him. He wanted photos of Rachel, her vital statistics and anything else Fred could think of that might help. These simple demands would force him to do something to help his granddaughter. The frightened grandfather poured thanks through the phone lines, showering Nick with appreciation for his help, speed, and action on Rachel's behalf. The sound of hope rang clearly all the way from Florida to Nick's Toronto home.

When Nick finally got loose from the grateful Fred, he settled back at his desk to think about the problem facing him. From all angles, it seemed one hell of a lot bigger than the problem he had helped this gang of very active retirees solve only a year ago.

Then, they were out to steal their own money away from a very slick group of confidence men working their way across the country. The police were unable to help so Nick and Harry, along with LJ and the other victims, made up their own rules. They operated on the edge of legality and conned the conmen; 'doing unto others as had been done unto them.' This would be very different.

Grenada was a sovereign country with a system of government much different from that which most of the retirees knew. Although similar to Nick and Fred's homeland of Canada, with a Prime Minister instead of a President, most of Grenada's systems would be alien to all but a few of the Florida group. It had a different system of justice where titles such as Barrister and Solicitor meant more than just plain old lawyer. Their courts were places where you addressed a judge as M'Lord, called other lawyers "my learned friend," and always asked "if it please the court," when addressing anyone in the room. It was indeed very different from the rough and tumble legal system of the United States which most of the retirees knew.

Their approach to policing was different as well. Constables, as members of the Royal Grenada Police Force were called, carried nightsticks instead of guns to control almost any situation they met. It was a different land with a different lifestyle. It moved at a much slower pace, seemed a much gentler environment and above all, was much more polite. Nick and his friends from Florida would be way out of their element trying to do something this time.

Getting up from the desk in his home-office, Nick decided to chat with the lovely Ann, his wife. She was the best listener he knew and always seemed capable of helpful and intelligent suggestions. Besides, neither of them had been to Grenada and Nick knew she'd jump at the chance to go, no matter the reason.

Chapter Two

Day Two: 12 Noon, Florida.

Noon found Nick sitting in Ed Fisher's Bradenton, Florida restaurant patiently awaiting the arrival of his host. Beside him sat Harry Stanton, LJ Livingston, and across from them, Fred Lusinski, all sipping beers at a long wooden table in the rear banquet room of Ed's seafood eatery. It had been forty-eight hours since Rachel had disappeared and less than twenty-four since Fred's panicky call.

The superb little cafe was conveniently located on Highway 41, known locally as Tamiami Trail, the main north-south road through the area. It wasn't far from the airport or Nick's usual hotel and everyone knew where it was. Besides, Ed, the proprietor was a nice guy and usually sprang for their beers.

Nick had caught the early flight out of Toronto that morning, picked up his rental at Tampa airport and drove the fifty miles south with time to spare. As always, while driving, he mouthed a silent prayer of thanks for the day his wife started working for Air Canada. It sure helped make these spur of the moment activities possible.

To use their waiting time constructively, Fred shook open a large manila envelope, spreading the contents across their table. In the mix was a large, colored graduation picture of Rachel, complete with the mandatory bundle of red roses and a perky mortarboard atop her blonde head. There were wedding photos with Rachel as bridesmaid, plus a bunch of snapshots taken around her home in Canada or on some beach. Included were several school photos with the young lady in sports outfits, usually with laughing, happy classmates. Large or small, all pictured a very pretty girl: no, best call her a very attractive young woman, in a wide variety of dress and poses. The four men studied the pictures, memorizing the pretty, happy face. In most photos, her long blonde hair was carefully brushed smooth over one shoulder. Some were more candid and casual with her hair swirling about in the wind on a beach or in some friend's backyard. She was one of those women who's bright personality came through in the pictures as much as her physical beauty. Rachel Lusinski had all it would take to be a fashion model had she wanted.

Included with the pictures were several copies of a fact sheet with all Rachel's vital statistics. Fred had her age, birth date, height and weight as well as a long list of her likes, dislikes, and favorite things. He had spent an hour on the phone with his former daughter-in-law Irene, and then another hour talking to his son Tony, Rachel's father. He had put together a large amount of information and Nick thought he had done a bang-up job.

All the pictures clearly showed Rachel was the kind of young woman men looked at twice, three times, or even more. One particularly caught the attention of Fred's three companions and demanded a little extra time for study. It was taken on a beach and Rachel was wearing a tiny, red, two-piece bathing suit specifically designed to leave little doubt that she followed healthy eating habits and exercised regularly. They were looking at a very attractive woman and Nick knew she would catch the eye of any man of any age, including the bad ones, who had not yet gone through the embalming process.

"Anything new?" Nick asked Fred as they shuffled through the pictures.

"No," dejected and upset, Fred actually wrung his old hands as he spoke.

"I was on the phone with Grenada's Police Commissioner just before coming here and he as much as said the major part of their investigation was over, although he did ask me to Fax or e-mail the fact sheet and one or two pictures. He has them by now. It's a pretty small island, you know, and it seems the whole force has been involved." He turned from Nick, trying to gain control.

"They said they couldn't find a trace of her, or her bag, or her sandals or anything. There's absolutely no evidence of foul play. They know she didn't run with a disreputable element on the island, and there's no hint of drugs, excess booze or undesirable conduct. They've got nothing to go on and there's not much more they can do except assign the case to a couple of officers and hope they'll come up with something." Nick thought the old man was about to burst into tears.

"Maybe so Fred, but remember, you were told a long time ago there was nothing you could do about your lost money and look what happened. Give us a chance to check this out." Nick reached over and patted Fred's knee as he spoke.

"You've done a great job on all this information. What are Rachel's mom and dad doing?"

"Anthony's flying to Grenada today. He's not sure what he can do but says he has to be there and I understand; her mom's coming down here this afternoon to be with my wife, then she's going to Grenada from Miami. She's a good woman, Irene is; I could never understand how that dumb bugger son of mine ever let her slip away." This latter was a sore spot with Fred and all in the room knew the story of the breakup.

Ed walked in at this moment carrying a tray with five fresh beers and sat it on the end of their table furthest from the pictures. The tray was empty in seconds and

16

they all stood and shook hands with their host. Ed knew the rule, beer first, hand shaking second. Even Fred didn't deviate.

"How's it going guys?" he asked as he pulled up a chair, reaching over and shuffling through the pile of photos.

This was the first time in several months Nick had been south and seen any of them although the gang had become a social group and kept in touch with each other via golf games, tennis matches and the occasional dinner. All missed the excitement of the Phoenix caper and the thrill of getting their money back. Now word was out about a new job to be done and the excitement was spreading. It was a new opportunity for them to stop vegetating and do something useful. They sensed action, something better than striving to think up new ways to kill time.

Even fresh blood; people who hadn't been involved in the effort to retrieve the stolen cash but had heard about it from the cocktail circuit and other seniors gatherings, were calling, offering help and expertise.

Harry Stanton, known around town as 'The Chief', was surprised at how fast the word had spread and told Fred so. "Don't worry, my old friend," he said, "we're going to find your granddaughter alive and well, and we're going to bring her home."

"OK," Nick said, bringing the small band to order. "This is going to take some doing and we don't have very much time. LJ, you're first."

The weathered, old, retired, printer/soldier leaned his six foot plus frame forward and simply said "Yes Sir" to Nick. Things had come a long way in the many months since Nick was introduced to Louis John Livingston. At that time the ramrod straight, grizzled old man had told that Nick his friends called him LJ, but that he could call him Mr. Livingston.

"We need to move some people to Grenada quickly, within the next twenty-four to thirty-six hours. We need someone there to meet and greet them." Nick glanced at his watch "it's not twelve, can you leave today?"

"If there's a flight, yes," LJ said.

Nick looked across the table and straight into LJ's eyes. "I think I remember something about you having visited Grenada some time ago. Is that right?"

"Yes," LJ said again.

"Could you enlighten us on that visit?" Nick prodded.

"I was working for Ronald Reagan at the time," he said, pausing before going on.

"Some local thugs, backed by our friend in Cuba, assassinated the Prime Minister of Grenada and seven senior members of his government, one of them a very pregnant lady. The killers took over the island and declared martial law. This communist coup caused a lot of concern and several of Grenada's nearest neighbors feared it might be the start of a series of Cuban-backed domino type takeovers across the Caribbean.

"Edward Seaga, the Jamaican leader, Eugenia Charles, Prime Minister of Dominica, and the PM of Barbados, I forget his name, asked my boss to do something." This was the longest speech Nick had ever heard LJ make. He was fascinated.

"We were actually on our way to Lebanon when the word came through from 'The Boss' to go in and clean out the scum", LJ continued. "We did the job in a few days and within weeks my visit ended." He sat back in his chair, obviously not wanting to talk further.

Harry butted in, saying quietly, "LJ is a retired Marine and landed with his unit in the north of Grenada. They did much of the heavy lifting, and a few units moved south to aid a group of SEALS pinned down with the island's Governor in his official residence. Good men were lost in the few days it took to clean up the mess."

Nick softened his approach. "LJ, we're going to need accommodations in a strategic location. We'll need enough for a large bunch of people, thirty, maybe forty, and it seems you're the only one who really knows anything about the place. Can you help us?"

"Don't be stupid, of course I can. That was the past. Who and what I left behind on that island has nothing to do with finding this young lady. Now, I want everyone to forget about how I know anything; let's just use what I know." The steely glint of an old officer laying down the law flashed through the room and all knew not to question LJ Livingston.

"Thanks," said Nick, "now let's get started. Harry, I need you to get on the phone and find out how many can go to Grenada now. And Harry, I mean now, like this afternoon if possible but no later than tomorrow. Ask your wife. By the way, say hello to Kitty for me; ask her to get on her computer and find every possible airline routing to Grenada. We may all have to go to Miami and fly to Jamaica, or Puerto Rico, or some other place for connections. Tell her we'll need each airline's name, their inbound schedule, and their reservation phone number." Nick then turned back to LJ.

"We'll need rooms in a place we can use as a base and none of us have a clue about the island. We know she was staying at a private guest house somewhere south of the capital city, and we know where she was last seen. You're the only one with some idea of where we might stay, relative to those sites. Fred will give you the details. Find us something handy because our efforts will have to start from where she disappeared."

LJ finished his beer, stood and pulled his cell phone from his pocket. "The wife and I will fly out today. This type of thing is best done with boots on the ground. When you know, e-mail me on how many may be coming, how they're coming and whether they need singles or doubles." He turned and headed for the door while calling home with instructions on packing. Just as he stepped through the doorway, he asked his wife to hang on and turned back to Nick and the group.

"Find some maps, Nick. Good maps of the island. It's one of the things we didn't have the last time I was there and the lack of good maps cost us dearly. Good men died because we had no maps. Find some and bring them with you tomorrow," he ordered, and turned, disappearing through the doorway.

Nick turned to Fred, "That's a job for you. There's an aviation map and book store at St. Pete's airport. Harry, you know the one, you've been in it several times and you took me there once. Draw a map for Fred on how to get there and we'll buy everything they have, you know, tourist, aviation, topographical, just get everything available. Now Fred, go and get it done. Keep your receipts and we'll give your granddaughter a bill when we find her. We'll meet back here at four."

Turning to Harry, who was passing a scribbled map to the store at St. Pete's airport to Fred, Nick flipped to a new page in his notebook, and then called out to the departing Fred Lusinski.

"Fred, while you're at it, stop by the Books-A-Million store down at the corner of Cortez and see if they have anything on Grenada. You know, like a Fodor's, or Thomas Cook, that type of book, the kind filled with the islands tourist details. Pick up a couple of each if they have any." Fred called back 'OK', and kept moving.

Now Nick turned back to Harry.

"Do you still have any connections in Washington?" Nick was referring to Harry's efforts over the years on behalf of local Republican senators and congressmen. These connections had come in handy in the past, even getting Nick invitations to both of George W. Bush's inaugurations.

"I can still call the odd person, and believe me, some of them are pretty odd, and they'll still come to the phone, why?"

"Find out if they can get us any maps of the island, good ones. You know. The type the CIA or the military would use. If they didn't have them in 1983, as LJ said, I'll bet they sure as hell have some now.

"Also, see if they can give the local embassy a heads up on our arrival and intent. We may need some help getting the locals to take us seriously, so explain our problem and tell them we're going in to help the locals in their efforts. I'll call a friend of mine in Ottawa. You'll love his title. He's the Second Secretary to the High Commissioner of the Organization of Eastern Caribbean States." Nick took a deep breath. "Man, that's a mouthful. Can you imagine the length of the envelope he uses to send mail? Anyway, he may be able to help smooth our way a little."

Turning at last to Ed Fisher, their intrepid host, Nick smiled. "Well Ed, if you were thinking there was nothing left, I've got a surprise for you. You're now our materials man and it won't be easy. Remember, we all have to fly, and you know the restrictions that puts on us and we only have twenty-four hours to gather all the goodies.

"We'll need two-way radios, cell phones that can work in Grenada, and computers, laptops, as many as we can find. Ask everyone involved if they have one. We'll also need a bunch of transformers. I checked the web last night and discovered Grenada's power system is 220 volt, 50 cycle and we'll have to step it down for all our electrical needs." Ed was scribbling all this on a sheet of paper. Nick forged on.

"Look around and see if you can find a long-range router so we can set up our own wireless network. I doubt there's much on the island so we may have to hook into a local internet café or work with one of the better hotels." Nick stopped to let Ed catch up.

"Get in touch with some of the old gang; call Vince Strong, Herb Sayer and John Hardy. They'll help you figure out what we need. From what I can make out, this is a pretty sophisticated island and we should be able to get what we need there but it will be easier and faster to set up if we bring a lot of the stuff with us.

"Also," Nick continued, "keep all your bills guys. Like I told Fred, when we find Rachel and get her home, we'll figure out how she's going to pay for all our efforts." This brought out the first smile he'd seen on any of the group that day.

Nick stood and started gathering his papers and the material Fred had laid out across their table, looking at the photos, wondering which would make the best shot for a missing person poster.

"OK guys, you all have your marching orders so let's get this ship on the rails", he said as he headed out through the restaurant's back door.

Chapter Three

Day Two: One P.M.

After the meeting, Nick headed back to his usual haunt, a Hilton near the airport that was just a couple of hundred yards from Ed's restaurant. He had much to do over the next few hours and stopping at the front desk to pass on some instructions was the first of them.

He and Ann stayed at the same hotel every time they came down to visit Harry and Kitty, usually one of their birthdays.

For the past twenty-five years there had been no way for Ann to get out of working every holiday on the calendar including Christmas and New Years. She also had to work every weekend for the first fifteen years, but in return, she and he spouse got unlimited reduced fare flights on a standby basis. The rule was 'if there's no bum in the seat, employees fly cheap'. It was how he could go fifteen hundred miles just to take some friends out for dinner.

Nick was in the car business, specifically the car moving business. Over the past fifteen years he had moved hundreds of vehicles across the borders of Mexico, the U.S. and Canada for dealers, brokers, and the occasional private citizen. There were very few spots in all three countries he hadn't visited at one time or another and his knowledge of the highway systems and where the cheapest gas could be purchased was legend. His work gave him a freedom most men never enjoyed and his wife's job allowed him a hobby he loved, seeing the world. Nick considered himself a very lucky man.

The front desk clerk smiled as he approached, recognizing him as one of their regulars. Nick picked up a pen and reached for a notepad.

"If anyone calls for me and I'm not here, please give them this number or take a message and call me right away. This is my cell number, its long distance for you but it will get me anywhere in North America. If you do call me, just bill my room."

"Don't worry sir; I'll post it for the night clerk as well as everyone else." She smiled as she taped the note above the main phone console. Knowing he would get all his messages, Nick then moved on toward his room. As he did, his cell phone rang.

"Hi Hon, are we going to Grenada?" asked his wife Ann.

"You bet we are so pack your bag and don't forget your teeny bikini."

"Oh sure, like women over fifty should be wearing a bikini. I'm pretty sure there's a law against it. If there isn't, there damn well should be."

Ann laughed, knowing she still had a pretty good figure for someone just shy of fifty-five but she was also smart enough to know that as the years increased, so should the amount of material a woman used to cover herself in public. "My old reliable one-piece will do just fine, thank you."

Nick sighed, "Oh well, I guess I'll have to be content chasing you around the hotel in your nightie."

"That's OK by me, but I hope none of the staff see you in my nightie. They'll figure you're some weirdo or pervert," and she laughed at her witty retort.

After several seconds their laughing subsided and they both hung on, enjoying each other's company; although twelve hundred miles apart, it was one of those good moments.

"What's happening? Is there any news?" Ann asked, breaking the silence.

"Nothing," Nick mumbled as he tried to find his room key. "Rachel's father is on his way to Grenada and her mother is coming down here to see Fred's wife before flying to Miami and then on to Grenada. When do you think you'll get in?"

"Late tomorrow afternoon. I'm going direct to Montego Bay on our regular sched and taking Air Jamaica. It's not a bad connection." He was not surprised she had it figured out already. Ann knew more about the airline business and how to move about the planet than anyone Nick had ever met.

Starting many years ago as a counter agent in Hamilton, Ontario for a now long gone regional airline called Nordair, she was required to learn everything about making a staff-starved station work. She had to calculate weight and balance sheets and process cargo to make sure the live things like dogs, cats and baby chicks went into the pressurized holds. She had even taken an exam and passed her radio license test so she could talk to the air crews as they flew in and out of the airport. It was much different in the seventies and eighties when the aviation industry still had a lot of glamour.

In the early days, Nick's wife carried the industry bible, an OAG, with her whenever she flew anywhere. The thick and heavy Official Airline Guide had all the information anyone would want to know stuffed into the tiny print between its covers. That book, plus a handful of validated tickets, could get you just about anywhere in the world.

Nick recalled asking an agent in some bug infested island airport what his company code was so Ann could complete writing the tickets to get them out of there. The everyday systems may have changed with the arrival of the computer but the knowledge of how aviation worked was still Ann's great strength.

"Make sure you get a hotel with an internet connection and e-mail me as soon as you get in. We may have to move but until we do, keep the bed warm for me." He knew she could imagine his grin from all those miles away.

"You should be so lucky. I might fill it with hot coals," she teased, and the soft and sexy laughter that got to him almost thirty years ago was again working its special magic.

"Damn, not on the floor again. You're so bad, you know." Both laughing again now, remembering long ago a motel vibrating bed they had put fifty cents into for a ten minute shake but found the thing wouldn't shut off. Eventually, after a great deal of fun and giggling, they pulled the mattress off the bed frame onto the floor so they could spend a hilarious night beside a bed with a terminal case of St. Vitas Dance.

When they had checked out in the morning they left the bed still doing the jitter-bug and couldn't explain the situation to the desk clerk between their hysterical fits of giggling. To this day, anything about hotel beds triggered the same response.

Settling down, Nick said, "just be careful and make sure you're there when I get in. I'll see you probably late tomorrow or early the next day. LJ is heading out today so e-mail him when you arrive and maybe you and his wife can connect up." His room phone rang at that moment. "Take care darling'. He said. "I have to go, work you know. Love you." He rang off, her special goodbye tickling his memory banks.

It took two more rings before he moved completely back to the job at hand and the jangling telephone in his room. Reaching for it, he shook off the last of the trip down memory lane.

"Hello, this is the Nicolas Archer residence."

"Not for long, exalted one," Harry said. "She who must be obeyed has booked you and the Fishers on a flight tonight into Barbados. You leave Tampa at five-thirty, have a forty-five minute layover in Miami and get into Barbados about twelve. Kitty arranged a hotel so you guys can overnight near the airport then fly on the world famous Leeward Island Air Transport, or LIAT to those of us in the know, to Salines at seven in the morning."

"Salines? I thought we were going to Grenada. What the hell are the Salines?"

Harry loved to stump Nick on anything and enjoyed stretching it out. "Why do you ask, oh font of all knowledge? Is it possible that the walking encyclopedia from the frozen steppes of Canada may have missed some tiny morsel of information? I'm shocked, shocked."

"Very funny, you old fart. And by the way, in case no one ever told you, the steppes are in Russia. We handsome, brilliant Canadians have prairies, with lots and lots of oil under them which we're going to sell to you rich American gringos for twice what it's worth, just like the Arabs do now. So there, smart ass. Now tell me about Salines?" Nick was laughing again.

"Salines is an airport built by Cubans so I'm not sure if it's any good but you have no choice. It's either fly into a Cuban made airport or swim. The main runway is situated beside Grand Bay and Hardy Bay on the south end of the island of Grenada a few miles from beautiful downtown St. George's. If you didn't know, and I'm sure you don't, St. George's is the capital of this splendid little nation of spice, palm trees, and great beaches." Harry was proud of his knowledge of their destination and Nick had to acknowledge his great wisdom.

"OK, you've been a busy little devil. So everything's done?"

"Everything's taken care of, oh leader of the great unwashed, due to the wonderfulness of myself. We're still working on a rental car in Grenada but not the

27

hotel because LJ may have a place for you by the time you arrive. I'll e-mail you at your hotel in Barbados when we know about the Grenada car or LJ's hotel if we have it. I'll also e-mail a heads up to LJ." Harry stopped for a moment to catch his breath before continuing.

"I talked to Ed and he's turning all his information on supplies over to me and I'll carry the ball from here. We already have some stuff, so keep some space in your bag available, at least enough for a few two-way radios and a pile of maps." Harry finished, satisfied he was doing his part.

"Well done, my friend. After this is all over we'll all get together and help finance a lovely new travel agency for you and Kitty. Well, maybe just for her, because everyone knows she does all the work."

A loud and long Bronx cheer was the response to this last bit. "I don't care what you say, or how nasty you are, you can't hurt my feelings. It's just great to be back doing something useful and all your insults and mean words are not going to change that one bit. So there." This was followed by another, smaller Bronx cheer. Harry was enjoying himself.

"Okay, I'll start getting ready and check out of here. Thank the brains in your family for me. Tell her I think she's great."

"You tell her yourself. You'll have time before catching your flight and I may have more info for you. See you in half an hour, so long" and Harry hung up.

Nick laughed as he put the receiver back in its cradle. He marveled at how someone hovering around the eighty year mark could sound so young and enthusiastic. Picking up his notebook, he made his way to the door and the front desk to make his change of plans known, all the time shaking his head in wonder at the vitality of his old friend.

Chapter Four

Day Two: Early Morning, Grenada

Manuel stood in the dirt and moaned quietly, stretching both arms over his head. He swung each up and down, twisting his upper torso and turning his head hard to the left and right trying to work out the kinks out of his neck, back and shoulders. During these exercises he slowly shuffled through the dust, away from the front of his small sleeping shack. He couldn't call it anything else because all he ever did in it was sleep, and not that well either, he thought. He didn't cook in it. It had no washroom facilities because they were down the trail in the bushes, and the only piece of furniture, other than a sleeping hammock, was a small stool to help one get into that hammock. It was simply a sleeping shack in the middle of the jungle, surrounded by palms, brush and noisy damn birds.

He couldn't complain though. He had picked this base camp after many days of carefully searching the countryside, pouring over maps and stomping through the bush, always knowing exactly what he wanted.

He had stumbled on the small clearing one day while following a stream high in the hills. It was old, run down but looked like it had been used in the not too distant past; possibly as a base for a grow-op, now driven out of business for a while by a vigorous local anti-drug effort. He knew instantly when he came upon the clearing that it was exactly what he was looking for.

The small open area in the underbrush contained two tiny buildings, a fire pit in the ground between them, and a clear stream splashing down through the lush jungle less than twenty yards away. Dense brush enclosed it on all sides, hiding it so completely from view one could be within twenty-five feet of the huts and not know they existed. Best of all, the closest home or farm was almost a mile away. It was the perfect hiding spot.

Manuel had brought in two hammocks, cooking utensils and what he thought were adequate supplies for the one or two weeks he expected to need the place. He was no fool, and the effort he put into preparing for this project would have impressed a military leader. Twenty-five years of revengeful dreaming tended to make one a very detail oriented person.

Manuel Fernando Ruiz, at six feet one inch, was unusually tall for a Cuban and just as strong and athletic as most of his countrymen. At thirty-four, even after spending more than fifteen years in the hotel industry, the effects of his early years of working dawn to dusk in the sweltering cane fields of his homeland still showed. He had the kind of physique most North American men only dreamed of having. Manuel knew how good he looked and wasn't shy about working with his shirt off, showing his strong arms, shoulders and flat stomach to the young girls at home. But now he wasn't home, he was high in the hills of central Grenada many miles north of St. George's Town, the centuries old capital of this tiny island nation. Here his strength and stamina would be put to the test achieving his lifelong dream, and that dream didn't include impressing girls with his sleek body.

Stacked between his sleeping shack and the fire pit opposite the other building in the tiny clearing was a small pile of firewood. Hacked into manageable pieces with the machete Manuel carried on a leather strap slung over his shoulder, it was another of his preparations. He stooped, sorting through the firewood and picked out a several pieces. Stepping to the fire pit he tossed them all onto the smoldering coals knowing the fire would be well up for coffee when he got back from the privy just twenty yards down the trail.

Taking care of nature's demands and carefully washing his hands in the stream as his mother had taught him, Manuel returned to the clearing and placed his remaining small piece of soap on a stump near the closed door of the second shack.

It was time for breakfast so he picked up his galvanized bucket, large coffee pot and a cast iron fry pan. Today would be a big day for him, a day people would talk of back home in Cuba for years to come, and it must start smoothly and properly. He looked around to assure himself all was as it should be before starting the short trek up the path to the stream above the camp.

He headed for a place where the stream from higher up in the hills had created a tiny pond before racing down the slope near the sleeping shacks and on down past the privy. Joining another stream further downhill, the two would eventually band with others like them to form a small river winding its way through the village of Birch Grove.

During his search for this hide-away, Manuel had spent considerable time in Birch Grove, posing as a student researching tropical plant life and undergrowth. He was amazed at how open people were, how willing to give him information, and how ready to help. They offered details of the town, the hills, their history, and anything else they thought one might like to know. He learned the bridge on the main street over the river from the hills was built with Japanese money donated after the destruction of Hurricane Ivan several years before. Manuel considered all he had discovered of this land in which his father had died and liked the place much more than he had thought he would.

31

The galvanized bucket of cold water went straight onto the fire and the coffee pot was placed on a metal grill set on rocks. Manuel disappeared into his shack, returning with coffee, a bag of oatmeal and a small container of sugar. After setting up the coffee and putting the fry pan on with some water, he went across to the second shack, only twenty feet beyond the fire pit, and gently knocked on the wooden door. He waited and then knocked again.

"I heard you the first time," an unfriendly female voice called from within. "Just unlock the bloody door."

"It's unlocked," said Manuel, and he moved back to the fire to add oatmeal to the bubbling water in the cast iron fry pan.

Rachel Lusinski slammed open the wooden door of her shack and stepped out into the morning sunlight. Squinting, adjusting to the glare, she looked toward the fire, where Manuel was stooped down stirring oatmeal in the large fry pan.

"Oh no, not more oatmeal. Can't you cook anything else, for Christ's sake?"

"Oatmeal is good for you. It keeps well and won't go bad. With coconuts, bananas and some breadfruit you can thrive and live forever on it, and it is easy to make. Don't you read your history? Everyone in Scotland has lived on it for centuries. If an American gringo like you does not want it, that's okay, because eventually you'll get hungry and want some. And also, watch your language. There is no reason to use the Lord's name the way you do." Manuel turned to his pan of oatmeal and continued stirring.

"I'm Canadian, you Cuban halfwit. Stop calling me an American. I'm from Canada, the second largest country in the world. Hell, we could drop your crappy little country into one of our lakes and you would sink out of sight. No one would know you ever existed. Didn't they teach you the difference between Canada and the United States in those bloody communist schools you attended?" She stormed back to her shack but couldn't resist one last shot.

"And another thing, I know they've been eating oatmeal in Scotland for centuries. That's why they're called dour Scots and run around throwing hammers and telephone poles all over the place. It's from eating that crappy stuff so much it makes them all a little crazy." And she plunked herself down on the step of her shack.

Manuel just shrugged and ignored her jibes. He moved from the pan to the bucket, tested the water and seemed pleased at how hot it was. Carefully lifting it from the coals, he carried it across the clearing and set the bucket down three feet from Rachel.

"Yesterday, you complained about needing a hot bath. This pail has hot water and there is some soap." He pointed to the piece he had set on the stump. "I will take the pail behind your sleeping shack and you can wash. I will not look. I will not bother you. After, if you want, maybe you will have some oatmeal." He handed Rachel some towels, lifted the heavy pail with both hands and lugged it the short distance to the side of the shack and then around the corner to the back, out of sight.

Surprised, Rachel watched him disappear with the bucket but didn't move a muscle. She knew he was trying to make a little peace but she also knew he was a kidnapper and she was his victim and she had no idea where this would end. What was she to do?

When Manuel returned from the rear of her shack, she grabbed the soap with as much dignity as she could muster and stomped away from him, heading for the bucket of lovely hot water. Trailing from her ankle was the reason she couldn't get away. A long cord of nylon securely fastened with small bolts and nuts trailed from her long slim leg. It ran back to a point on her shack's door jam where the line was expertly fastened with much larger bolts. Holding up his hand, Manuel stopped her.

"I will undo the rope from the door and you can pull it through to remove your bathing suit and put on your shorts. After doing so, you will throw the rope around the corner of the hut so I can retrieve it and re-attach it. Do not try to escape, I will catch you."

Glaring back at him, all she could say was "If I catch you peeking, I swear to God I'll kill you. Do you understand?" and she stormed around the hut, small hand towel and larger drying towel draped over her arm to the fabulous, wonderful, dreamy bucket of hot water.

She knew she had won a small point with this morning bath project and she looked forward to being clean. Quickly pulling her shorts and bathing suit down and stepping from them she thought this was going to be perfect. Now stark naked, she pulled the cord through her clothing and slid her shorts back onto her tether. A nearby bush became her bathing suit holder. She stooped low and crept to the corner of the hut and tossed the curled up cord around the building as hard as she could. Hearing him move through the underbrush to pick it up, she held her breath, hoping she had thrown it far enough. When she was sure he wasn't going to walk around the corner, she returned to her pail of beautiful hot water and dropped the small towel into the bucket. Reaching in to retrieve it, she pulled out the dripping piece of cloth and stood up straight, laying it gently across her chest. With eyes closed she let out a long soft sigh. It was like being in heaven, she thought.

Three full days without a bath or hot shower was an absolute first for her, the longest time she could ever remember going without a good cleaning. Standing naked in the early morning sunshine filtering down through the palms she felt the deliciously warm water running down her belly to trickle the length of her long legs. She was surprised to find herself thinking of her kidnapper. This peace offering of his come completely out of the blue and was the best idea he had had, maybe in his whole life. She really didn't care if he did sneak a little peak; he had earned it. She was just going to enjoy the luxury of the next few soapy minutes; the smoldering dark eyes of a good looking Cuban stealing a quick peak through the bushes was not going to spoil them. Actually, she would be a little disappointed if he didn't.

Chapter Five

Day Two: Early Morning

Sitting on his heels, Manuel quietly stirred the pan of oatmeal placed on a stone at the edge of the fire. He was concentrating hard on the cooking task, ignoring the urge to crawl through the bushes to spy on Rachel. He knew she would be standing naked behind the shack as she washed herself and the temptation to peek was almost overpowering, almost.

He was well aware of her many physical attributes, having carried her to his car after taping her up when he grabbed her three mornings ago. He had ample opportunity to check her out very closely.

She was young, probably about twenty-one or twenty-two, with long, very beautiful blonde hair sweeping halfway down her back. She was athletic, healthy, and strong, much like the many young women from Europe and Canada who vacationed at the resorts in Varadero. Manuel had thought she was capable of running from him, or even striking him, had he not held the blade of his glistening half-meter long machete threateningly near her face. It had made all the difference when he originally met her.

Wearing a one piece bathing suit, white shorts and leather sandals, her slim body was an easy burden as he quickly made his way through the tall grass and bushes near the water's edge to the stolen car he was using. He had slid her gently onto the back seat and quietly told her to be calm and quiet and she wouldn't get hurt. The blanket he used to cover her didn't blot out the image of her lying wide-eyed and terrified. It was burned into his mind.

That image stayed clear as he drove carefully north, taking the long route around the east side of St. George's through the early morning traffic and up into the hills. How could he not think of her? He was thirty-four, and though brought up by a widow who made him attend church when home, he was at the peak of his manhood. He was healthy, normal and not made of stone. Now as he stooped by the fire, stirring the pan of oatmeal, she stood naked, out of sight, just twenty-five feet away, washing herself.

Manuel shook his head and stirred breakfast violently. Enough, he thought, pushing the image of his captive's lovely young body from his mind. There was work to be done.

Rachel cleared her throat; startling Manuel and making him look up from the fire. She stood ten feet away, in front of her shack, wearing her white shorts but holding the small towel across her chest, attempting, with some small degree of success, to cover what the towel wasn't designed to cover.

"Would you have a spare shirt of some kind I could borrow?"

"Yes. Yes. Of course," he sputtered, jumping up and disappearing into his sleeping shack, reappearing several seconds later with a red T shirt in hand. "Here," was all he could muster as he handed over the shirt, fighting to keep his eyes diverted from his captive's barely covered front. His fumbling embarrassment almost made Rachel feel sorry for him.

Turning her bare back to her kidnapper, Rachel calmly dropped the towel and pulled the T shirt over her head, slipping it down over her torso, tugging at it and smoothing it out. To finish the little show, she leaned forward, reached behind her head with both hands and pulled her long blonde hair from beneath the shirt, shaking her head to make it fall free down her back.

She knew how good it looked and it never occurred to her she might be stoking a fire she wouldn't be able to put out.

She then picked up the towel and her bathing suit and hung both on some nails sticking out from the shack. Almost happily she turned and strolled back to the bubbling coffee pot on the fire, knowing the tight shirt covered her like a second skin and left nothing to the imagination. 'So what' she thought. 'Let the dummy blush and squirm. At least I'm reasonably clean, out of that damned bathing suit, and I don't care.'

Fortunately for her, Manuel's embarrassment was far greater than his lust and he just kept his head down and his eyes averted.

"Tell me Pedro," she started.

"It's Manuel. My name is Manuel," he interrupted.

"Sure, whatever; your name is Manuel. OK, Manuel, tell me something will you? Why would a Cuban come all the way to a place like Grenada to kidnap a Canadian student out minding her own business? And why would you then chain her to a ramshackle hut in the middle of this bug-infested jungle for days and feed her nothing but oatmeal. Is this some kind of scientific experiment or something?" She stopped for breath, standing, hands on hips, while he stooped at the fire. "And another thing," she continued, "where did you learn to speak English so well?"

Her captor looked up at her for a moment and returned to pouring coffee. She may look good, he thought, but he didn't like the way she talked. He didn't like her foul language nor her constant use of the Lord's name in vain. Manuel considered her a smart-mouthed, bad-mannered spoiled brat whose parents should have given her a few good spankings as she was growing up.

"Hotels," he said. "I worked in hotels serving drinks and food to tourists and businessmen from Canada,

England and the United States. Yes, you Canadians come to Cuba just like all the rest; fat, rich, and thinking you own the world. I listened, studied, and practiced so I could know what they were saying when they thought I was just some stupid servant who could not understand. It's surprising what gringos tell each other around those considered ignorant staff, and it was easy to pretend I didn't understand the language." He gave her a wry look and handed her a plate of oatmeal. She took it without thinking.

"So you learned English working in the tourist industry. Good for you. That still doesn't explain what you're doing in Grenada, involved in some kind of skullduggery that will earn you a whole lot of time behind bars." She took a mouthful and hoped he wouldn't comment on her eating.

"That's a story much too long to tell here. It is enough to say my father died on this island and I have come to Grenada to settle an old family debt with an old enemy and to restore honor to my family's name." Manuel's eyes didn't waver as he looked directly into hers.

"How? By dragging me into the forest and making me eat oatmeal for breakfast, lunch and dinner for a bloody week? I don't know what the hell this old grudge is but you should have picked a fat lady. This diet would have done her wonders and she would have thanked you." Rachel angrily tossed her now empty plate on the ground at his feet. She was definitely over the euphoria of her bath and the freedom from her Speedo.

"You listen to me, you stupid Cuban twit," she said as she pointed and shouted at him. "Just you hope and pray the police find us before my father does. If he gets his hands on you first, you better believe he'll beat you 'till you look like a pile of red guacamole," and she turned and stormed back into her shack, slamming the door as hard as she could.

Again Manuel just shrugged. Slowly he stood, picked up her plate and spoon, setting them with his, and walked across the clearing to her hut. Hefting the steel pin in his hand, he decided not to slip it through the hasp on her door. There was no reason to lock her in while he was away. The tether on her ankle would keep her close to home.

"I must go to town for some food and do some business," he called to her through the closed door. "You have water in there and I'll leave some oranges. I'll be back in two hours, perhaps three," and he turned to leave.

"Well get some decent food, dummy, something like 'Kraft Dinner', maybe some chicken noodle soup, you understand? The next time you serve up oatmeal I swear I'll barf all over your damn cooking fire, your coffee pot, and you."

He just shook his head at her outburst and thought when he got back he'd have to look up the word 'barf' in the small English dictionary he kept in his bag. He never heard it before but he knew from her tone that it wasn't something good.

Chapter Six

Day Three: Early Morning

LJ stood at the counter of the Grenada Grand Beach Resort talking to the pretty German expatriate working behind the counter. He was making arrangements for more rooms because the Florida seniors were on their way. He had been up less than three hours this first full day on the island but had already received several e-mails from Harry, one from Nick and another from Ann, Nick's wife. Harry's e-mail listed the names of eleven couples who would be flying in that day at different times and on several different airlines. He needed a dozen rooms that day plus at least a couple more within a day or two, all preferably in the same section of the complex.

Edith, his ever-there wife, was at the moment driving to the airport several miles south of the hotel on the wrong side of the road, as she called it. LJ smiled to himself as he thought of his seventy-plus wife trying something she had never done. This was her first run to pick up some of the new arrivals and hopefully they'd be standing at the same counter within the hour, and the rental car was still in one piece.

"Sabine, do you think we could get these new people into block nine or ten, if possible?" he spun the plan of the complex around and pointed to the sections he referred to. "These old farts are like me and the shorter the walk to the restaurant or bar, the better."

Sabine leaned across the front desk and patted LJ's hand, smiling up into his weather-beaten old face

"Don't you worry," she said in her soft German accent. "We've set aside both blocks for your people and they'll all get rooms in nine or ten, either upstairs or down, it does not matter. You know I'll take care of them." She paused for a second and then threw him a curve ball.

"Another thing; you're not an old fart. In fact, if you hadn't brought your lovely wife along, I may have taken a shot at you myself before any of the pretty young tourists out on the beach got their hands on you." LJ almost blushed at the devilish wink she gave him.

"Thank you," he smiled "but I must say, looking into those eyes," and he pointed at her face, "if I was alone, I'd be tempted. But you know, fifty-three years of keeping me on the straight and narrow has taught her not to let me loose alone on a tropical island with a gorgeous German girl."

They both laughed; working together to reach a goal she considered now hers as much as his. The day before, prior to LJ and Edith's arrival; Sabine's boss, Samuel Roy, called her into his office, sat her down with the Front Desk Manager and explained to them both exactly what was happening. She already knew about the missing girl, as everyone else on the island did within hours of her disappearance, and she was thrilled their hotel would be involved in the rescue efforts.

After an hour-long meeting that morning, she had walked out of the General Manager's office on air, proud to be included at such a high level of decision making and confident she could make a difference. She was ready to do whatever she could to help.

LJ had been on the island less than eighteen hours but had managed to get everyone he contacted on side, striving to help. When he arrived, he was surprised that virtually every person in Grenada seemed to know about the missing girl. Not only that, they also were well aware that a contingent of family and friends were headed for their country over the next few days to help in the search. News certainly traveled fast in this land.

When he walked down the stairs from the Air Jamaica Airbus and past the smiling agent greeting them, LJ had stepped several paces away from the plane and moved three feet to his left out of the line of passengers heading toward the terminal's arrivals door. He stopped, set down his carry-on, and quietly stood, looking around, slowly taking in every inch of the vast area and all the buildings about him. There wasn't a military aircraft or anyone with a gun in sight. Everywhere he looked, LJ saw gently waving palms welcoming them. All across the front of the terminal, neat rows of hibiscus bushes ablaze with red, pink and white flowers greeted the passengers in the early evening sunlight. The place had changed since the last time he had been there.

Edith, following a step or two behind, said nothing. She simply stepped aside with him and stopped, quietly waiting in the fading light while her husband took deep breaths of the fragrant evening air, looking, noting, absorbing.

Edith Livingston, LJ's wife of more than fifty years, always seemed to be a couple of steps behind her husband and sometimes, a little bit flustered. This led many to think he was the brains of their union and that she was constantly having trouble keeping up. Only the few who knew the Livingstons well, understood how wrong an assumption this was. Theirs was a truly equal partnership in all ways. They discussed every detail of their life and knew each other like characters in a much read and dearly-loved book. Like all longtime equal partnerships, a moment of deep feeling in one always seemed to transmit without words to the other. Edith knew this was one of those times and was happy to wait patiently.

LJ finally let out a long sigh and turned to her smiling. "Nice, isn't it?"

"It's simply beautiful," she beamed, happy at how peaceful and relaxed he was. She took his hand and gave it a squeeze. "Come on, after we find Fred's granddaughter we'll take a couple of days to visit properly," she said and they started across the tarmac for the terminal.

As they walked into the arrival section and moved toward the custom and immigration booths, Edith turned and looked up at LJ, giving him the smile that had conquered him more than half a century before. They continued to a booth and presented their passports with Edith walking a little straighter than usual, knowing she was being escorted by a real man.

Edith had booked two nights at the Grenada Grand Beach Resort on Grand Anse Beach, a few miles south of the capital city of St. George's Town. She had found the hotel on the internet, phoned them directly and laid out the problem of their group truthfully to Samuel Roy, the hotel's manager. She knew LJ needed to check out the place before committing to a longer stay for the group and Mr. Roy had been very understanding and helpful.

It was dark when they arrived at the hotel and by the time they were finished checking in, followed the porter to their room and started unpacking, any idea of sightseeing beyond the boundaries of the hotel grounds was out of the question. Besides, it had been a hectic day and both were tired.

Edith told LJ to go look around while she finished unpacking, so he wandered out and around the property. The sounds of tree frogs above and the gentle rumble of surf rolling onto the beach filled the air and the mixed aroma of all the flowers on the property were so different from the first time he had visited Grenada. That was a time of gunshots, mortars, screams of pain, and great thundering trucks roaring past on the roads.

All of this, he recalled, accompanied by the ever present thump, thump, thump of helicopters overhead. What he now encountered was as different from that time as one could imagine. Now it was peaceful; 'beautiful' as Edith said, and LJ knew that this was how it was meant to be.

He stopped often during his stroll about the lush hotel grounds, taking in everything. The manicured lawns dotted with banana and palm trees rustling in the breeze looked the same as those in Florida but were different. These were island palms and bananas.

Looking out across the almost calm waters into the darkness of the Caribbean, he could see a distant thunderstorm passing, signaling that all should grant a wide berth with its lightning flashes.

To his right, toward the harbor entrance, the lights of St. George's and a glistening cruise ship berthed below Fort George reminded LJ this was a modern sophisticated place, unlike the last time he had been here, more than a quarter of a century ago.

Images washed over him as he stood ramrod straight, motionless, arms at his side as though standing at attention. He was remembering that time, sorting out feelings he thought had long ago faded into the past, to be gone forever. That was a time of fear and hate and death. It was a time whose details were best forgotten.

He was surprised how fresh and real the memories were and how clearly he could see the faces of those he had fought with. It was many minutes before he moved on.

Finally, he stood outside the open air restaurant just off the beach and it brought him back to the present. He remembered promising his wife supper and since food would be available for only the next hour, he turned, heading back to the room to get her. It was dinner time and a meal with his wife was far more important than wandering around with old memories.

Chapter Seven

Day Three: Early Morning

Edith Livingston silently hoped Grenada's medical facilities were top notch because she was positive she was heading for a major heart attack long before she ever got the rental car near the airport.

LJ's first job after breakfast had been to rent a car big enough to carry at least five people plus their luggage. He chose a Japanese four door with a decent sized trunk and a flimsy luggage rack perched on its roof. After completing all the paperwork, the rental agent drove them to a nearby police station where he and Edith each purchased a mandatory U.S. twelve dollar, temporary driver's license. Edith couldn't figure out why she would need one until an hour later when LJ came back to their room from the hotel's Client Computer Station with a sheet of paper sticking from his pocket.

"I got another e-mail from Harry. He says Nick, Ed Fisher and Ed's wife will arrive in forty-five minutes so you'd better be on your way" and he tossed the keys for the rental car across the room in her general direction.

"Are you nuts? I have enough trouble driving around Florida on the right side of the road in my own car," she laughed, and tossed the keys back. "If you expect me to drive on the wrong side of a road as narrow as a sidewalk, or share those crazy round-a-bouts with people determined to kill me while singing 'Day-Oh' on the way to work, you can forget it. You drive."

"Don't be silly, of course you can do it. It's a piece of cake" and he threw the keys back.

"Honey," Edith said "if we're going to play catch, let's go out onto the grass and get some fresh air and sunshine. Then we can throw these damn things back and forth all day." The keys once again flew over the bed on their way across the room.

LJ caught them, moved around the bed and put his arm around her. She looked up at him skeptically, knowing exactly what was coming.

"Ah, come on Hon, you can drive anything with wheels. You've driven scooters all over Bermuda, dune buggies in Virginia, bicycles in France where they really are crazy, and a large truck from Kansas to Kissimmee. This is no big deal." He put the keys in her hand and rolled her fingers tightly around them. "I have an appointment at the Police Commissioner's office in St. George's in one hour. I'll take a cab but someone has to pick up Nick, Ed, and his wife. Then you'll have to go get Irene and Alice when they get in. Don't worry, I have faith in you," and he leaned down from his six foot two to her five foot three and gently kissed her on the cheek.

He was doing it again; just as he had so many times over the past fifty years. He made her do things she didn't think she could, and didn't want to anyway, and he always talked her into it. What made her crazy was she always did it successfully, which, of course, always made him right. Now he was talking her into driving on the wrong side of the road in a country where everyone seemed intent on using her for demolition derby practice.

Her first real problem on the road was the 'Round-About' just two hundred yards from the hotel. Although she had a rough idea how it worked she had never driven into one and wondered if she did, would she ever drive out. Stopping at the entranceway she forced herself to look to her right to see if anyone was coming. It seemed like half the island's car and truck population was aiming for her door.

Behind her, a van driver tooted his horn, waving her toward an opening in the traffic not big enough for a bicycle. She shook her head and waited.

Soon a symphony of tooting horns rolled across the traffic circle playing a melody that sounded a little like the 'Get the Hell a Move-On Chorus'. Edith was no longer uncomfortable, she was in a full fledged panic sweat.

As the door to the van behind her swung open and the large driver stepped onto the pavement, Edith saw an opening big enough for a motor scooter and darted out into it. She was more concerned about escaping the van driver than reaching the airport and her maneuver worked. She was on her way.

As the airport entrance sign came into view Edith almost wept with relief. All the way from the damned hotel, while constantly reminding herself to stay on the left side of the road, she had been devising gruesome ways to pay back her smooth talking husband. For the moment though, parking the car was her main problem. She felt she had aged ten years and even with the air conditioner blasting away, she was still sweating as she signaled to pull into the terminal parking lot. And once again, her action started the windshield wipers going. The wiper switch was on the left side of the steering column and the directional lever on the right, exactly the opposite of her car at home. It was funny the first three times it happened but now, fifteen or twenty times later, she wanted to find a rock and beat the tar out of the damned wiper switch. The only thing stopping her was some very threatening rain clouds off in the distance. Notwithstanding the very stupid wiper switch, she managed to park without tearing off a fender, on hers or someone else's car.

Now free of the idiot car and its dumb wipers, Edith felt better, even a little proud of herself. Begrudgingly, she silently acknowledged LJ had been right, damn him; she could do it, and she knew it would be easier on the way back but it sure wasn't a piece of cake, and he would pay.

Walking from the parking lot, she spotted a small LIAT plane taxiing toward the terminal building. She wondered if it was Nick Archer and Ed Fisher's flight. She didn't want to keep them waiting so she hurried across the road in the direction of the building's main doors.

Within ten minutes Ed and Linda Fisher strode through the exit doors into the waiting area filled with cab drivers, tour bus operators, and assorted friends and relatives of those arriving. Instantly they spotted Edith, waved, and hurried over, dragging their luggage with them.

"Hi Edith," Linda Fisher called, "are you our chauffeur?"

"Yes, and you better hang on to your hat, I tell you. Better still, you may want to get a cab. Did you know they drive on the wrong side of the road on this island? This trip from the hotel is my very first try and it sure was one heck of an adventure." She looked around not noticing the look of terror on Ed's face and asked where Nick was. It was only then that Ed relaxed and laughed.

"He was sent into secondary. I think they nailed him for all the radios and other electronic stuff in his bag. Give him time, he'll be out when they're finished with him," and he took hold of their bags as they moved away from the crowded area into the quieter and cooler breezeway in front of the terminal.

Edith fussed over her two friends, making sure they had a seat on a bench under the canopy and offering to get them a cold beer from the concession stand nearby. Asking them to wait for Nick, she headed across the road toward the parking lot to get the car and bring it

49

around. Ed offered to come with her but she demurred. Edith sure didn't want them with her as she retrieved the car and drove it to the terminal. There was no way she was giving them the chance of seeing her driving around in glaring sunlight with her wipers dragging back and forth on a dry windshield. She knew the drive back to the hotel would be hair-raising enough.

It wasn't long before Nick came out into the breezeway. In fact, he ambled out through the swinging arrivals doors accompanied by a young customs official who was carrying one of Nick's bags. When Nick saw his traveling companions he walked toward them chatting to the porter as if he was a long lost friend.

When the young man left, after much hand shaking and polite banter, Ed asked what was going on.

"You wouldn't believe the reaction when they found out I was one of the group here to help find Rachel," Nick said with a grin. "The search of my bags immediately stopped, everyone gathered around, all with questions. Several offered advice and help. I have the names and phone numbers of a few who volunteered to search. Boy, I think this is the biggest thing to hit the island in years." At this point Edith chugged around the circular one way road and pulled expertly up to the curb and got out to greet him.

"Hi Nick, how was the flight?"

"I'll tell you on the way to the hotel. Have you heard from Ann? She's should be down here somewhere."

"I've heard nothing yet but LJ said he had an e-mail from her so when we get back to the hotel, I'll see if he knows when she's due. I know he got a pile of e-mails this morning so I expect I'll be back out here shortly. In the meantime, buckle up my friends; you're in for the ride of your life."

Later, standing at the front desk of the hotel, Nick had to agree. It had indeed been the ride of his life.

Chapter Eight

Day Three: Early Morning

After the meeting in the hotel lobby, LJ Livingston spent half an hour taking great care in his preparations for his next. He had brought his best dark suit from Florida, the one he asked Edith to bury him in, for this very important rendezvous. When he donned it with the white shirt and blue silk tie Edith picked for him, he knew he looked good. After giving his black shoes their second military buffing, he stood before the full length mirror, ramrod straight, making sure every snow white hair was in place. They all were, so it was time to go.

This was his first visit to Grenada's Police Commissioner's headquarters in Fort George high above the capital city. He wanted it to start well and go well. His military training taught him the amount of effort put into one's appearance could be construed as an indication of the amount of respect held for the person being met.

That old saw was true in this case because there was no question of LJ's respect for Grenada's top policeman and all the things he stood for. He was well aware how competent the Royal Grenadian Police Force was and the effort and good investigative work already put into the case. Also, he didn't want to come across as one of those obnoxious 'pros from Dover' types who arrive on the scene hell-bent on telling the local yokels how to do their jobs. This was a sensitive mission and he wanted to be seen as a friend offering some assistance if it was needed. The Commissioner was the one man who could make or break the effort of Nick and the entire group.

The taxi taking him to police headquarters wound its way around a body of water simply called The Lagoon.

The name then changed to Wharf Road which encircled a harbor area called the Carenage, a place where long ago sailing ships were pulled ashore to be rolled on their side for cleaning and repairs. Now the ancient stone buildings throughout the whole Carenage section contained local-fare restaurants and gift shops overflowing with souvenirs for all tastes and budgets but many were still used as well for the day-to-day business of the busy harbor.

They inched slowly along the water's edge past the tall 'Christ Statue of the Deep' with arms spread in welcome towards the open sea, and once beyond, crept around the next curve into the real working seaport part of the waterfront.

Everyday traffic drove right through the chaotic confusion of small rusty freighters tied up at the curbside. In a mix of motion, assorted materials were being moved to or from the trucks and vans double and sometimes triple parked beside the ships. Moving through this mess, assorted local businessmen and women dodged long two by fours, sheets of plywood and cylinders of gas while slipping between push-carts. With cell phones to their ears, none seemed to notice the chaos while going about their daily chores. Inserted into the mix were scores of tourists, most from cruise ships, wandering about in shorts and strangely colored shirts, taking pictures of anything that moved, or stood still.

LJ watched in wonder as the taxi eased slowly through the frenzy, his driver tooting the horn, mostly to friends or relatives working in the melee. There were more smiles than frowns and no anger in the shouts and calls of those moving about. The feelings of life and industry were infectious. This was St. George's and Grenada at their best.

The driver kept up a running commentary on the buildings they passed and the action on the streets but

LJ had trouble understanding many of the flurry of comments tossed from the front seat. The broad Caribbean accent, mixed with a patois of French and English was difficult for him to keep up with, let alone make any comments of his own.

They swung to the right onto a narrow street running away from the waterfront, passing the ancient public library building. Once beyond it, the entrance to the Sendal Tunnel loomed like a dark cave in the mountainside and the taxi was hurtling straight for it. This everyday part of the city was just another wonder of the wonderful old town. LJ was fascinated.

The tunnel was a long hole, hacked through a huge hill in the centre of St. George's Town at the insistence of the Governor, Sir Walter Sendall, more than a century ago. He felt sorry for the workers from the docks who had to climb up and down the steep sides of the hill laden with goods coming and going to the harbor they had just driven through. The incline was too steep for pack animals, so rain or shine, it was the men who slithered and slid up and down the greasy wet slopes. Governor Sendal could be called an early, true humanitarian.

His creation had a low ceiling and was wet and dank. Originally built for small carts and load-carrying men going both ways, it was only wide enough for a one-way small car lane and a very narrow lane for very cautious and brave pedestrians. LJ held his breath, wondering how his cab driver would navigate through without losing his mirror on one side, or killing a pedestrian on the other. He need not have worried.

Once out and into the blinding sunlight, he marveled at the vibrant activity around him. On his left was a new cruise terminal fronted by a shopping mall through which all arriving and departing passengers must pass. LJ surmised there may have been some Yankee know-how involved in the positioning of this gauntlet of shops between the ship and the shore. On his right reared the city of St. George's in all its crazy confusion of steep and incredibly narrow streets running up and down hills every which way from that cruise terminal.

The taxi moved slowly, its progress impeded by a mass of relaxed and happy people who ignored street traffic as they went about their work.

Music blared from shops or boom boxes set on tables in front of some stores. Friends shouted greetings from one narrow sidewalk to another, over, or through the windows of the cars clogging their streets. The amount of laughter, good natured jibes, and broad smiles surprised LJ, sitting in the car enthralled, taking it all in through the window. It was a very different world from the Grenada he had first visited a quarter century ago.

Then, the people cowered in fear. Scores of their fellow citizens lay dead or injured, struck down by ones they thought were friends, or in some cases, by members of their own families. In less than two weeks, their Prime Minister and a large part of his government had been arrested, set free, seized again after a bloody battle at the fort, and hours later, without a trial, executed. Those responsible imposed martial law and citizens were unable to leave their homes for food or supplies. Within days, forces of the mightiest power on earth encircled their island with warships, sent in troops, and after several days of fighting, were in complete control of the country. The people had every right to be afraid.

Now, LJ looked around and saw a far better world. It was cleaner, brighter, more prosperous, and best of all it was a much happier world.

The taxi only moved a hundred yards through this milieu before turning right into a slow moving line of traffic. Another hundred yards had them turning right again, avoiding a busy open air market on their left. Once again they were slowly snaking up a narrow street littered with people. LJ couldn't figure out exactly where they were headed.

"Are you sure this is the right way?" he hollered over the din from the street.

The driver, now stopped and waiting for the light to change, turned to LJ and grinned, "Have you met a taxi man anywhere who didn't know where police headquarters was?"

"No, you do have a point," conceded LJ.

"Good, so just relax and be cool mon." At that moment, the light turned green and the car behind instantly gave a gentle toot of his horn. The taxi jerked forward, up the hill and swung right where the driver navigated an impossibly steep and narrow roadway into the fortress where the Police Commissioner was stationed.

LJ climbed out and passed a handful of Eastern Caribbean bills to the driver. The tip was a great deal more than necessary but it had been an excellent ride, both informative and enjoyable. He was in a good mood, ready for the police officer sitting in the building overlooking the spot where the taxi had left him.

Turning from his view of the city spread out below him, LJ looked toward the building his driver had pointed out and was overwhelmed by the rush of memories that swept over him. It was as though he had stepped back in time.

He had only been in Fort George once before, as a soldier. The eighteenth century complex was then called Fort Rupert, in honor of Rupert Bishop, the father of Grenada's dead Prime Minister Maurice Bishop, whose assassination had triggered the events responsible for LJ and his unit being there.

After the liberation of the north, LJ's unit had been ordered south toward St. George's to help some Navy Seals with the evacuation of the Governor General, Sir Paul Scoon, the Queen's representative on the island. The move south took about twelve hours and by the time they arrived, Sir Paul was safe, the war was over, and people were dancing in the streets. The scenes in towns all over Grenada were reminiscent of liberated people welcoming troops towards the end of World War Two. Once convinced the danger was past, Grenadians poured out of their homes with food, flowers and gifts for the invading U.S. forces. The invasion and end of the insurgency was very popular locally.

LJ had wanted to visit the fort, before leaving with his unit to continue their interrupted deployment to Lebanon. The fortress was where great events had occurred in the life of this small nation.

This was where the communist insurgents sent a force with three armored vehicles fitted out with 14.5 mm heavy machine guns. Reports later said no negotiations were offered, no call was made for Prime Minister Bishop to surrender, and no attempt was put forth to peacefully settle the problem. The commander of the communist force, Conrad Mayers, a young inexperienced officer cadet simply ordered his men to start shooting, mowing down forty or fifty innocent men, women and children who stood between the vehicles and the attacker's target, the Prime Minister.

When the killers seized their man, they marched him and seven others, some members of his government, up into the area of the fort called 'Top Square' and within an hour lined them up against a wall in front of four medium machine guns and shot them all. One of them, Jaqueline Creft, the Minister of Education, begged for mercy because she was pregnant. It didn't matter; these revolutionaries were equal opportunity killers. She died in the same hail of bullets as the seven men.

Within ten days the revolution was over, the island was securely in American hands, and allies from three neighboring island countries were patrolling streets and keeping the peace. Sir Paul Scoon was back in the bullet scarred Government House while most of the bad guys were in prison, awaiting trial and the judgment of their countrymen.

Just before leaving for Lebanon, LJ decided to visit the place where it all began, and now, after all these years, but for a fresh coat of paint and a few late model cars parked around the square, the place seemed exactly as it had been twenty-five years ago.

Slowly he made his way across the square to the iron steps leading up to the balcony serving the second floor. Halfway up he stopped and ran his right hand along the steel railing, fingering the nicks and cuts in the metal. After all these years, the bullet holes and cuts in the railings were still there, sharp points hammered flat, painted over several times, but still there, remnants of a bloody ten minutes when citizens of Grenada were killing other citizens of Grenada.

LJ found the door on the second level with its brass plaque instructing one to knock first and then enter. Doing as told, he stepped into the outer office of the island's top policeman.

The receptionist in her small booth to his left smiled and asked how she could help. When he gave his name and mission she immediately transformed from a slightly bored civil servant to an officious, professional front line staff member of some very important people.

"Of course, Mr. Livingston; right this way please," and she came out from her cubicle, walking past him to a door down a hall on his right. With a gentle tap she opened the door part way and spoke to someone unseen. In an instant, the Commissioner of Police was standing in front of LJ, a broad grin of perfect teeth on his handsome black face.

"Mr. Livingston, how nice to meet you," he said and seized LJ's hand in his firm grip. "Your call yesterday intrigued me and I've been looking forward to our getting together. Come in, come in, please," and he stood aside letting LJ in.

The man wasn't what LJ expected. Commissioner Frank was about forty five-years old, the same height as LJ and appeared to be in very good physical condition. His diction and accent, as well as his manners, suggested an extensive education in some of the better schools in England and LJ's own country.

His dark uniform, complete with broad red stripes running down each leg to perfectly polished regulation shoes, looked like it was hand tailored on Savile Row and pressed ten minutes before LJ arrived. The white shirt he wore said custom made in every stitch and his hair may well have been trimmed that morning. LJ was very glad he had spent extra time getting ready because this man understood the importance of presenting the proper image.

The next hour seemed to fly by as both men got to know each other better while exchanging views and swapping suggestions on the Rachel Lusinski case. LJ sensed no resentment or protective posturing on the part of his host and had no trouble getting information on how things were progressing. Any assistance offered by the gang of seniors seemed eagerly welcome. LJ felt the key moment of their discussion was the posters.

Prior to leaving Florida, Nick had scanned a couple of very good photos of Rachel and emailed them to LJ's two sons in Paterson, New Jersey. They ran the family printing business started by LJ on his retirement from the Marines. He had turned it over to them on his second retirement several years ago, and they had grown it into something much bigger than LJ believed possible. He was very proud of them and they worshiped the ground he walked on. They also did anything their father asked without question, and they did it quickly. This was one of those times.

Nick had asked them to make a few hundred posters, twenty-four by eighteen inches with Rachel's picture and some message like 'HAVE YOU SEEN THIS GIRL' and instructions to call the police. The posters arrived that morning and had to be cleared through customs. LJ suggested his people were prepared to start putting them up all over the island as soon as they were cleared. The posters certainly interested the Commissioner.

"I may be able to help you on this one if you give me the details," he said and reached for the telephone sitting on his desk. He thought a moment, and then dialed a number which was answered almost immediately.

"Winston," he grinned into the phone, "how are you my old friend? Excellent, excellent, I'm so glad to hear that. Winston, I have a small favor to ask and I need a little extra effort to get it done quickly." He listened quietly to Winston's reply.

"I knew I could count on you. I have a shipment of posters, yes posters, coming in from the States. That's right, posters of the missing girl. I need them right away so we can start getting them up." There was another pause. "Yes, yes, they're the ones. Damn, nothing gets past you at that airport, does it Winston? You're right, they're from Paterson, New Jersey, the Livingston Printing Company. I'm so glad you're on top of things out there." He waited again.

"Great, put up a few around the airport and send the rest to the Grand, care of LJ Livingston. Thanks

Winston. This is a big help and for it, I'll let you beat me at tennis this weekend." Laughing at some retort from Winston, he hung up the phone.

"They should be at the hotel when you get back. Winston is the head of customs at the airport, a very nice man."

LJ was impressed. "I'm beginning to believe this island is full of very nice people," and stood to leave.

Commissioner Frank stepped around the desk and stuck out his hand. "If your people have any trouble when putting up the posters, tell the troublemakers to call the police. We'll set them straight." He reached for the door to let LJ out.

"You may want to bring a couple of your top people around tomorrow at eight a.m. and I'll have my men lay out the search program we're operating at the moment. It's not perfect but it's the best we can do with the staff we have. We have maps, a grid layout, and some high priority areas. You may be able to take one or two of the sectors and we'll move our searchers into other spots. You could be a big help."

They both stepped from the room, moved down the hall and out into the bright sunshine on the balcony. LJ couldn't help but feel the police officer didn't do this often and was subtly telling everyone in sight that the elderly man with him was an important person.

Standing at the railing overlooking Bottom Square, the two men stayed motionless for several moments.

"You've been here before, haven't you?" the officer asked.

"Yes, a long, long time ago when things were bad and the island had many problems," LJ said, turning to his host. "How did you know?"

"After you called yesterday, I phoned an old friend I know from my days at your FBI Academy. He called me back just before you arrived this morning. He told me you were a friend of my country and you were here when we needed help many years ago. All of us appreciate what you and your country did for us.

"He also told me you were a fair and honest businessman, a person who could be trusted. Therefore we will work together and find this girl, believe me," and he offered LJ his hand once again, this time putting his left over their two clasped right hands. LJ quietly thanked him, turned, and walked to the stairs.

"Oh, by the way," Commissioner Frank called out to LJ as he started down the stairs. "My friend in Washington said to make sure no one on the island tries to steal any money from you or your group. He said not to be fooled by the white hair. Sometime, over a cool drink, you will have to tell me the story behind his comments."

LJ stopped and slowly turned, a large grin on his face, but the balcony was empty, the Commissioner was gone.

Chapter Nine

Day Three: Mid Morning

Manuel thought deeply about his dilemma as he worked his way down through the dense tropical growth on the mountain side. The physical effort of using his machete to hack through some of the sections of the hill had made him sweat, and helped him think. Manuel was a physical man, at his best using his large hands or strong back. When doing so, his mind would run free, allowing him to dream, plan, or, as in this venture, to plot.

Now he had a problem and needed the exercise to help him figure a way to solve it. He had come to Grenada with a detailed plan to kidnap a female American citizen and hold her until all his demands of the American Government were met. Everything had gone according to plan perfectly except for one major point. He had mistakenly grabbed a bad-tempered, foul-mouthed Canadian girl instead. He needed time to think.

Manuel was born in Isabela de Sagua, a tiny village of less than a hundred souls in the agricultural province of Villa Clara on the north coast of Cuba. His father, Louis Fernando Ruiz, had marched with the Great Leader Fidel from the very beginning of the revolution, and had been assigned to the northeast sector of the country by the new government after the fall of Batista on December 31st, 1958. The job he received for his loyalty and bravery was to assist in the rebuilding of the area's totally destroyed infrastructure.

Louis' role in the fight leading to the bastard Batista running from the country on New Years Eve was as a foot soldier in a small 300 man column led by Che Guevara.

Manuel's whole family knew of how Louis Ruiz never wavered in his dedication to the revolutionary struggle and the story was told many times of how three days before the victory, Che and Louis faced federal tanks and soldiers while being strafed by government aircraft. Many died, and many paid the lifelong price of the revolution by spending their remaining years on crutches or in wheelchairs.

The battle for Santa Clara was finally won after two bloody days when the soldiers in Batista's derailed armored train surrendered to the rebels who held the city. Since then, Che Guevara had become a worldwide legend, and Louis Fernando Ruiz had become a damn good road builder.

It was not long before the abilities of Manuel's father propelled him up through the ranks to be appointed area supervisor in charge of all road building and maintenance in the northern sector of Villa Clara. It was considered an important position and, under his direction northern Villa Clara soon became renowned throughout the province and across Cuba for the fine quality and excellent condition of its roads.

The Ruiz family lived well compared to other families in their village. The head of the household was an important man, a man of substance, often driving home in an old government pick-up truck confiscated from some capitalist exploiter who was thankfully now out of business.

There was always abundant food, much brought home by Manuel's father at the end of a day's work, but often delivered by people who worked for Senor Supervisor. It was a good life for Manuel, his younger sister Luisa and baby brother Roberto, but it all started to end after he turned nine.

On that day, while Manuel still basked in the glow of his birthday celebrations, his life started to change, although, at the time, he was much too young to be aware of the many grand events in far off places shaping that change.

On the fifth day after his birthday, a big black automobile stopped in front of their little home in the village of Isabela de Sagua. The driver got out and opened the door for his two passengers. One was a high ranking military officer whose chest was emblazoned with several rows of colored ribbons and many medals. The other wore a crumpled business suit that didn't fit too well. Even a casual observer would realize it was the crumpled man who was in charge.

The driver of the long car was another military man but he wore no gold braid, had no medals and wore a different style of hat. He didn't enter the home.

Manuel was shuffled out of the house with his little sister while the two very important looking men met with his father and mother. Intrigued by the car, he kept one eye on the soldier-driver and another on his little sister as the military man moved about his charge, wiping off dust from the road, and polishing the chrome until the whole car glittered and sparkled in the sunshine.

Time passed slowly and finally he collected enough nerve to speak to the soldier who surprised him by smiling and being friendly and informative, willing to show the boy how much he knew. Patiently he walked his young inquisitor around the car, telling him it was a Mercedes Benz and was made far away in a country called Germany. He opened the hood and helped the boy up to stand on the bumper so he could stare at the huge engine.

Warming up, the soldier explained how after the exploiters and criminals were driven from Cuba, the government seized the car and many other things from the closed casinos in Havana. He also bragged how it was the best car in the world; far better than the American Cadillac's everyone seemed to think were so great when they were also seized at the same time. Manuel, car crazy like any nine year old boy in any place on earth, was wide-eyed and fascinated.

Opening the driver's door, the soldier told Manuel to remove his sandals and climb up in behind the steering wheel. It was a little boy paradise as the slight child sat grinning, gripping the wheel with both hands and studying all the dials and buttons spread before him as though he might have an exam the next day about everything he saw. It was a different world from the old pick-up his father sometimes drove and, to this day, his thoughts slipped back to that beautiful black Mercedes Benz every time he got behind the wheel of a motor vehicle.

When an hour had passed, the front door of the small Ruiz home swung open and the two important visitors emerged, followed by Manuel's father and mother. The young soldier waved the small boy out of the driver's seat and hurried around the car, opening the gleaming rear door for his important cargo. Manuel, scrambling on his hands and knees in the dust, gathered up his sandals on the driver's side of the car.

Within minutes, after getting his hair tousled by the driver as he climbed into his seat, Manuel stood, still in awe, as the majestic auto growled to life and pulled away, disappearing in a small cloud of dust. Only then did he turn to his parents, who, like Manuel, stood motionless, silently watching the great car vanish as it passed through their village on its trip back into the unknown world of the government.

The first part of the family's evening meal was quiet but near the end, Manuel's father explained that he must go away for a while. Their Great Leader Fidel had bestowed upon him and his family the honor of helping the cause of socialism even more then they had already. Louis, the great revolutionary hero, had been asked to go away to a place called Grenada, where the poor people of that poor island had wisely installed a socialist government and needed help to build a new airport. The Cuban patriots were going to provide that help.

The Ruiz family was being called upon to take care of themselves for many months; perhaps as long as a year, and he, Manuel, must assume the position of family head, the man of the house, until his father returned.

Filled with pride, the small boy solemnly swore he would work hard keeping his mother, brother, and little sister safe and secure until his father returned. Even for ten years.

Three days later, an older car with many dents and much rust in many places arrived at the little house in Isabela de Sagua to take his father away. Manuel's mother stood outside their home, proud and solemn, the small baby Roberto in her arms, flanked by the two older children. The father emerged from the house in his best suit and a clean white shirt, carrying two old suitcases. He purposefully walked out to his family and turned to face them, setting his bags on the ground. For a long time he stood very still, looking at each one in turn as though trying to burn this particular image into his memory. Then he spoke.

"Manuel, you are a fine boy with a strong body and a good mind. Use your body to help your mother, brother and sister, and improve your mind at every opportunity. That way, some day, you can be the man who orders people to leave their family and go off to faraway lands." He held out his hand to shake Manuel's hand, the way men do.

He turned to his daughter, stooping down to take the small bundle of smiles and curls into his arms so he could hold her tight. She was six, unaware of the moment, giggling as her daddy squeezed her.

Standing up, he reached to brush a wisp of wayward hair from his wife's face, pretending not to see the tiny tear slowly sliding down her cheek as she held Roberto close. He leaned forward, smiling, and whispered something into her ear that caused a small sad smile to flit across her face. Gently, he placed a small kiss on the tear streak on her cheek, turned to pick up his bags, and strode to the waiting car. Manuel walked beside him as an escort.

As the driver helped put the bags in the trunk, Manuel struggled with the rear door of the car. After some effort he managed to get it open, and stood straight beside it as he had seen the soldier do three days before, waiting for his important cargo. His father stepped to the opening and before getting in, turned once again to his son.

"Thank you son; already you are the man of the house," and he slid into the seat and helped Manuel shut the door. As the driver walked around to the front, the rear window slid down and Manuel's father reached out, smiling, and ran his fingers roughly through the boys hair.

Laughing, he said "man of the house or not, I can still do that because you are still my son." The car then pulled away.

Manuel never saw his father again.

Chapter Ten

Day Three: Late Afternoon

It was after three o'clock and the entire hotel was buzzing. LJ had worked miracles in the few hours since his return from the Police Commissioner's office. An outsider would never believe the organized confusion he was seeing and that it had started less than three days before in a country more than a thousand miles away.

Commissioner Frank was correct regarding the posters from New Jersey. When LJ got back to the hotel from Fort George, he saw what looked like a dozen or so large brown paper wrapped bundles stacked high beside the front desk as he walked through the lobby. Attached to the top of the pile was a note to him from the Airport Customs Officer. Obviously written in haste with a large felt pen, it simply said:

Dear Mr. Livingston, we kept twenty-five or thirty posters to put up around the airport and over at the Medical School at True Blue Bay. My men also put some on poles on the roads to the village of Frequente and east toward Calivigny as well as on the road west to Grand Anse Beach. The staff volunteered to do this and if you need more help, please call. Also, everyone is taking a poster home to put outside their properties.

The note ended with a large GOOD LUCK scrawled across the bottom and the one word signature, WINSTON.

LJ carefully folded the note and slipped it in his pocket. It was something to be saved.

The posters weren't the only delivery from the airport that day. Edith, bless her nervous driver's soul, was on her third trip in her shuttle service and so far had dropped off John and Beth Hardy, Herb and Thelma

68

Sayer and Vince Strong and his wife Isabel. She also brought in Bella Brown, who was on the same flight as the Strong's. The Strong's and Bella agreed that Edith had wheeled the car around like a local which made LJ grin and Edith stick out her tongue at him.

On top of Edith's efforts, several arriving seniors picked up rental cars at the airport, went around to the police station for their licenses, and drove to the hotel ready for work.

Ed Fisher had established the poster brigade minutes after the bundles arrived from customs and, ever since, his gang of installers had grown with each new arrival from Florida. At the moment, there were four cars on the road slapping up signs as fast as they could. Two were in St. George's; the other two had gone east into St. David's Parish.

His system was simple. Whenever someone drove in from the airport and asked if there was anything they could do, Ed arranged to have their luggage moved to their room, asked the wife to start the unpacking while he talked to the husband, and then sent him out putting up posters. It worked like a charm.

At the moment he was instructing two new crews where to go; one toward Goayave on the west coast, the other north through the middle of the island toward Grenville. As they loaded posters, hammers, roofing nails and rolls of duct tape into the cars, Ed was stuffing maps and notes into their hands while giving directions to places he had never been.

When the last crew left and a lull swept through the place, Ed spotted LJ on the grass between the lobby and their rooms. He waved him over.

"How'd it go at the cop shop?" he asked, stopping to wipe his brow in the shade of a banana tree.

"I think it went great. The 'man' himself called customs and basically ordered them to deliver the posters ASAP. I'm glad to see you got them."

Ed laughed, "Two uniformed young men roared up the driveway in a Grenada Airport Authority pick-up with the posters neatly piled in the back. They jumped out and wasted no time lugging all the bundles into the lobby. The guys fussed all over us, wondering if the bundles were in the right place, should they set them somewhere else and did we want them in two piles, that kind of stuff. I guess they had orders to be helpful and they were determined to be as helpful as they could. It seems you have friends in low places, eh?"

"Let's just say this commissioner appears to have a lot of clout. I have a good idea he and those above him would love to see a quick and happy ending to this problem," LJ said. "He's worried it could turn into something like the fiasco in Aruba a few years ago when a girl disappeared and they never found her and never arrested anyone. The Aruba police and tourist industry both ended up with a large black eye. I don't think the authorities here want the same in Grenada. It's my guess they figure any help from outside, even from a bunch of decrepit old farts like us, is welcome. How are you making out?"

"Come on, you look like you could use a beer, and besides, like always, I'm buying," and with a big grin, he guided LJ past the dining area to a bar near one of the pools. Finding a couple of seats away from some relaxing hotel guests, he ordered two Caribes and sat back with his feet stretched out in front of him.

"This feels good," he said as he poured half the bottle down his throat. "Now, I'll tell you what I've been up to if you'll tell me what you learned from the fuzz." For the next half hour they swapped details on the project.

Ed figured the job of signing the whole island would be done by dark the following day, when the country would be plastered with over a thousand large blue bordered color reproductions of Rachel's smiling face. He told LJ his sons in New Jersey had sent twelve hundred posters instead of the two hundred and fifty Nick had asked for and that it must have cost them a bundle to ship so quickly.

LJ just grinned and said "I guess when they get that new giant press of theirs running, it spits out things faster than expected. Anyway, it sounds like you can use them."

What surprised Ed were the reports back from the crews of almost one hundred percent co-operation from the citizens of Grenada. Everyone the sign workers encountered was aware of the plight of the lost girl and wanted a poster. One crew in St. George's came back to restock and said they were putting one in every store window in town.

Everyone also seemed to know that a band of seniors from Florida had arrived on the island to help in the search and everyone wanted to be part of the venture. The signs were flying up onto poles, walls, on houses and in shops. They were even stuck onto the mini busses that sped around the narrow winding roads picking up and dropping off passengers. Within twenty-four hours you wouldn't be able to open your eyes without seeing Rachel's face. If anyone, anywhere had seen the beautiful young blonde, their memory was sure to be jolted and they would have a phone number to call.

LJ was pleased. "So you think you'll be done by tomorrow night?" he asked between sips.

"Maybe sooner; I might go out myself later today and hit a few of the more remote areas west of here in St. David's Parish. Don't worry, it'll be done when I say.

71

Now, what did you learn?" He leaned back, signaled the bartender for a couple more, and became a listener.

"First off," LJ started, "the police seem to think that if she hasn't had some unfortunate accident, you know, like falling down a cliff into some remote crag or hole; or swam off shore to look at coral and met up with a shark or something, she must have met a stranger, someone from off island, and took up with him, or her."

"I asked him why a stranger and not a local 'ne'er-do-well?" LJ knew Ed would ask that as well.

"He said the first thing they did after checking her belongings and gathering items to be sent to an off-island lab, was to start working all the usual suspects and lowlifes. Anyone with any form of brush with the law, particularly over something like women, young girls or tourists, was hauled in for a grilling. This is a tiny country, it has only one hundred thousand people and I think the Commissioner has the name of every villain memorized. There are very few secrets in a place this small and it didn't take them long to figure out it wasn't some local dude out being bad." LJ thanked the waitress for his new drink.

"He claims there isn't a hint of anything foul or unusual occurring the day before, or in the three days since she disappeared. With a population as small as Grenada's, the degree of separation is a hell of a lot less than back home. I would think almost every person on this island is a distant relative of almost everyone else in some way, shape or form. If he says no hint, I really think he means no hint."

Both men sat quietly for several moments, considering the implications of the police officer's conclusions.

"So he's saying she either had an accident, which narrows the area we have to search, or she's been scooped up by someone who has done something to keep her from re-appearing." Ed thought for a minute. "Well, if we accept the Commissioner's first premise, we check an area you can walk through in four or five hours. Accepting the second means we check the whole damned island. What do you think?"

LJ didn't hesitate. "We check the whole damned island."

"Why?" Ed prodded.

"Several reasons," LJ pulled a sheet of paper from his pocket and sat quietly, thinking, putting his thoughts in order. He then wrote number one on the paper and looked at Ed.

"First, the police have already conducted a search of the area where she was last seen and if we search the whole island we will also search that area again. We'll take extra care in her walking area, but it will be as part of the whole operation.

"Second, and this is pretty gruesome, but the cop said it, and I know he's right. He claims a dead body in this climate gets pretty rank in two days. You can smell it from quite a distance and believe me, I know, there is nothing that smells worse." LJ stopped, away somewhere, remembering.

"Anyway," coming back to the present, "if you mark a map with the spot she was last seen, and draw a circle taking in the greatest distance one could walk in four or five hours from that spot, we'll know where she could be and it's not a very big area. Not only that, it's a fairly well populated section. There are people and homes and small farms spotted all over the place and the police would know pretty quickly if something big, like a human, was lying around decomposing. Happily, they've had no reports or complaints."

"Thank God for that." Ed bowed, crossing himself.

"I didn't know you were Catholic," LJ said.

73

Ed laughed, "I'm not. I learned to do that for a wonderful young lady I dated more than forty years ago and every once in a while it just pops out."

"A girl taught you how to cross yourself forty years ago. What the hell for?" LJ asked between sips.

"Her name was Elsie and she had the most beautiful head of red hair and the longest legs on the planet. Man, she was gorgeous.

"She came from a family of devout Irish Catholics and I had to fake the religious routine for them whenever I visited for dinner. They would have disowned the poor girl and thrown her out on the street if they knew she was dating one of those 'bloody Protestants', as her father would say. So, she bought me a rosary, drilled me on how to cross myself, and gave me a crash course on what to do in church. She made me one of the Pope's own and it worked like a charm."

"Was all the trouble and play acting worth it?" LJ grinned.

"You bet your life it was. Her old man figured a good Catholic boy like me could do no wrong. Elsie and I got away with just about anything we wanted." Ed sighed.

"I would have converted for her, hell I would have crawled over broken glass for her, but even that wouldn't have satisfied her father so marriage was out of the question. You know how it was in those days. It was unthinkable to live together, and we knew marriage was out, so we broke up and went our separate ways. I've never seen nor heard of her since." Ed took a long pull from his beer.

"I still have a soft spot for redheads though; I guess always hoping one will sashay over and whisper 'ooh la-la' in my ear, the way she always did," Ed had a faraway look and LJ knew the feeling of going back and remembering something, or someone, very special.

"Oh well," sighed the old restaurateur, "we live in different times with different rules. Still, every time a long, lean redhead with great legs and bright red lips strolls by, I'm the one who says a silent 'ooh la-la' and whispers a quiet and heartfelt 'fare thee well' to my dear Elsie."

They both sat in silence for a few minutes. LJ knew exactly what Ed was talking about.

"Enough of the reminiscing," Ed finally said. "What else did the cop say?"

"Not much more. He's happy about the posters; says to call him if we have trouble getting them up. He did ask me to drop back tomorrow morning with a couple of the top dogs here and he'd introduce us to the officers in charge of their investigations. I thought maybe you and Nick. That way we can coordinate our efforts. Otherwise, all seems smooth." LJ drained his beer and sat quietly.

"Great," Ed said standing and stretching. "I've got some work to do and I know you have too, so I better get my butt in gear. Will you be around later tonight?"

"Affirmative."

"I'll see you then. By the way, Nick and Ann are here. I sent them out with some posters. They should be back about eight. You should have heard him. Claims I wouldn't give him a chance to unpack. Poor baby." Both men laughed.

Ed finished his beer and moved away but LJ hardly noticed. He was deep in thought about the big search that would start tomorrow.

Chapter Eleven

Day Three: Late Afternoon

Manuel stood quietly in dense vegetation just fifteen feet from the edge of the road but well out of sight. He was as still as a post, white plastic bags of provisions hanging motionless in each hand. With eyes tightly shut, his labored breathing and the tiny droplets of sweat streaking his face were the only indications of life. He was stunned, in a state of total shock, fighting to maintain control, determined not to let out a long howl of anguish.

Earlier that day, he left Rachel in the small compound high in the hills and slowly worked his way down toward the village of Birch Grove. It had been a slow trek across the northwest side of the peak through dense bush but he had been in no hurry. He took his time, thinking about his unbelievable problem caused by being stupid enough to kidnap a young girl of the wrong nationality.

At times, deep in thought and not paying attention to the task at hand, he would find his descent barred by impassable tangles of brush and vines or rock outcrops leading to frightening cliffs, forcing him to double back and search out another route. Persevering, he managed to move through an area where few wandered and no trails existed, marking discreetly with the sharp blade of his machete, distinctive trees that could help him find his way back.

Drawing close to Birch Grove he slowed down, taking time to find the best place to emerge from the jungle and enter the village. He knew a white stranger appearing out of the undergrowth might cause some unwanted investigation and he didn't want that. This forced him to make detours around several small homes on the outskirts of town in order to enter the community by one of the three roads running through it.

Convinced his entry was undetected, he set about his shopping and took his time. He wandered from store to store; not wanting to appear hurried, carefully checking off each item on his list. He would stand quietly reading the labels on cans or packages, deciding what he needed and especially what might keep his captive quiet. When the food was all collected plus the bar of soap and tube of toothpaste along with two new toothbrushes were all bagged, he moved up the street to what appeared to be a clothing store. He needed to buy a shirt.

The shop had exactly what he wanted. Among the rows of neatly folded jeans and dress trousers was a shelf with piles of T shirts stacked by color and according to size. In an instant he spotted the one for Rachel. It was white, came in a large size, and had a red bordered green and gold flag of Grenada emblazoned across the front. He discussed the size with the clerk because he thought the red shirt he gave her that morning was far too small and tight. He wanted something to fit loosely, to be less revealing, therefore less provocative. The clerk held it up for consideration and Manuel smiled and said thank you. It would be perfect.

Leaving the tiny shop with his head down while arranging his parcels, Manuel turned to his left without looking and bumped into the open rear door of a car parked in front of the store. There had been no car there when he entered the shop.

Somewhat upset, he spun around to see who could be so inconsiderate as to leave his auto like this and found no one near. Searching about, he glanced into the car and recoiled as though slapped in the face. Smiling up from the back seat of the car stared the blue eyes and perfect teeth of Manuel's beautiful blonde captive. Frozen in stunned horror, he failed to notice two elderly gentlemen approaching him on his left and his right. Each carried a hammer, tape, and additional posters of the girl, identical to the ones mocking him from the back seat of the car.

"Hi," one called out, "pretty, isn't she?"

"Yes sir, in fact she's very beautiful," answered Manuel, surprised he could even speak, let alone carry on a sensible conversation as he stood trapped between the two old men.

"Haven't seen her by any chance in the past few days, have you?" one of the seniors asked as he placed his bundle of posters onto the seat and tossed his hammer and other tools and tape on the floor.

"No sir, I haven't, and I would certainly remember someone as lovely as her, believe me. Why do you ask?" He was surprised at his exterior calm as compared to the inner shock and cold terror he felt, standing there fully exposed in the sunny street of the small town.

The one still holding his tools answered, "She's missing; no one has seen her for several days so we're here to find her."

"Well, I certainly hope you're successful. Is there anything I can do to help?"

"Sure. Take one of these and put it up at your place, and call the number on it right away if you spot her or know anything else that may help. That number on it is a direct line to the Police Commissioner's office." And he handed Manuel one of the posters.

"Thank you. I certainly will call if I hear anything or see the young lady, believe me, I will." And he put the poster under his arm as he turned away from the two elderly gentlemen who had closed the rear door and were now climbing into the front seats.

The Cuban's heart was pounding like the drums of the street entertainers in Old Havana as he forced himself to walk calmly and slowly away from the car. As it passed, the driver gave a little toot of his horn and Manuel raised one arm laden with grocery bags in salute. Not until it disappeared over the new bridge did he seem able to breath. Still, he walked calmly toward the bridge, not picking up the pace until just before the span when he turned to his right onto the road out of town.

Manuel had to think, to assess this new development and plan his next move, but he knew his first priority was to calm down, relax and get control of his emotions. Slipping into the bush well after passing the last house on the road, he found a spot out of sight where he could just stand and worry.

At the same time, as the sign crew maneuvered their car through the curves of the road south of Birch Grove, the driver commented to his passenger, "That guy had a strange accent, don't you think?"

"I don't know, maybe a little stilted, almost formal, I'd say. Probably one of those spoiled, wealthy, well-educated Latinos, up here from some South American country squandering his family's money," the man sitting beside him said casually as he searched the roadside for another place to slap up a poster.

Chapter Twelve

Day Three: Late Afternoon

Cursing the mud and brush, Manuel slowly clawed his way up from the village, at times on hands and knees, desperately trying to get back to his hideaway in the hills. He had missed his machete mark on a large tree at the bottom and now wasn't sure he was climbing in the proper direction. Every few moments he would stop and check his bearings, turning around, trying to recognize familiar places or tree groupings. The posters had him rattled, had broken his train of thought, and altered everything.

He had dropped the poster early in his climb but the plastic bags of provisions, including the shirt for his captive made the job very difficult, acting like anchors holding him back. This was not how he had planned things and he couldn't help but think how his mother would be appalled at his foul language as he slid, slipped and fought his way up the steep hillside.

The poster had unnerved him. He was shaking, feeling physically ill, almost in a state of panic. His mind raced, sorting things out and trying to reset priorities. He needed to succeed but he knew deep down, with each step back up to his tiny cabins, that he may have failed. The possibility was alien to him, a scenario he had never given a moment's thought because his cause was just. There was no need to consider what to do if his efforts were unsuccessful and no need for an exit strategy. Now, if he didn't adjust his plan, he'd never be able to extract the revenge he had dreamed about for these past twenty-five years.

Manuel was depressed almost to the point of tears. Worries whirled in his head about his future, his mother's future, and that of his two dear siblings. As he slowly worked his way up through the dense underbrush, he worried also about how his government and fellow Cubans would view his failure. He would be returned home not as a hero waving high above his head an apology from the hated Americans, but with hands bound, a captured, failed, kidnapper, hunted down like an animal in the mountains of Grenada.

He stopped, sweating, and once more checked his bearings, worried also of his other major concern; the young lady, whose pretty face with its dazzling smile was now on posters most likely spread across the island, calling on people to find her. Something would have to be done about her, up there near the top of these hills, tied to her shack with a stout piece of cord. He would have to make some very important decisions about Miss Bad Manners very soon and they might have to be unpleasant. Manuel was again almost sick with fear and panic, wondering if he could ever make those decisions.

Manuel Ruiz wasn't a bad man, just a misguided one. Misguided by a blind faith in his government's propaganda, by a belief in the anti-American ranting of his country's leaders, and by a lifetime of stories from his own family.

His mother, whom he remembered crying quietly in her room late at night, spoke little of the passing of Manuel's father. She simply said he was a very brave man who valiantly died serving his country on an island far from home.

His father's brother, a large man whom Manuel respected and feared, claimed many times, usually after a large amount of rum, that it was the hated and bloodthirsty Americans who were responsible for his beloved brother's death. He would stand in the middle of the room, ranting on about jackbooted American troops, roaring about them goose-stepping across a tiny island; an island of innocents being helped by freedom loving Cuban patriots working to bring modern socialism to its downtrodden and exploited people. Everyone present would stand and loudly shout agreement, spitting into the dust of the dirt floor of their home, cursing the hated enemy.

Manuel believed every word and his loathing and hatred of all those responsible for his father's death festered inside him over the years, his uncle's ravings authenticated by government leaders who said basically the same things in speeches on the radio as well as in newspaper articles.

His plan was born during the evening of his sixteenth birthday when all his family gathered at his home where the beer ran plentiful and the rum flowed like water. As the celebration progressed into the night, the levity was tainted by the sadness that the birthday boy's father was not there for such a great day. The sadness slowly turned into anger as the rum continued to flow and the stories became more frenzied. Verbal rampages raged throughout the gathering against the great Satan sitting fat and rotten just ninety miles to the north across the Straits of Florida. Led by Manuel's hulking brute of an uncle, the rant against the U.S. soared to a peak when he stood, towering over all, swaying, a drink in hand, demanding who in their family would, or could, restore the honor ripped away by those bastards to the north. No one answered, especially not the bellicose speechmaker.

Manuel soaked it all up. He thought, standing there in that house, now sixteen and a man, that he could right this great wrong. He could restore honor to his family, and he would.

At night he would lie in the dark, sometimes with the soft sound of his mother's crying drifting through the curtain separating their beds, and he would plot his revenge. Plan after plan was concocted, mulled over, and then discarded, mainly because of one basic flaw common to them all. He could not speak the language of his enemy and that was a disadvantage far too great to ignore. If he was going to achieve his dream, he must learn English. Once he understood this, he set aside all plotting and schemes of vengeance, and set about figuring out how he could learn to speak English, a language no one could speak in his village of Isabela de Sagua.

Manuel's village was so small, news of the young man's desire to learn another tongue spread to every corner in less than two days. An older man, one who traveled often to buy materials for many of the local farmers, heard of Manuel's search and came around to his home to pass on something he heard in his travels.

Over coffee, he told the boy that in Santa Clara, a very large city many miles to the southwest, a local hotel received permission from the central Government in Havana to install a huge special television satellite dish antenna on its roof. The hotel was allowed to pick up the BBC foreign broadcasts from London, two Chinese news and culture stations in Spanish and English as well as the Havana based stations. The old man suggested Manuel might want to investigate the possibilities of looking for work in a place with English television. The young boy agreed, knowing he had to go there.

Now sixteen and considered a man, he told his mother he was taking a few days off from his work in the sugar fields so he could go to Santa Clara on very important business. Treating him as the man of the house should be treated, she offered to pack some food and wished him a safe journey. She walked with him to the roadway in front of their home and looked up with a tear in her eye. Standing on her toes, she kissed his cheek and wished him well. As she did so, she slipped one hundred pesos into his hand. Mothers are the same in any country, in any language, all over the world.

The trip to Santa Clara was an adventure in itself. Manuel had never spent a night away from home and never traveled more than ten kilometers from his village. Now he found himself in the back of a beat up pick-up truck, or wedged between members of a family and their chickens in their rickety old car bouncing down the road. To save money, he hitched rides, as many Cubans did, and although he sometimes had to wait hours for a lift, the people he met were always pleasant, generous and very accommodating. One family took him home to lunch and when finished, the father drove him back to the main road to continue his trek. It was a good coming of age trip for a young man.

Santa Clara was a shock. Manuel came from a village of much less than two hundred people and no building was more than one story tall. Everyone lived off the land or did something for a living related to the land, like blacksmithing, or farm machinery repair. There was a one room school with one teacher, no medical facility, no gas station, and no post office. He was certainly unprepared for Santa Clara.

The city had paved roads with many rotundas, or traffic circles. It had buildings so tall they required lifting devices called elevators, to get you all the way to the top. Santa Clara even had lights on poles everywhere on the streets that came on in the evening and stayed on all night. It was a revelation.

After wandering the streets asking directions, Manuel found the hotel with the television dish for foreign language stations. For an hour he stood across the street watching patrons push through the front door before getting his nerve up to enter.

He had never been in a hotel. He had never heard of a hotel or what the word meant before this moment. He only knew that a hotel, this hotel, held the answer to his dilemma.

Shyly looking around the lobby, he decided the man behind a large counter was the one to speak with about English Television. He went to him and explained what he needed.

The young boy was devastated to discover the hotel seldom tuned the big television in the bar/restaurant to the BBC or any other English channel because few in town spoke English and very few English-speaking people stayed at the hotel. In fact, the man informed Manuel the only English language people who came to Santa Clara usually just visited for the day to see the 'wrecked train and bulldozer' memorial to Che Guevara commemorating the great victory during the revolution. Even though his father fought in that battle with the great Che, and Manuel had intended to visit the site himself, he was heartbroken, standing in the hotel lobby wondering what he was going to do next.

Crestfallen and fighting back tears, he slowly turned to leave when the manager, a shrewd manipulating exploiter of people, saw an opportunity not to be missed and called the boy back to offer a suggestion.

If Manuel wanted, he could work around the hotel, sweeping, cleaning and doing odd jobs to help other staff during the day. Then he could watch his English channels after the bar closed at eleven. Seeing his hesitation, the manager also offered a small cot in the basement's service room where he could sleep if he wanted. Unfortunately, he said, there could be no pay, but any tips were his to keep. That clinched the deal. The hotel manager got his free laborer, and an elated Manuel got his English television.

The weeks rolled by and Manuel became an invaluable part of the hotel's infrastructure. There was nothing he wouldn't do quickly, happily, and usually better than anyone else. He learned how to operate the elevator, make a bed properly, clean a washroom, and carry several suitcases at a time. Whenever any staff member asked for his help, Manuel would smile, say 'Si', and get to work. Soon everyone loved the young man.

By the end of the second week, he had also learned that running small errands for hotel guests meant getting tips, sometimes as much as five pesos for only one small service. It was wonderful. At the end of the third week, he carried all of the hotel's mail and several guests' postcards and letters to the post office. Included in the bundle he proudly carried was his own letter to his mother, his first ever, explaining what he was doing. It contained a crisp, clean, twenty peso bill for her, to help with household expenses. It was a new bill and was carefully placed within the note.

Within two years, Manuel moved from his unpaid job in Santa Clara to a large hotel on Varadero Beach where his growing skills in English were an asset no hotelier could overlook. He got a job in the hotel's main restaurant, was paid a regular salary, and made much more in tips than he ever did in Santa Clara. As before, he was ever helpful, always cheerful, and never stopped looking for ways to learn English. He read anything and everything in English he could get his hands on. Soon the prettiest young girls in the complex were shyly bringing him English magazines and pocket books the guests had left behind.

Manuel grew adept at sidestepping the advances of those seeking a handsome well-paid husband, as he accepted with a smile the many books left mostly by Canadians and Brits. And as always, each week a letter went home to his mother with at least twenty pesos, sometimes even fifty.

His last move was to Havana after he wrote a letter of application in both Spanish and English to the Ambos Mundos Hotel in the heart of the old city. His letter so impressed the manager that he took the time to drive down the coast road to Varadero, spend an hour interviewing the young man, then hiring him on the spot.

Two weeks later, Manuel was working in the hotel that Ernest Hemingway had called home for over seven years. This master of the English language had stood at his typewriter and written 'Death in the Afternoon' and part of 'The Old Man and The Sea' high in a corner room, where he could look out onto the busy street below. This was a great attraction and large numbers of English-speaking tourists constantly visited just to stand where the great writer had once stood. The hotel's management preserved Hemingway's room just as the writer had left it after moving out to get married and charged a small fee per visit to the hordes of tourists who were drawn to 'El Papas' place.

Manuel refined his language skills so well during this time he would be occasionally taken for a Canadian because of his soft eloquence, and he was often heard saying 'eh' in his speech, a habit he had picked up while working in Varadero.

He loved the old hotel and decided this would be where he finished his education in English. One heard the language in the hotel all the time, especially throughout the lobby, in the rickety old iron elevator and around the bar when the grand piano wasn't being played. It was the perfect place for a student of English to finish his education.

Manuel was now in his late twenties, fluently bilingual, hard working and leading a frugal and solitary life. His diet consisted mostly of black beans and rice, oatmeal, and what he could scrounge from the hotel's kitchen.

He didn't smoke and seldom touched alcohol, unlike many of his co-workers. He also kept away from the many very friendly young ladies who strolled along the streets amid the tourists. They would call to him with coy smiles when he made his way to his small apartment after each shift but Manuel just politely ignored them.

These habits, or lack of bad habits, enabled him to save much of the money he earned, sending it home with the weekly cash for his mother. Often, this extra cash was in Euros, British Pounds, Canadian dollars, and even the green dollars of his enemies, the hated Americans.

This horde of currencies grew steadily. During a recent trip home to visit his mother, he pulled a small wooden box his father used for family treasures from behind a large wardrobe. In it, along with some family papers, two old photos and a medal given to his father by the great leader himself, was Manuel's stash. He had managed to sock away the equivalent of over seven hundred US dollars in five different currencies.

It was at that point, while counting his cash, that he decided he had overcome two of his problems; language and finances. The third problem was a plan. It was now time to devise his plan and put it into action.

Manuel shook his head and came back to the present. Nothing could be gained by sitting in the rain on a Grenadian mountainside, reliving the past and feeling remorse.

His main job was to get back to the clearing, prepare a meal for his captive and himself and start working on a solution to his dilemma. He stood, picked up the plastic grocery bags and moved slowly to his right, climbing steeply upwards along a break in the bushes. He moved carefully, aware of the slippery mud underfoot and the drop on his left that seemed to be getting steeper and deeper with each step. His progress was slow. Often, he was forced to move both bags into his left hand as he needed his right for grabbing hold of branches or vines to help him up.

Half an hour later, he was two hundred feet further up the trail, lugging both bags in his left hand again. The going was slow and the footing treacherous but he knew he was only a few hundred yards from the level area not far from the clearing. He was almost there.

Stopping for a moment to catch his breath, Manuel looked down into the gorge on his left and shuddered at how deep it was and how many treetops he could see. He thought this would be the last time he would use this route.

Eager to finish, he seized a vine to help him over a rough spot and felt it pull loose just as a large rock beneath his feet moved, slipped away, and silently disappeared over the edge. Manuel knew he was following it.

He wasn't afraid. As he fell from the path and sailed out into space, he was more overwhelmed by sadness. He had failed.

The first pain came when he crashed through the tree tops well below the edge. That didn't last long. Suddenly, his head hit something hard and everything flashed from bright red to black. Then there was nothing.

Chapter Thirteen

Day Three: Early Evening.

Edith wheeled out of the hotel's driveway onto the main thoroughfare to the airport as though she had done it a hundred times. At least, that's the way it felt as once more she made her way through the early evening traffic.

She smiled as she thought of how LJ continuously teased her about her driving on the wrong side but he had to admit, with badly hidden pride, that the rental car was indeed surviving. It had no dents, scratches or other damage resulting from her many trips to pick up new arrivals, and the wiper switch and directional lever were still working.

This journey was to pick up Alice Lusinski, Fred's wife and their still much-loved former daughter-in-law, Irene.

Nick was concerned about Fred's health and wanted Alice present to keep an eye on him and Irene said she was coming as well. Besides, they all figured it would be cheaper to fly Alice in to be with Fred at the hotel before long distance fees bankrupted everyone. Nick said the flights would cost less than the phone calls between Florida and Grenada and LJ joked that he'd heard a loud groan from the phone company when word got out that Alice was heading to the island to help.

Parking was a breeze for Edith now, as she wheeled between the rows of cars searching for a spot. She thought she should ask for a name plate on the fence for her personal slot, given the number of times she was there. Maybe the fact all the staff knew her by now, waving cheerily in greeting as she strode into arrivals, made up for the lack of her own private parking spot.

"Hey, over here," Edith hollered as loud as she could as the two women exited the immigration area. They had come through the swinging doors together, both looking a little haggard from their trip. Alice, somewhat into her sixties and well dressed for the heat reached just to the shoulder of her former daughter-in-law.

Irene Lusinski, in her forties, would stand out and attract attention walking through Reagan International in D.C. Here she caused people to stare.

Tall, regal even, Irene walked out through the throng of the airport much the same way as a Princess would exit Windsor Castle. The chaos of a Caribbean airport had no effect on her as she reached out to take Edith's hand, smiling warmly.

"How was the flight?"

"Which one? The first, second, or third." Irene laughed from beneath her mildly disheveled three hundred dollar hairdo.

Edith laughed. "Come on. I think you both need a good stiff drink and if you don't now, you will after you've seen my driving," and she grabbed one of their bags and herded the two travelers toward the parking lot.

Alice was quiet and serious as they left the lot and said almost nothing until they were well on their way toward the hotel.

"Have you heard anything Edith?" She asked quietly and calmly as the car roared around a traffic circle and shot down hill toward a shopping plaza.

"No. It's as though she's gone up in a puff of smoke. The police have been great and there are lots of good signs she's being held somewhere and doing fine but as to finding where she's sitting at this moment, we're not much further ahead now than when we started." Edith spoke slowly as she worked her way around another traffic circle and then stomped the gas as they hurtled down toward the water, her passengers holding their breath and checking their seatbelts to make sure they were secure.

Irene called from the backseat during a brief break in her terror "Have you heard from my good old, not-so-reliable ex-husband?"

"Not a peep. We don't know where he's staying or what he's doing."

"Just as well," Irene sighed. "He'd just be his usual obnoxious self and get in everybody's way."

"Now, now Irene," Alice the peacemaker soothed, "he's just as worried as you and I'm sure he's trying his best to find Rachel. Just try to remember that when you see him, and be nice. After all, it has been only twenty some years since you and he made the girl and I know you have good taste so he couldn't have been all that bad. Try and be nice when you meet Anthony. This is a hard time for him too, you know."

"I'll be nice, I promise. And no, he's not all that bad and yes, I know he's worried. I'll make you proud of me, mother."

This seemed to satisfy Alice and she sat back, relaxing a little, possibly a little less afraid of dying in a flaming car crash on a Grenadian back road.

Closing her eyes, Alice mused on how Irene, her ex-daughter-in-law was more of a daughter than Anthony was a son. On their very first meeting, Alice jokingly asked if the beautiful young girl hanging onto her son's arm knew what she was getting into. Irene had shot back that she'd call her for instructions any time Anthony became too much to handle. They were fast friends from that moment.

Now, almost twenty-five years later, Alice talked to her ex-daughter-in-law far more often than she talked to her son and felt much closer to her. During the difficult time of their divorce, there had been times when Alice

92

could have used a whip on her son for being so stupid. When she found out the details, she'd have gladly traded the whip for a baseball bat.

Anthony had had a great job in a large company where a sweet young thing in his office, not much older than Rachel, decided he needed to spice up his life with a younger woman. She worked on him and as the old saying goes, 'familiarity breeds consent'. He didn't stand a chance.

Eventually, Irene found out and politely told him either the mistress had to go or she would. Like the dummy he was, he moved out of the house and into his girlfriend's apartment. Because there was no contest, the decree absolute was issued nine months later. The romance with the youngster lasted another three months.

Alice refused to speak to her son for a year after the divorce and only relented after Rachel begged, nagged and threatened not to come for her annual summer visit if she didn't talk to her dad. Alice spoke to him, although their conversations were still somewhat reserved.

Now safely stopped in the hotel's parking lot, Alice jumped from the car, opened the rear door for Irene, and waited while she stepped out. Standing erect, Irene was surprised when Alice stood on her tiptoes and kissed her on the cheek, whispering, "I know you'll be nice dear. That's your way and I'm so pleased you've passed it on to my granddaughter. Thank you".

Chapter Fourteen

Day Three: Evening

LJ, Harry and Nick knew time was running out. All three were aware of articles over the years quoting police officers saying the first three or four days represented the best time in the life of a missing person search. After that, what the authorities were doing was no longer a search and rescue operation, but a victim recovery effort. They all knew they were fast approaching that point.

"OK guys, what do we have?" asked Nick.

Ed Fisher entered the room and he didn't look any less dejected than LJ and Harry. They all hated going to a meeting where the only news was bad.

"I hate to say it Nick, but it's not looking good," LJ was the first to speak. "Ed's done a super job getting the signs up all over the place. Hell, you can't move without seeing one. I spoke to a Constable two hours ago and they're thrilled by them, but from what I heard from the same cop, there has been no action from them at all," and he turned to Ed and gave him a light punch on the shoulder.

"How about you, Harry, heard anything yet?"

"Not a peep. All day we've had teams going into every bar and restaurant in town with pictures but can't come up with even the slightest sniff. It's as though she just vanished from the earth in a puff of smoke." Harry was very unhappy.

"How's Fred taking all this?" Nick asked all of them.

It was Ed's turn to jump in. "I'm worried about him. You know he has a bad ticker and has to take pills all day long, so I've informed everyone to nag him to make sure he does. I also gave them a list of hospitals and clinics throughout the island and their phone numbers, plus numbers for ambulances and EMO units, just in case. There's no way we can slow him down or get him to take it easy so I figure plan B is get ready if he has a problem. Hell, I think half the posters we've put up on this island were done by him." He glanced at his notebook, jotted something in it and turned back to his friends.

"Now that his wife Alice is in with Rachel's mom Irene, they may be able to slow him down. We should grab both and make sure they stick close and keep tabs on his pill taking.

"I'll print up a bunch of copies of the medical list and get one to each member of the gang. I doubt anyone will have any use for it but you never know."

"Good idea, and make sure all the wives get their copy. You know how guys are about things medical." Nick drew a line through an item on his list and looked to the three men in front of him.

"Well, here's what I've found out and it doesn't make for good reading," and he flicked to a new page in his notebook. "The police have run up against a brick wall. This is a small island with about a hundred thousand people on it, that's just a couple thousand less than Sarasota and Bradenton combined. Believe me, there's little that goes on that the local police don't know about.

"They know every lowlife, bad dude and wannabe bad dude in every nook and cranny of this land. I'm told they've questioned over two hundred people not presently being held in custody and drew a blank. They've even discussed it with some of the prisoners in their jails in case they might have heard something and again, nothing, absolutely nothing."

Nick turned a page in his book and continued "They gave me a list of all the criminal acts investigated everywhere on the island in the days leading up to her disappearance and there appears to be no connection with any of them. A house was broken into in St. George's around midnight before she went missing but they have the guy and the cop said he wouldn't have the brains to kidnap a fence post.

"The back door of a rum shop was kicked in and some booze stolen up in Victoria, a town way north of here on the coast. The cops are pretty sure they know who did it and they're waiting for him to come out of the bush for fresh stock. It would be too much trouble to go after him and this is not the first time it's happened. He's the north island drunk; old, harmless and too far away to be involved.

"The only other thing to occur was a rental car being stolen from the airport but it was discovered the next day, out of gas, near a little village south of Grenville, let me see," and once again Nick went to his notes. "Ah, here it is. The village is called La Digue, I'm not even sure I'm pronouncing it right. Again, it's a common occurrence. These car thefts are usually done by someone employed at the airport with no bus fare who is heading home after work. They check the rental parking area for anything with keys, drive close to home and park it, knowing someone will pick it up in a day or two. It isn't like they have a big crime problem in this country." Nick snapped his notebook shut.

"We may have to accept the possibility she ran into a problem in the water that no one saw. You know, a shark or manta or cramps, and got herself washed out to sea. When you look at all the work that's been done, it may be the final conclusion we're stuck with." He stood, tired, depressed, and ready for some sleep.

"The hell with that," said LJ, standing and gathering his papers. "I don't believe she was ever in the water because no one in a bathing suit ever swims wearing shorts and sandals with a backpack slung over their shoulders. Those items were never found so she sure as hell didn't leave them lying around. I know damn well she's alive and needs us and I'm sure as hell not ready to throw in the towel yet. Let's get a good night's sleep and meet back here at six to plot our next move. All agreed?"

Three tired faces looked up at him and all shot back a firm 'agreed'. Standing, they all left the meeting in silence, each lost in thought on how to solve their problem.

Chapter Fifteen

Day Three: Close to Midnight

To say Rachel was concerned would be a gross understatement. She was very close to outright panic. Every little sound, every rustling leaf, every bird squawk or tree frog's croak made her jump nervously to look about, trying to see something.

She had been sitting on a stool outside her sleeping shack for hours waiting for Manuel to return. A great cloud mass blotted out any light from the stars and, with no moon that night, it was like sitting in a coal mine. In fact, it was so dark, her hand disappeared when she held her arm straight out in front of her. It had been like this for hours and she was afraid to move. Rachel was scared, hungry, angry and scared some more.

"Where the hell is that damned Cuban twit?" she yelled into the darkness, wishing she had a bowl of his rotten oatmeal in her hands. She was so hungry she probably would have thanked him for it with a pleasant grin.

Manuel had left early, to get some needed provisions he said, and told her it might take him several hours to get back. He left her two oranges and a full bottle of water for her lunch and discreetly placed an old bucket at the side of her shack not far from where she had bathed. No words were necessary to spell out the reason for it being there.

Stuffing some Eastern Caribbean Dollars into his pocket, he crossed the small clearing and started down the path, calling out a goodbye to her. Rachel answered in her normal manner.

"Just bring back some decent food, for Christ's sake," she shouted, watching his back stiffen and his step hesitate a little. She smiled; glad she could still hit a nerve and unsettle him when she wanted.

Manuel didn't turn nor throw back a retort and, within seconds, the sounds of his trek down the trail faded to nothing and Rachel was alone, tied to the shack with a rope just long enough for her to move about, but short enough to keep her within twenty feet of it at all times.

It was her first time alone for more than a few minutes since her kidnapping and she thought it would be a good time to check out the place without Manuel's dark eyes following her every move.

She could reach the cooking pit with the smoldering remnants of the morning fire but the pile of twigs and wood was beside his shack, well beyond her reach. It didn't matter. The sun was already high and hot, suggesting another scorcher, and a fire was the last thing she needed. He would relight it when he got back from shopping, hopefully to cook something other than his damned oatmeal.

She carefully explored all four sides of her shack, inside and out, getting down on her hands and knees several times to have a look underneath. There sure wasn't much to see. Made of rough hewn floor planks, thin side boards and a centre peaked corrugated roof she could see through in several spots, she knew her shack was certainly not the Grenada Plaza. After completing the inspection, all she could think of was how wet she was bound to get if any kind of rain storm blew in, whether she was inside, or out.

The hours dragged slowly by and when the sun had slipped past its peak she ate her two oranges and drank most of her water. She was bored, having nothing to read, nor paper to write on. Mischievously she took a piece of charcoal from the fire pit and with a grin, whimsically marked the door of her hut with large black letters--RACHEL'S MANSION. This done, and being unable to find any other trouble to get into, she adjourned to her mansion, climbed into her hammock, and was soon fast asleep.

The sound of light rain tapping on the metal roof penetrated Rachel's sleep and she was soon standing at her doorway, wondering how bad the rainfall might be. Happily, it was only one large dark cloud and seemed to be almost past so she stepped out into the clearing to stretch and see what Manuel was up to. She figured from what sunshine she could see beyond the large cloud it must be about six o'clock and she looked around for her captor. There was no new fire in the pit, just a tiny wisp of smoke rising from the damp ashes, fighting against what little rain had fallen. The place was eerily silent.

"Manuel, you crazy Cuban, where the heck are you?" she called many times. The only reply she got was a whispering from the palms as the gentle breeze moved through them. Several birds high in those trees also answered, telling her she was not really alone. Rachel stood, listening, concerned.

He had said several hours but this was ridiculous. He left long before noon and it was now about six and in a couple of hours it would be dark. Besides, she was getting hungry and her water was almost gone.

Turning toward the path he would use to enter the clearing, she stood, hands on hips, wearing her most fearsome face and hollered out into the bush as loud as she could. "You better get your sorry hide back here and get this fire going and my supper ready, do you hear me, you Latin nincompoop." The only reply was silence and she turned back to her hut, feeling better, but still lonely.

She sat and waited and worried all night long and as the sky began to grow less black and a soft half light slowly spread across the clearing, she could see further and further, confirming what she already knew; no one was there.

What am I going to do, she thought? She was very hungry but knew she could go days, even weeks, without food, but she couldn't go anytime without water. She needed water, and soon. You can't last many days without water and she had none and couldn't get to any. Deep down inside she knew Manuel wasn't coming back.

She had never felt so utterly alone or helpless in her life. Even when her kidnapper accosted her on the road to the seashore and carried her to his car, she believed she would be rescued and reunited with her family and friends. This was different, she knew now that she was in very real trouble.

Rachel sat on her stool for several more minutes letting the fear sweep over her before she shouted 'no' and stood up. There was no bloody way she was going to die chained to a rickety shack in the jungle, so she better start thinking about how she could get herself out of this mess. She was intelligent, well educated and resourceful. As she paced back and forth in the growing light, she knew she could figure something out. She had to come up with a plan.

Chapter Sixteen

Day Four: Six Thirty A.M.

The eight members of the search parties management team plus Irene and Alice Lusinski sat around a large table strewn with coffee pots, mugs, spoons and assorted papers, maps and notebooks. They were in the far corner of the open air dining section of the hotel where hotel staff had blocked off an area with a velvet rope to keep uninvolved tourists out of the way.

For almost half an hour, Nick and LJ led the group through everything they knew or had learned up to this point. To some, like Ed Fisher, the old restaurateur and Harry Stanton, Nick's buddy from Bradenton, it was a rehash of the night before. For the others, most of the information was new or updated.

Nick's wife, Ann, sat on his right with a large notebook, ostensibly to record the meeting but everyone knew Nick depended heavily on her insight and good sense. LJ was on Nick's left and Ed at the head of the table. Harry was at the other end, opposite Ed.

Across from Nick sat Fred Lusinski, the missing girl's grandfather, and tiny Bella Brown, the ninety-some year-old widow who was as tough as nails and bright as a new penny. She asked to be included because, she said, Fred was there for her when her husband died in Phoenix during their last caper, and she was damn well going to be there for him now that he needed help. That settled it because no one was dumb enough to argue with the Sergeant Major, as some secretly called her.

The eighth person at the table was the hotel manager. He had also asked to be let in, suggesting he might be able to offer some advice or insight into the island and its people. He wanted to help and Lord knew they could use all the help they could get.

Nick was finishing off his little presentation, "That's the story folks and we have to decide where we go from here. We've covered the whole island with signs; we've visited just about every watering hole and hang-out in this land and the police have put the collar on every villain they have ever come across. Actually, they have bent over backwards to find Rachel and I don't honestly think we could ask for more.

"The people of Grenada have been superb. We couldn't ask for more co-operation, help, or sympathy, and yet we haven't moved one inch beyond where we were when we first heard from Fred almost four full days ago. We've reached the point where we must put on our thinking caps and try to figure out where we are going. The floor is open for discussion, suggestions, flights of fancy or anything else."

Bella Brown spoke first. "My husband Richard loved reading mysteries and the Sherlock Holmes stories were his favorites. Most of you know that, and he read them all more than once. Whenever he had some problem to solve, he always used a line Holmes used that goes like this 'if you can eliminate the impossible, whatever remains, however improbable, must be the truth.' Maybe we should start eliminating everything we know didn't happen to find out what did happen."

There was a silence around the table as each digested what she had just said. LJ was the first to speak.

"You mean, Bella, if we know she didn't own a boat, or rent one, or borrow or steal one, and none are known to have disappeared, we can eliminate the suggestion she went out in a boat and overturned, or sank or was involved in some other tragedy like that?"

"That's exactly what I mean," Bella said.

"Well, hell, that makes a lot of sense to me," the old warrior said and sat back.

Nick picked it up from there. "OK, Bella seems to have a plan and you're right LJ, it does make sense. Let's go back to the beginning and start all over again." He picked up a pencil and pulled several sheets of paper to him.

"Let's start at where she could be. She's either in the water, on land, or off the island all together." He spread out three sheets of paper in front of him and put a heading at the top of each; the first title WATER, the second, LAND, and the third, GONE. Then he drew a line down the middle of each of the three pages and wrote Pro at the top of the left column and Con at the top of the right one. All eyes were on him as he worked.

"Let's start with the water. If someone was studying marine life, needed to conduct some research before lunch, and walked to the water's edge early in the morning, what would they do?"

"Get in a boat," said LJ.

"We know for sure she didn't do that. She didn't own one. She made no arrangements to rent one, and the Police confirmed there are no boats missing so we know she didn't steal one. What then?" Nick prodded.

LJ said, "OK, so she didn't get in a boat, maybe she waded out or swam out to do her investigations."

Bella Brown jumped back in at this point.

"If she swam out or waded out to do her studies, did she take her backpack with her? I doubt it; and what about her shorts and sandals? If she was going in with shorts on, why wear a tight bathing suit for the walk to the shore, and would she want to walk back in wet sandals? She's a woman, clothes conscious, she's sure not going to get those things wet or damaged if she doesn't have to. She must have left them on shore."

"Wouldn't the police have found the backpack, or her shorts and sandals by now if she'd left them on shore?" Ann asked.

"I would think so," LJ chipped in, knowing how much effort the local Police had put into their investigation. "She would have no reason to hide the stuff. She was just a few yards off shore, out for a couple of hours to study. I would doubt she ever got very far from her bag. You're right, I'm sure the police would have found some of her stuff."

Harry spoke quietly "Well, we know a boat being involved is out so she didn't go down to the shoreline, get into a boat and sail out to sea and disappear. We're also pretty sure she didn't go down to the shoreline and walk out into the water wearing sandals, white shorts, with a backpack slung over her shoulder. I think we're safe in eliminating the water as a place to look for our little lost girl."

Seven heads bobbed up and down while Nick marked the page entitled WATER with a large 'X' and shoved it aside.

"Well Bella," he said, "your idea seems to work. I guess you're not just another pretty face like we all thought."

For a fleeting moment, more than seventy-five years of life gave way to a pretty young smile and sparkling eyes. Some said later they were sure Bella Brown actually blushed.

"What about leaving the island altogether?" Ed asked.

LJ, sitting quietly on Nick's left, leaned forward and flipped open a notebook. Because of his close relationship with the Commissioner of Police, one of LJ's jobs was to work with the authorities on those things the gang of seniors couldn't do, and gather information for the group.

"The Police have questioned every airline and that's a no go. Also, the exit system on this island is so precise it's almost a reverse immigration procedure. The airport officials would know if she did skip. At least she didn't do it through the airport. You can't get to an airplane without going past Grenadian Immigration Officials and they keep very good records." He turned back to his notes for a second and then proceeded with his report.

"Every private aircraft leaving the island since Rachel disappeared has been checked out by the Police. They even went so far as to call the first port of entry the flight plans named, to see if the craft arrived, and if all was as it should be. There is no joy for us in what they found.

"We did have some luck regarding yachts and power boats around the island," LJ continued. "A storm watch was posted on the day she went missing. It extended through the night and into the following day. There was a storm, but it veered south of here, passing much closer to Trinidad, completely missing Grenada. There was some fear it could swing north again so the warning was maintained, keeping almost everything, including ferries to Carriacou and Petit Martinique, in port for a couple of days. The Police also doubt she could have left by private boat on those days. I think we can eliminate her leaving the island." He closed his notebook.

"Could she have been spirited away out of some small port quietly, on a boat not known or detected?" Harry asked.

The hotel manager raised his hand here, indicating a desire to contribute.

"Please!" was all Nick said, offering him their attention.

"I started in the hospitality business as a galley hand on an old inter-island freighter almost thirty years ago although I know I look too young for that." His deep voice made listening a pleasure.

"After several years, I moved to a restaurant kitchen on the waterfront of St. George's, then to a hotel and slowly worked my way up to this," he waved his hand about him proudly presenting the largest tourist resort on Grenada. He had every right to be proud.

"This is a small island and I swear, everyone on it is related in some way to everyone else. They know what's going on and if they think anything will hurt their homeland, they will make a big stink about it, you can be sure of that. I can tell you the people of Grenada are deeply concerned about this missing girl. It's not just that many are thinking it could hurt our tourist industry; they're very upset because something like this should not happen here at all.

"A cousin of mine called to say CNN and a Canadian broadcaster, I think CTV, he said, called the Best Western just next door to see if there were any rooms available. My cousin's sister-in-law works at the Best Western and I don't think those TV people are coming down for our jerk chicken festival."

"Hell, that's all we need," LJ said "a gang of bloody reporters with mikes and cameras wandering about getting in the way."

The manager nodded in agreement, "Anyway, about boats, and slipping off the island. It happens all the time but please believe me, it never happens without someone knowing about it. Whether it's the people who sell the fuel, or the ones who supply provisions or the repair shops all along our coast; someone knows.

"In a lot of cases, those who know have no interest and don't care. In some cases, those who know have a vested interest and it's better to say nothing. None of that applies here. If someone knew of a ship slipping out after all the publicity, and all your posters, the

Police would have received an envelope over the transom or an anonymous phone call.

"Besides," he said in closing, "if by chance a ship did slip away, our shore patrols are amongst the best equipped in the Caribbean. Our friends, the Americans, have seen to that with training, equipment, and several high speed patrol boats. It would be hard to get away undetected." The manager sat back, hoping he had helped.

"Well," Nick sighed, "after a report like that I think we can all agree we can eliminate Rachel leaving or being taken off the island against her will."

For the second time that morning, seven heads bobbed up and down as Nick put a big 'X' on the sheet marked 'GONE'.

"Then she's still on the island and we better devise a plan to find her. I'm open to any and all suggestions." And he looked around the table.

Bella spoke up again. "I think we're safe in assuming she has disappeared against her will. Nothing in her background, style, manner or temperament suggests this is a voluntary thing. Someone kidnapped her." All at the table hung on her every word.

"I also believe the kidnapping was carefully planned," the ninety year old said.

"Why would you say that, Bella?" Harry asked.

"If it had been an impulsive thing done by some young drunk who had the hots for a good looking blonde in tight shorts, it would have happened closer to the time young drunks get drunk. This happened at eight or nine in the morning when young drunks are snoring somewhere or nursing a raging hangover. Now, old drunks may be out early, but they're not interested in sweet young things prancing down the road. Old drunks are just interested in where their next drink is coming from.

"I believe she was kidnapped by someone who carefully planned the crime, knew who his victim was, and was stone sober when he did it." Bella Brown sat back waiting for some reaction.

Ed called from his end of the table, "How the heck would you know all this about young drunks and old drunks and kidnappings, Bella?"

The old lady smiled sadly. "I told you how my husband loved mysteries but I never mentioned so do I. I read everything he read and, many times, over a glass of sherry, we discussed the nuances and intricate details of one murder story or another. I miss those times with him but I still keep up my part and read every mystery I can get my hands on.

"And I'll tell you something. You can pack in a lot of learning from the likes of Agatha Christie or Dick Francis or Tony Hillerman or Arthur Conan Doyle during eighty years of reading."

"I'll be damned," muttered LJ beside Nick.

"So will I" Nick whispered back with a grin.

"OK," said Nick "she was kidnapped and it was planned. Now let's all pretend we're the kidnappers and try to figure out how we would do it and most importantly, what would we do with her once we had hold of her?"

For the next half hour, the oddly mixed group of ten tossed ideas back and forth. There was some argument over details, but also some laughter over a comment or two tossed on the table either in jest or seriously. Bella Brown received more than her share of attention and her respect level around the table went up with each contribution she made.

By eight A.M. a consensus was formed and work started on an action plan for a physical search of part of the island. LJ was assigned to Police Headquarters to present the groups premise and to enlist the aid of the locals in concentrating on their search plan.

Ed's job as sign manager was finished so Nick asked him to set up the search party program and put together several teams to start later in the day.

Bella was asked to organize the women into a support auxiliary to shuttle food, materials and people between the hotel and the search area.

"OK," Nick said as everyone prepared to adjourn to a quick breakfast before getting to work. "This is the start of the fifth day Rachel has been missing. We're nearing the time to really start worrying so of all things, time is of the essence. We need everyone working on this."

He then turned to the hotel manager. "We need bodies to search the bush, young ones preferably because not all of us are capable of doing that part of the job. We'll hire vans, we'll provide drivers, we'll feed them, but we need bodies this afternoon to get out and start searching an area. Can you help us?"

"I'll provide a team of five of my staff and one of the hotel's vehicles. They'll be at the front, ready to go at noon."

Bella, sitting beside him, placed her tiny, ancient white hand on his great black forearm and smiled up at him, saying "You're a good man, Mr. Roy, thank you."

It was a splendid way to end the meeting.

Chapter Seventeen

Day Four: Eight A.M.

Anne Baxter reached to her left and poked her husband Peter discreetly but firmly in the ribs as a tall elderly man strode by their table toward the breakfast buffet. It was his second trip to refill his plate during the couple's meal and each time the old fellow passed, Anne's eyes followed him, tracking his every move.

"He's the one," she said quietly. "He's the leader. For the past few days, he's been directing people all over this place like a general arranging his troops on a battlefield. Haven't you noticed all those serious looking old folk who keep coming up to him asking questions, getting instructions and exchanging papers?"

"You mean the Marlboro Man's grandfather?" Peter grinned at his wife.

"Be serious hon, I'm not kidding. Something unusual is going on around here and that old guy is right in the middle of it. I think he has something to do with that girl who disappeared," as she discreetly pointed toward LJ with her fork. "If you don't find out what's happening in this place, I'm just going to march up to him and ask."

"I promise," Peter chuckled between mouthfuls of bacon and syrup soaked pancakes. "I'll go to the front desk and make some inquiries, OK?"

"OK, but do it right after breakfast, please?" and she gave him her sweetest smile, knowing he couldn't resist that.

Peter laughed. He and Anne had been relaxing at the hotel for two days now, oblivious to the outside world, but he was beginning to see signs of how all the serenity and peacefulness was starting to make her just a little bit crazy. Anne was an 'A' type lady from the golden horseshoe of Ontario and all the peace and relaxation was getting on her nerves. She was an action girl, one who got involved, did things, helped charities. Anne was a go to girl when problems needed solving. She was not one to sit in the sun and vegetate for more than twenty minutes. Peter on the other hand could vegetate for twenty days and he loved the place.

Grenada was far from his high octane life; made up mostly of jetting around the world overseeing the installation of his award winning kitchens and bathrooms in the homes of people with far too much money. The island was so different it took him a full two days to even start winding down. Now, though, he was in cruise mode, relaxing his way through the first half of James Clavell's 'Shogun' and looking forward to the other half.

Anne, a bundle of energy, was another matter. Easily bored, she already felt a bit edgy and was now spending way too much time checking out what others were doing at the resort. She had walked every square inch of the place at least twice. She knew where the laundry was, how often the grass was cut, and how many pounds of chlorine the pools used each week. She had visited the gift shop so often she knew the price of each item and how many were in stock. He husband half expected her to be offered a job and put on the payroll before their vacation was up. The place was a little too quiet for Anne.

Their holiday was a twenty-fifth anniversary gift from their son Mathew and daughter Mackenzie who thought a week on a romantic tropical island would be just the thing to add a little zip to the lives of their ancient parents. Mathew had even laughingly told his father the trip might inject some spice into their old humdrum life. That's why he had picked the spice island.

Well yuk yuk. Peter didn't feel old, having just passed the half century mark a year or two before, and his life sure as hell wasn't humdrum. He also didn't think his son was all that damn funny.

Then again, these past couple of days had been kind of nice. Anne, his beautiful blonde wife for those twenty-five years, did look pretty darn good under the palms with a hibiscus bloom behind her ear. He also liked the new black one-piece bathing suit she bought just before they left. He noticed it tended to turn a few heads here at the hotel whenever she strolled by.

He also liked the way her Canadian whiteness was rapidly turning to a rich warm Caribbean brown and how the fine lines around the eyes of this working mother had all but disappeared. She looked younger each morning when she rose. Maybe his smart assed son knew what he was talking about.

As Peter sat eating and musing on the quality of his son's weird thought process, Anne stood for a return trip to the buffet.

"Want anything, hon?" she asked, and when Peter shook his head 'no' she turned and made her way through the tables to the fruit and dessert buffet. As she moved across the restaurant floor, blonde hair gently touched and moved off her shoulders by the Caribbean breeze, Peter noticed men's heads turning and eyes following her. Smiling, he turned back to his plate, silently thinking 'eat your heart out, fellows.'

Anne was piling small pieces of pineapple beside long slices of papaya already on her plate while absentmindedly humming a tune from South Pacific when she bumped into a tall elderly gentleman spooning peach halves onto his plate.

"Excuse me," he said, looking down with smiling eyes set in an old weather-beaten face. "I should be more careful," he said.

Anne looked up into that face and saw the man who twice passed her table that morning and whom her husband called the Marlboro Man's grandfather. She instantly loved what she saw. He was tall, maybe six three or four, fit and well built, possessing a quiet sadness in eyes that could still twinkle when he smiled. With one look, Anne knew it was a good face.

"No, no, it was my fault," she smiled. "I was busy deciding what to gorge myself on and not watching what I was doing. I'm sorry."

"Don't be silly, young lady. Bumping into you is the nicest thing that's happened to me since I got here. In fact, I look forward to the next breakfast in the hope it might happen again. Do you think we could arrange it?" His grin and laughing eyes made her feel great.

"Sure," she smiled. "Consider it arranged, on one condition."

"Name it, young lady. Your wish is my command," and he snapped to attention and bowed at the waist.

Anne took a deep breath and decided, what the hell, why not, and jumped in. "Well, kind sir," she said with mock sternness, "if what you say is true, maybe I could command you to answer a few questions for me."

Keeping the joke going, he again bowed at the waist and told her to ask away.

"I couldn't help noticing you, sir, and your many friends in the hotel, and I don't think you're just plain ordinary tourists. It seems as though you may be here out of necessity. If you tell me who you are, why you're here, and what you're up to, I promise, I'll bump into you every morning this week." And she gave him a smile that could melt icebergs, and clinched the deal with a friendly nudge of her shoulder. He was toast.

Captivated, LJ said "I'll tell you what, show me where you're sitting and I'll get my wife and if you like, we'll join you for coffee. I promise I'll give you all the information you want and answer all your questions," and with a wink he strode away to his table. Anne walked back to Peter with a 'cat that ate the canary' look, once again humming the South Pacific tune.

Within minutes, LJ and his wife Edith were standing at Anne and Peter's table. "Hi, I understand you belong to this young lady here," he said, pointing at Anne.

"Yes, I'm guilty as charged. I do belong to her," and waved over a waitress to order a couple more coffees while standing to greet the newcomers.

"She told me we were going to have some guests then smiled her 'I'm so smart smile' before clamming up so please sit down, have a coffee and we'll get to know each other. I'm Peter, she's Anne and it's nice to meet you." Peter stuck out his hand with a wide grin.

"Sorry Peter, she conned me over here. She told me if I didn't do as she said and give her a pile of information, she wouldn't bump into me again. Now you may not realize it, but at my age, you welcome bumps from beautiful young women so I guess I'll do as I'm told". This last made them all laugh as the waitress poured their coffee.

"Well sir, she was nagging me to find out what was going on and I promised to ask at the front desk but she seems to have outfoxed me, as usual," and he reached over and gave her a playful poke in the shoulder. Anne just kept grinning.

"I know the feeling. Wait till you kids have been married as long as Edith and me, nothing will change. She'll still nag you and she'll always outfox you, every time." It was now Edith's turn to poke her spouse in the shoulder but not quite as gently as Peter. They all chuckled as they sipped their coffee and LJ rubbed an imaginary pain in his upper arm. There was a good feeling around the table.

"OK. I made a deal with this young lady and I guess I have to pay up. She wants to know all about our not-so-secret mission on this island." LJ was enjoying this.

"Get on with it," Edith said.

"All right, all right, let me have my fun, will you," LJ said, waving his hands. "I have to make this as dramatic as possible, you know." He turned grinning to Anne and spoke directly to her.

"To answer your first question, we're a bunch of Florida retirees here to help find the missing granddaughter of one of our group. She's a student of marine biology from Canada down here for a few months doing some post graduate research. She went AWOL a couple of days ago and we mean to find her." LJ silently sat and waited for the next question.

"What kind of group or club are you?" she asked.

LJ laughed. "We're actually a motley crew of old fogies who were cheated out of a lot of money just over a year ago. Few of us knew each other before that but now we're as thick as thieves," and he laughed hard here. "When this problem arose with one of the crew, it was just natural for the rest of his friends to saddle up and ride, hopefully, to the rescue."

"Lost a lot of money, eh? I guess you're all bound together by that loss."

"No, what binds us together are the several weeks of planning and effort we put into stealing our money back from the devils who stole it from us in the first place. It was necessary for us to commit larceny to get back our dough and believe me, it was the most fun any of us have had in years." He sat back, arms across his chest, a satisfied grin on his face.

"You guys sound like a pretty good bunch to know," Anne said. "Tell me, in this effort of yours to find the missing granddaughter, is there anything Peter and I can do to help?"

LJ looked at Edith and then turned to Peter. The smiling husband just sat there and gave a shrug of his shoulders. He knew Anne better than anyone and this didn't surprise him at all. Leaning forward, he simply said "Tell her what we can do to help, and we'll do it." Anne reached over and put her hand on his.

LJ checked his watch and then settled in to outline the details for the two new helpers.

He explained who the missing girl was and some of the details about her. He told them how about thirty people, all in their late sixties, seventies and a few somewhat older were at the hotel or on their way. He explained about Nick, the mid-fifties youngster advising them and how he was helping in the planning. He also touched on how helpful Nick had been in getting their money back over a year ago.

LJ then went into the details of the police investigation and how they would be out helping the police look for Rachel while others would help in research, transportation, distribution of information, feeding, cleaning and shopping. Like a grand army of old warriors, each of LJ's dedicated foot soldiers had a specific job to do.

At that moment, a little old lady who looked to be about a hundred and ten purposely approached the foursome at the table and pointedly tapped a large watch on her wrist. "It's about time LJ, we're all ready," and she turned away, briskly walking out of the restaurant.

"OK Bella, we're coming," and he stood while finishing his coffee, saying to all at the table "When Bella Brown speaks, I listen, and jump. If you two want to help, and I must say, we need it, come on and meet the gang," and he strode out across the lawn that spread from the restaurant to an open air thatched roof concrete pad about fifty yards away. Gathered in the shade of the

117

palm roof was a group of the older hotel guests, all members of LJ's small army. Edith, smiling, put down her coffee cup and said 'see you' before following her husband.

Peter looked at Anne with a 'what the hell' expression and rose from the table. He had seen the look in his wife's eyes when LJ was speaking and knew they could, and should help. Taking Anne's hand, the two followed LJ and Edith out of the restaurant onto the grass, wondering what the hell they were getting into. As they stepped onto the lawn, LJ, a dozen yards ahead of them by now, stopped and turned and waved. The old warrior had the feeling this was the start of a beautiful friendship.

Chapter Eighteen

Day Four: Eleven A.M.

The entire area in front of the hotel was a beehive of activity and anyone arriving for a quiet, restful vacation might have had reason to reconsider.

There were at least forty people milling around the multitude of vans, cars, police vehicles and pickups parked all over the place. Under the canopy immediately in front of the hotel was a white Toyota pickup with the hotel's logo on the doors. Two men sat in the cab and another three leaned on its sides, jumping to help or lend a hand where needed.

Behind the hotel pickup was a police car. The two officers were standing to one side looking over some papers handed to them only a few moments before by an ancient grey-haired lady moving about shoving bundles of papers into any hand that appeared empty.

Parked along the driveway that ran toward the street was a mix of rental cars, interspersed with a couple of vans. The parking lot, on the left between the tennis courts and the roadway, had its share of cars as well. This was a formidable force getting ready to head out. People were moving in all directions throughout the area loaded with boxes, bags, blankets and other assorted goods, making it look like the evacuation of a village in the face of pending disaster. Into the midst of all this organized confusion stepped Ed Fisher with a small Boy Scout whistle. He took a deep breath and let go one hell of a blast. Everyone stopped moving.

"Thank you" he hollered. "My wife said this was the only way to get your attention, when she loaned me this whistle. Thanks, hon." And he turned to his wife and made a small bow.

"Now that I have your attention, gather round".

Ed was standing at the hotel's main entrance on the low wall of a raised landscaped area filled with tropical flowers. While he was calling his flock to him, LJ and Harry were setting up a large easel on his right and placing a four foot square map of the island on it. In moments, all had moved in close and the noise had subsided.

"First," Ed said "I want to thank everyone for being here and ready to do some hard work, and believe me, it will be hard.

"You all know why we're here and you know what we want from you, so let's get to the details.

"Now folks, we have decided the most probable area to look for Rachel is in the Parish of St. Andrew, just south and west of Grenada's second city of Grenville."

"Why there?" a male voice from the back of the crowd called out and all turned to see who it was. The question came from a stranger, a man of forty-five or fifty, tall, well-dressed, with movie star good looks.

Not missing a beat, Ed smiled and was about to ask who the speaker was when someone else angrily spoke out.

"Where the hell have you been?" It was Fred Lusinski, and he sure didn't seem to be very happy.

"Looking for my daughter over these past few days, which I would have thought you might be doing instead of hanging out at a resort hotel with this gang of over-the-hill losers," and he swung his hand dismissively toward the crowd between him and the makeshift podium. The dark looks he got from the last comment clearly showed that though the ensemble may be getting on in years, they certainly were not deaf.

Fred, red of face, stepped forward and Ed saw a nasty public father and son battle shaping up. He gave LJ a shove toward Fred and leaned down to Harry, quietly suggesting he go and help LJ calm this down so they could all get back to work. He then turned back to Fred's son and like any good restaurateur dealing with an unhappy customer, put on his best 'I feel your pain' look.

"In answer to your question, if you'll take a look at the map, I'll show the rationale for our decision. A decision, I guarantee, that has been vetted by this country's police and given the green light. So come on up, take a look," and he waited for the girl's belligerent father to make the next move. When he didn't say anything or step toward the front, Ed knew he still had some control of the meeting.

"OK folks, here's the situation. The night before Rachel disappeared, a car was stolen from the rental car parking area at the airport. Cars are often left with keys in the ignition and one going astray for a day or two isn't unusual. It was a small item on the police blotter and became even smaller when they found the vehicle two days later. The car was found out of gas, on a side road in St. Andrew Parish near the little village of La Digue." Ed stopped to see if the loud-mouthed, bad-mannered father was listening and was glad to see he was. He carried on.

"We're convinced this was a planned kidnapping. It wasn't a spur of the moment act by a passionate drunk gone over the edge when he spotted a footloose beautiful blonde. Hell, it happened at seven in the morning when most passionate drunks are sleeping it off. We figure Rachel was the target of one or more people, followed, then whisked away.

"Assuming this was what happened, how could the kidnappers hide her in broad daylight so quickly? How could they move her undetected away from the last place she was seen, unless by car? Secondly, if this was planned, they must have had some obscure place to take her. If you know this island, it better be an obscure place because if it wasn't, some person out there would know about it. So we're sure they had a car and we're sure they drove to an area well out of the way." Ed let this sink in.

Not hearing any comments and seeing LJ and Harry had Fred well under control, he pressed forward.

"The police have checked every car rental on this island for a week before the kidnapping and there's nothing of interest. Just tourists who are still here or have left and can be checked plus a few businessmen who also check out clean. This is a small island with a small population. This stolen rental appears to be the only possible car the kidnappers could have used to move Rachel to some out-of-the-way place. We think they may have been trying to get it back to the airport, or near it. Unfortunately for them, the car ran out of gas and they had to abandon it. We think if there is a place to look for Rachel, it is in the area the car was found."

"How do you know the stolen car was used to transport my daughter?"

"We don't. It's been rented once since they found it so a forensic check would be of little value."

"Then this is just guesswork and you don't know a damn thing for sure," the father shot back.

"Yes, it is guesswork. It's guesswork by a pretty damn sharp group of people with one hell of a lot more years dealing with their fellow humans than you," Ed was beginning to get a little irritated.

"Now, if you have any suggestions based on better assumptions, now is the time to shout them out. Believe me, we'll listen. Otherwise, I would suggest you give us some much needed help, or shut up and get the hell out of the way."

"Listen asshole, who the hell do you think you're talking to?"

"First off, that's Mr. Asshole to you, and I damn well know who I'm talking to. I'm talking to the father of a girl who is missing on this island. And I happen to be trying to co-ordinate an effort by about forty over-the-hill losers who came to this island at their own expense to find her."

No one said a word, and the silence of the crowd seemed to last forever with all present waiting for the next verbal blow. Finally, a soft female voice from Ed's left helped calm everyone down. It belonged to a tall classy-looking lady in her early forties standing with several other women involved in loading the cars. She left her little group and moved through the crowd toward Anthony.

"I hope you all will forgive Anthony and me for being a little uptight about this. We're both distraught over these events concerning our daughter and at times we tend to lash out." Irene Lusinski calmly defused the situation in a very ladylike and disarming way.

Anthony Lusinski stood his ground for several seconds, looking first from Ed to Fred and at last to his ex-wife Irene. The looks must have told him to do as suggested and he turned back to Ed.

"She's right," he said to all of them. "I should be thanking you for all the effort you're putting into finding our daughter, instead of flinging insults around. Please forgive me and tell me if I can help," and he stood quietly, seeking some understanding.

From the sidelines of the group a firm voice called out "well, now that that's settled, lets get on with the job. I'm not getting any younger you know." It was the sergeant major, Bella Brown, and in one swipe she dispelled all tension and caused some laughter. Ed let out a quiet sigh of relief and moved on.

"Good. Now listen up, and refer to the notes and maps Bella handed out over the last many minutes.

"We've drawn on the map a diamond-shaped area with Mount St Catherine as the northern point, Mount Granby on the west, and South East Mount as the southern tip and the City of Grenville on the east. This area is the most mountainous, difficult terrain, and is the least populated section of the country. If you were going to hide someone, this would be the place. Remember, the stolen car was found in this area, at the side of the road out of gas. It had almost made it out of the diamond."

The rustle of paper could be heard throughout the group as couples sorted their maps and studied the described zone and the stolen car location marked with a red 'X'.

"As of now, we have seven search teams set to start looking. I'll go over them now." Ed was impatient to get the gang started.

"First," he called out, "we have the Grenada Grand Beach Resort group, better known as Team 1, headed by Raymond Redhead. He's accompanied by four other staffers of the hotel. That good-looking fellow standing over there to your right is Mr. Samuel Roy, the hotel's manager and he is ready to help even more, if we need it." There was a loud round of applause as Mr. Roy beamed and waved.

"This group will work from Birch Grove, where one of the men was born and raised. Their territory will be to the east of Birch Grove, south of the road that runs to La Digue, where the car was found."

Ed flipped a page and pointed out the next group. "John Hardy, from Harry Truman's home town of Independence, will lead Team 2. They will start from Adelphi and move east into the hills, arc south toward Seven Falls and include the village of St. Margaret."

"Team 3, headed by Peter Baxter, who didn't see the Queen's shilling in the bottom of his drink and was pressed into service, gets Lower Capital, where he will be based, just south of the main road running from Gouyave to Grenville. Team 3 will stay north of the road to La Digue, while Team 1 will be on the south side. By the way, Peter and his lovely wife Anne are from Canada and are here on their twenty-fifth anniversary holiday. They won the right to do this job simply by volunteering and we appreciate their help." Ed stopped for a moment so the second round of applause could die down.

"Team 4, led by Vince Strong, will cover the eastern half of the section Team 3 is searching and will be based at the village of St. James. Have you all got that?" Ed waited for any questions.

A hand went up deep in the crowd and a voice asked "who can I work with?" It was Anthony, quietly wanting to know how he could help.

"LJ needs a fifth for his team, and I don't mean a Fifth of Bourbon, 'though I doubt any of the team would refuse that. He's the tall one over near your father, go see him," and Ed moved on.

"Teams 5 and 6 will work west of the Felix Park to La Digue road, up near the north end. Team 5, Harry Stanton's gang of 'ner-do-wells' should set up in Richmond, and Team 6, with Fred Lusinski trying to ride herd, will set up in Plaisance. Both of your teams will comb west of the road, working your way toward John Hardy and his Team 2 operating out of Adelphi. It's a huge area, so I think it will take at least two full days, so don't get separated or lost and be sure to mark where you've been on your maps.

"Last but not least, is Team 7 led by LJ Livingston. He and his gang are going to the west side of the main highway from Beauregard, northwest to Belvidere and back to Castaigne. This is a large section, probably the most desolate on the island, so they have their work cut out for them."

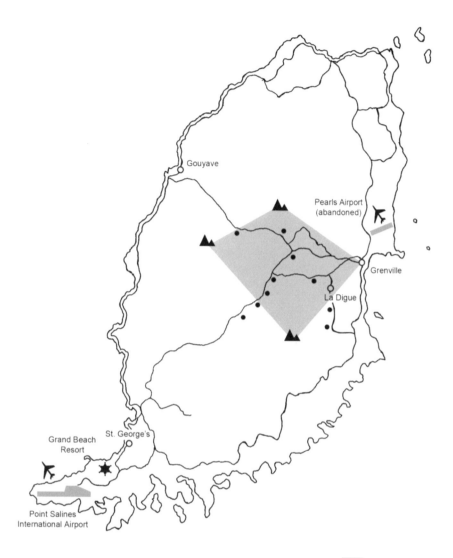

Gouyave

Pearls Airport
(abandoned)

Grenville

La Digue

Grand Beach
Resort

St. George's

Point Salines
International Airport

grenada

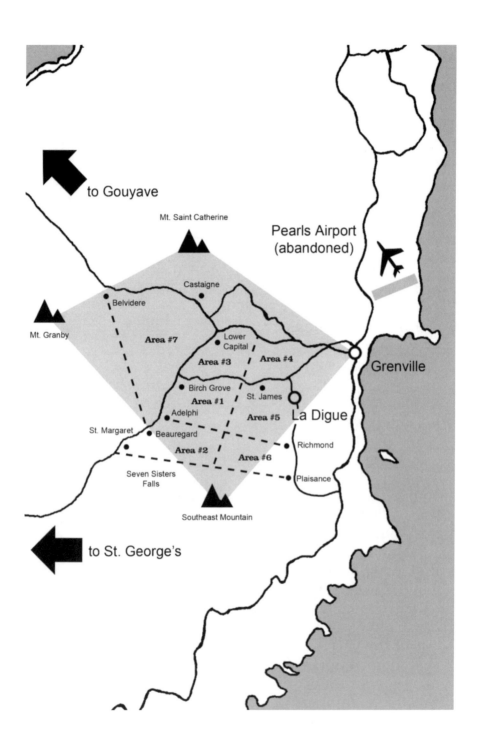

to Gouyave

Mt. Saint Catherine

Pearls Airport
(abandoned)

Castaigne

Belvidere

Mt. Granby

Area #7

Lower
Capital

Area #3   Area #4

Grenville

Birch Grove

Area #1   St. James

Adelphi

Area #5   La Digue

St. Margaret   Beauregard

Richmond

Area #2   Area #6

Seven Sisters
Falls

Plaisance

Southeast Mountain

to St. George's

It was time now to get moving and Ed sensed it.

"OK folks. We have assigned two vehicles to each team. One is to act as base camp with provisions. These will include food and water, emergency first-aid supplies, spare batteries for the radios, and a friendly face if you need one. The other vehicle is the runner. Their sole purpose is to provide mobility. They will deliver things, pick things up and transport team members out or to another area. You name it and they will do it. Just remember, they are there to assist you. Now let's get going." Ed hopped down from the flower bed wall and walked over to LJ, Nick and Harry. He was still concerned about Anthony.

"How are things going?" he asked, expecting a problem.

"Oh fine," LJ said and handed some papers to Anthony. Still playing team leader, he turned to Harry and gave him a sheet of paper. "Why?" he asked over his shoulder.

"Just wondering."

The cars and vans started to move out for their designated base locations and the level of noise and confusion was dropping like a stone. Ed was pleased at the smooth way things had gone, hoping they had guessed right.

The teams moved out in groups of three vehicles. The first usually had the team leader and a couple of his gang. The next car was generally piloted by a wife with at least one, and usually two, support members. The third vehicle was the runner and it too was driven by one of the wives. Each team was a self-contained unit of searchers, supporters with food and other provisions, and a communications and procurement element. It was an impressive operation. As the last car disappeared through the gates, the grounds once again grew silent save for the rustling palms and the soft call of the birds.

Chapter Nineteen

Day Four: Early Morning

Rachel studied the tether around her ankle, but couldn't get down close enough to figure out what it was made of without shoving her big toe up her nose. This wouldn't do, so she dropped it, stood up, and moved to the spot on the door frame of her shack where it was fastened.

Her kidnapper had done a good job.

The door of the hut was flimsy but the builder, many years before, must have considered a doorway and its framework to be the heart of a well-constructed building. The woodwork around the door was strong enough to withstand a hurricane and would surely outlast the rest of the old shack itself. Manuel must have realized this because he had drilled a hole two feet above the floor through the double two by sixes, tightened in a long bolt with a ring on the outside, and looped the tether through the ring, affixing it with a double clamp using lock washers and double nuts.

Rachel's inspection left her with no doubt that the long bolt to which her leash was fixed was new, securely held, and could not be undone without proper tools. Dismantling her anchor was not an option. She also discovered the rope had a metal core made up of a thin multi-strand wire. Breaking, cutting or sawing her tether without a hacksaw seemed beyond her as well.

Slowly walking back to her stool in front of the hut, she sat down facing the building and stared intently at the doorway.

"If you think I'm beaten, think again, you dumb door," she said, pointing a long slender finger at the offending woodwork. "This is just a temporary delay in me getting out of here and if I have to, I'll figure out a way to burn you to the ground. So look out!"

Having shouted at her opponent, she felt better and got up to wander about to see what could be used as a tool or hammer. She knew there had to be a solution; all she had to do was find it.

Rachel's problem-solving abilities didn't come naturally. She never needed them until her parents decided they couldn't live together anymore and filed for divorce.

She was eighteen at the time, just out of her London, Ontario high school, holding a letter of acceptance from the renowned marine biology course at Guelph University, about fifty miles from her hometown. The news that the seemingly perfect family unit to which she belonged was breaking up, came as an incredibly devastating shock.

Her parents had acted very civilized about it all, sitting down with her at their dining room table, opening a bottle of Beaujolais, and pouring her a glass as well as their own. After some sipping and very light small talk, they proceeded very politely to explain how her world as she knew it was crashing into pieces around her feet.

Thinking back, Rachel knew she sure hadn't acted either civilized or polite at that table. She sat open mouthed, stunned by the horrendous news these two calm, well-dressed, sophisticated people tossed into her lap.

Her first reaction had been to demand 'how could you' over and over. With each repeat of the phrase, her voice rose in pitch and volume until she was literally screaming at them. Then she stood and banged both hands down onto the table so hard, one of her mother's treasured crystal wine glasses fell over, broke, and dumped its contents across the table and onto the incredibly expensive Afghan carpet beneath their feet. Neither her mother nor her father seemed to notice, which in retrospect was the most bizarre occurrence of the whole evening.

Rachel couldn't stay another moment in the same room with them and had to get away, so she stormed from the dining room, then the house, only pausing long enough to scream how they could both go to hell for all she cared, and even hell, in her opinion, was much too good for either of them.

Now, over three years had passed since that stormy get together and she had grown up a lot. Her parents were still her parents and although they didn't live together anymore, they worked together to take good care of her.

She found a small apartment in Guelph, after 'The Meeting', as she would always think of it, and had been living alone there ever since. She did this because she couldn't bring herself to decide which parent she wanted to live with. She loved them both and now felt more sorrow for them than she ever could feel for herself. She knew she was just starting out in life and would have been gone within a couple years anyway. The divorce simply speeded things up. What bothered her was how neither parent seemed inclined to remarry and she feared they might end up living alone the rest of their lives.

Rachel thought about these things as she rummaged around her shack but all she could come up with during the search were some short pieces of wood, a small bit of wire and a couple of nails. She knew she was no 'MacGyver' so there was little comfort in what she found. She then moved the search into the hut.

Getting down on hands and knees, Rachel tried every board in the floor to see if any were loose. There was no joy there.

Wondering what the heck she was going to do, she sat in her hammock, swinging back and forth, pushing herself with her foot as she had done a hundred times in the past, on a swing in a tree at her grandparents summer cottage, out on Long Point on the north shore of Lake Erie. For some time, she was lost in those dreams of nicer times with bonfires and marshmallows and mosquitoes.

As she swung and dreamed, she noticed that the post to which her hammock was attached in the center of the shack shuddered every time she pushed the floor with her foot to keep it swinging. Soon this shudder had all her attention.

Getting out of the hammock, Rachel started a close inspection. One end of the hammock was fastened to a ring in the corner post where a side wall joined the back wall. She saw she could, with patience and much work, untie it from the ring if she wanted. She then took a close look at the shuddering post holding up the other end.

Set in the middle of the hut, the center post was a stout piece of wood, approximately seven feet tall, about eight inches in diameter at the bottom, maybe four at the top, nailed to the floor in a box of two-by-fours. Looking up, she saw it attached to a ceiling beam with the same type of box holding it in place. The setup was simple but effective; under normal use, the pole would go nowhere and neither would the hammock.

Rachel sensed a tingle of anticipation and slowly moved around her hammock several times, studying the door, the ceiling, the floor and the material used to make the hammock. She was cooking a stew in her head and with each slow step, kept adding more and more ingredients, knowing that deep down she was right. Finally she stopped. It was now or never, she thought.

First, she went out and grabbed her stool. Bringing it inside she set it in the corner, stood on it and started to undo one end of the hammock from its wall fixture. It took her over an hour of sweaty work and cost her several broken nails but no matter, she thought, the hammock was undone and the nails would grow back.

After a break outside, she returned to her now one end undone hammock and moved the stool over to the center post, climbing up to see if she could touch the ceiling beam. She was close, but couldn't quite reach.

Stumped for the moment, Rachel headed outside, swinging the door open with a bang as she did so. The door itself was far more flimsy than the door frame, shuddering and shaking, so she gave it another sharp swing to again bang against the outside wall. She thought it seemed ready to fall apart and grabbed one of the boards, giving it a yank. It came off in her hands. 'What do you know' she thought; the only thing I didn't check is the easiest thing to tear apart. It took her only ten minutes to rip the whole door to pieces.

Now she had four six foot long boards and three shorter pieces all about eight inches wide and an inch thick. With them she knew she could get her stool up another four inches. And then if she could break the boards in half, she could get eight inches closer to the ceiling beam. It might just be enough.

Rachel's experience with lumber was as limited as her experience with Cuban kidnappers, so it took her a good hour banging one board with another just to get all of the short nails bent over so she wouldn't start poking holes in herself.

It took another half hour of experimenting before she got the first board to snap. Trial and error taught her the board needed to have one end higher than the board's bending capability. This meant there were many attempts before she found the right combination of stacking other boards and a few rocks combined with a good running jump and a leap in the air before she heard the wonderful crack of a piece of wood breaking as she came down on it. When that happened, she bounced about like some primitive doing a fertility dance, whooping joyously and waving her arms in the air.

Now, after all that work, she had eleven pieces of wood, each roughly three feet long, to put under her stool in the shack. Time was getting on but Rachel was on a roll and she knew it.

Carrying all her broken boards into the shack, she stacked them tight against the center post, then set her stool on top of them, checking it all for stability. There was no movement, so she shrugged, and barged on up with no concern.

Reaching up, she easily touched the ceiling beam and within a half hour had the loose end of the hammock she had untied from the corner, snuggly secure and hanging from the ceiling beam overhead. It was time for another fertility dance.

The center post was another matter. Jammed firmly against the floor and nailed to the ceiling beam, it appeared immoveable. It didn't matter, she wasn't ready to quit.

Close examination revealed one of the two-by-fours boxing in the base of the post was a little loose. With brute force, using a board from her pile to bang it, she sent the piece flying with one final great whack. The post now sat in a square box with only three sides and she knew she was getting somewhere.

Going around to the side of the post opposite the missing two-by-four, Rachel sat down on the floor, placed both feet on it and slid her bum forward about eight inches. With her arms stretched behind her for support, she pulled her feet from the post, bending her knees in toward her chest. Taking a deep breath and clenching her teeth, she kicked both feet forward with all her might, hammering the post a foot above the floor.

The damned post moved. She couldn't believe it. It had shifted away from her about a half inch and when she jumped up to look, she could see it was on a very slight angle. Rachel let out another whoop and did her best native dance of the day.

She figured if she kicked the post out far enough, the top would pull free and it would come crashing down. She hoped its fall would be restrained from hitting the floor by the hammock tied to the ceiling and around the middle of the pole itself. Taking time to check everything out and satisfied she was on the right track, she sat down again for more kicking.

Slowly, with much groaning from her and the ceiling beam above, the post crept out of its holding box on the floor and assumed a more pronounced angle toward the ceiling. When it was clear of all the nails holding it down, she got up, took a deep breath, and shoved it with all her might. The base moved a foot and the top broke loose from the ceiling and came hurtling down, yanking the bottom violently off the floor and knocking Rachel half-way across the room.

When the dust settled and the groaning of stressed wood in the ceiling stopped, an amazed Rachel Lusinski got up off the floor and stood open mouthed, watching her hammock post swing gently back and forth on its very odd looking tether attached to the beam above her head. She didn't whoop or dance about the room. She just stepped over to the pole and patted it gently.

"You lovely piece of wood, you," she said with a big grin. "When I am safely out of here, I'm going to come back and take you home as a souvenir," and she bent over, planting a tender kiss on it.

Rachel now had the perfect battering ram. It took only a couple of tries to see how it could be swung back on the hammock/rope attached to the ceiling, and then pushed forward, making it slam into the part of the door-jam she had been bolted to by her kidnapper.

"I've watched a lot of medieval battle scenes at the movies and I know this battering ram will work," she muttered, as she strained to pull the post back as far as possible to test it for aim.

Drenched in sweat from the heat of the room and the effort needed to move the pole, she rested for a moment before hauling it back, then pushed it forward with all her might to end its short pendulum-like swing with a deadening thud against the door frame.

Slowly she did it again, and again. Over and over she repeated this until the noise of the thud against wood was accompanied by a groan from the frame, then the cracking of wood. Soon a splinter or two flew outward into the clearing. She was getting there.

Finally the battered wood gave up and broke in two about four feet from the floor. Rachel let out a feeble cheer but couldn't dance about because she was near exhaustion and able only to stand, bent over, hands on knees, gasping for breath. She then staggered out into the clearing carrying her stool and flopped down to proudly survey her handiwork.

The next hour was spent working the broken bottom piece of the door frame back and forth, finally getting it completely free of the spikes holding it to the base of the building. She still had the rope around her ankle and it was still twenty feet long and it was still attached to part of the door frame, but she was free. She was free.

She could, and would, drag that piece of doorway to hell and back if necessary but first, she needed some water, so it was off to the stream, dragging her chunk of door frame, for some much needed refreshment.

Chapter Twenty

Day Four: 3:30 PM

LJ and his team had been in the bush for over an hour, slowly working their way up toward a high point so they could look over the terrain with binoculars and plan a search strategy, much like he had done a long time ago and in much the same area.

He had felt strange ever since leaving St. George Parish and entering the Grand Etang Forest Reserve because this was where he and his fellow Marines had operated, back in '83.

LJ was a Marine and although retired, he still thought and acted like a Marine. One of his many duties during his career was to go into Grenada to help clean up a mess set in motion by a gang of communist thugs. They had seized and assassinated Maurice Bishop, the island's Prime Minister, several members of his government, and a few of his friends for good measure in a bloody coup.

Bishop, also a communist, was not communist enough for some of the hardliners in his own party, so they solved their problem by standing him against a wall in a fort in St George's Town and shot holes in him.

It was a nasty piece of business and outraged many, including the leaders of several other Caribbean nations who thought they could be next.

These leaders made their case for help in a joint appeal to the U.S., prompting President Ronald Reagan to send in the Marines. He also sent in Army Rangers, Seals, the Navy, and just about everything else he could get to move there in short order. Using Barbados as a base of operations and with the help of the Barbados

Defense Force and contingents from other islands, the U.S. set about to make things right.

The assassinations took place on October 19th and six days later, on the 25th LJ was on the ground at Pearls Airfield, helping to seize and secure the place before moving into Grenville, Grenada's second largest city. Both the now abandoned airport and Grenville were within five miles of where he was looking for Rachel. It was no wonder he felt odd.

Ed had discussed the plan with him earlier, asking if LJ would mind leading one of the teams. The old Marine had insisted on the sector he was now sitting in. It was the most desolate, least populated and most hostile part of the island, and LJ had trekked it with full battle pack, hunting down bad guys who had gone to ground after the invasion. He knew exactly what was in store for his team but figured this time there would be no one shooting at him. At least he hoped not.

Each team was setting up the same way. They would first establish their base, find a convenient place to park their supply vehicle and communication car and then strike out for several hours to get a feel for their area and plan their search for the next morning. The Marines had taught him to find the high ground, seize it, and use it for any future operations. His five men were within minutes of achieving that goal.

Several miles northeast of LJ, Raymond Redhead and the members of Team 1, from the hotel, had already set up in Birch Grove. This was a town much larger than most area villages with many small shops and stores. Their plan the first day was to go house to house, systematically questioning every person in the small community. Nick, Ed and Harry figured if Rachel had been taken into the vicinity of Birch Grove, it could have been used by the kidnappers as a point of supply. Someone may have noticed a stranger in one of the shops or food stores. It was also thought that since one of the search team had grown up in Birch Grove, more of the locals could be talked into helping in the hunt.

All across the area, teams were setting up, with some already in the bush or moving up dirt paths to higher ground. In every case, locals, eager to help, were joining in the search. They sometimes acted as guides, some offered cool drinks or food, but most offered to be searchers, ready to take instructions and do whatever was necessary. Soon it wasn't seven teams of five searchers each; it was seven teams of anything from twenty-five to fifty searchers each. This slowed things down a bit because the new volunteers needed instructions, but they were eager and willing and would be a big help. In no time, almost two hundred searchers were out beating the bushes looking for Rachel.

Nick, playing general manager and coordinator, drove from one team base to the next offering encouragement, looking for problems, and smoothing any ruffled feathers he encountered. There weren't many.

At the first stop in Adelphi, John Hardy complained he had forgotten bottled water so Nick opened his trunk and told them to help themselves. He had six cases.

Next stop was Birch Grove, just a couple of miles up the road where he found the supply car and communications vehicle parked by the town's new bridge. The two drivers, young hotel staff, were sitting in the shade with several locals. They told Nick how the rest of their group was spread out through the town, banging on doors. Assured that all was fine and that they didn't need anything, he moved on along the road.

His third stop was in Lower Capital, a strangely named collection of homes north of Birch Grove. Here, Anne Baxter managed the supply car and communications vehicle for her husband's Team 3 with efficiency and good humor. It wasn't easy, being

140

surrounded by a gang of noisy local children scurrying about wanting to see what was going on. Off to one side lounged several older ladies, probably grandmothers keeping one eye on their charges, and another on the curious people parked in their village.

Nick spent a pleasant half hour here, going over the plan and getting a close introduction to Anne's preparations for the search.

She had bundles of sandwiches; both egg salad and ham and cheese, wrapped in cellophane. With them was half a watermelon and cold drinks stuffed into a cooler packed with ice. The cooler also contained a dozen hard boiled eggs. Besides all this was a great bag of local fruit on the back seat next to a box containing paring knives, spoons, salt and pepper and a jar of mustard. She had even brought along a package of white serviettes.

"Sorry, but I couldn't eat here." Nick deadpanned.

"Why not?" she said, crestfallen.

"No tablecloth, no candles, no vase for flowers and where's the wine?" Grinning, Nick climbed into his car and drove off, leaving the bemused lady laughing.

The next two hours saw Nick driving around the back roads, stopping at Vince Strong's base in St. James, then on to Harry's and a little south of Richmond to Fred Lusinski's operation. In each case the search teams were out in the bush, the support ladies were dealing with the locals and all seemed in place. Nick felt pretty good about the operation and had a feeling deep down inside that they'd get the job done. It would just take a little time.

Speaking of time, Nick checked his watch and was surprised to see how late it was. Six o'clock had come and gone and it would be dark soon. He stepped on the gas to close the distance to Beauregard, LJ's base, in order to be there when they returned from the bush. There would be a lot to talk about.

Chapter Twenty One

Day Four: Eleven A.M.

Manuel lay, unable to move, enveloped in pain but very sure he was not dead. Long ago, a priest told him you would feel no pain when you died, at least not until you were judged for your deeds on earth while you were alive, and then you'd know why you were feeling pain.

So Manuel was glad he was not dead but was very unhappy about the pain. It ran through his hips, his legs, across his shoulders and each time he took a breath, no matter how shallow, it shot in great sheets, like lightning, through his chest. His head hurt as well but that seemed the least of his worries. He had no idea how extensive or life threatening his injuries might be. He just knew he was in great pain, all over.

What he did not know was how long he had been lying unconscious, his head slightly lower than his feet, in soft earth and crushed underbrush. He could not know he had been there, in the same spot, beneath towering trees, almost eighteen hours, floating between life and death.

For the first six or seven hours, he lay motionless, one would think dead, unconscious from a series of blows to his head as he fell. Looking up, he could see what he fell through on his way down to crash into the soft wet earth. He knew he was out before he hit the ground.

During the long night, Manuel drifted in and out of consciousness, with each visit from the darkness to the real world around him getting a little longer than the last. These short awakenings made him wonder anew where he was, why he was there, and what could have happened to place him in this strange situation. He knew who he was, but not where he was and he knew he was injured but not how he got that way. Finally, each time he would close his eyes to rest, he drifted back into a coma-like sleep.

An hour passed before Manuel floated up to the surface of consciousness again and started once more to take stock of his situation. This time, he was able to remember the previous lucid moments and his thoughts of not being dead. He was now sure he wasn't and realized some memories were starting to seep back, like slow bubbles rising to the top in a quietly simmering pot of thick, delicious, oatmeal.

He remembered shopping, buying fruit and other food and some clothing. Not much clothing, but he couldn't remember what and he lay quiet, hoping the throbbing pain in his head would go away.

He remembered leaving some town, or village, and walking along a road and then into the bushes at the side of the road. He remembered pausing in the undergrowth, upset about something, but he couldn't pierce the dark clouds shielding him from his memories. Again, he was quiet, trying to calm himself, trying to breath slowly, as shallow as possible, trying not to hurt himself even more. He closed his eyes and drifted away again.

It was less than an hour this time and Manuel awoke with a reflex action to get up. The explosion of pain from his chest and hips screamed through him, making him gasp, causing tears to pour from his eyes. He wasn't just in pain; he now knew there were some very serious things damaged inside his body and he needed help.

He rested, knowing rest would help, and the time spent resting could be used to think, plan, and try to find a way out of this mess. He relaxed his muscles, slowed his breathing and started taking stock again.

From his position on his back he could see up between his feet to a wall of stone covered in tropical bushes rising up out of sight. Straight overhead he could see the blue sky through the limbs of several great trees stretching fifteen to twenty meters up all around him and near the stone wall. Gently, and very slowly, he turned his head to the left and saw the same landscape spreading away from him. After several minutes of rest, he managed to turn his head to the right and got a view of the same, except there was a small stream splashing down the side of the hill to disappear from his view further to his right.

Resting from the effort, he lay back and the memories started rolling in, filling his head. One caused him to jerk stiff, sending sheets of white agony raging through his body. It was the memory of a girl, rather the picture of a girl, smiling up at him from a poster on the backseat of a car. Now he knew, now he remembered everything, and he almost threw up.

Manuel dozed for half an hour, a welcome respite from his pain, both the physical, and mental.

During this mending of the mind process, Manuel was slowly checking his physical being as well. For some time he had been working each finger on both hands to see if anything was functioning properly without making him sick with pain.

Nothing seemed broken or wrecked in either hand and soon he was able to grasp a handful of earth, lift it slightly, then open his hand and drop it. This small victory raised his spirits.

He was now able to move his head with some ease and found his left hand, arm, elbow and shoulder capable of quite extensive movement. His right hand and wrist also worked well. Everything above that on his right wouldn't move and made him cry in pain if he tried. It seemed his right shoulder or collarbone, or both were badly smashed. His arm and elbow could be as well.

His lower extremities were an entirely different matter. Manuel was unable to move his feet, or legs without almost fainting. They would move; they just hurt a lot when he tried. He knew this meant he wasn't paralyzed, just badly broken up and he would need attention soon.

All these efforts to assess his situation took a toll. He was exhausted, aching, and in despair. He had a good idea where he was and that caused him all the more concern. In his effort to get back to the camp quickly, he had taken the direct route through the bush, straight up the steepest side of the small mountain. Had he not been so upset by developments, he would have shunned the untested short cut and returned on the much longer path, a route circling halfway around the hill. The sharp incline he used had been made slippery by rain and the instability of the path had caused him to fall. At the time of his tumble, he had been only about five hundred feet from the clearing and possibly a hundred and fifty feet below it.

Now he lay, broken and immobile, much further away from the clearing, knowing his prisoner wouldn't be able to help her even if he could call to her. He knew he must rest and when he did, he must think, for he knew that an answer must come. As his eyes closed and he drifted into a fitful sleep, he could see her face and he wondered how she was doing and what would become of her.

Chapter Twenty Two

Day Four: Six P.M.

Rachel was bone tired, but felt like a million dollars.

Hanging onto her tether, she dragged her doorframe up the path to the small pool in the stream above the clearing, stretched out on her stomach and stuck her head in deep, letting the water flow through her hair.

It was wonderful; cold and refreshing. She drank some, splashed some on her face, then drank some more. Sitting up, she swung her feet into the water and just sat there, up to her knees, enjoying. Automatically looking around to assure herself no one was watching, she off pulled her red T shirt to rinse it out in the icy water and, with a gasp, splashed it all over her upper torso. After the hours of hard work in the oppressive heat of her shack, this was like heaven. She closed her eyes in sheer pleasure, leaning back on her arms and relaxing, knowing only her God and the birds in the trees could see her. A long time passed with the sun drying her hair and the euphoria of freedom charging her batteries before she put her semi-dry shirt back on and moved to get up.

Grabbing up her tether to drag the chunk of wood back to the clearing, she laughed out loud, and pulled the wood closer.

"Come here," she commanded. "I should give you a name, you know. What do you think it should be? Wilson is already taken. I know, he wasn't wood, he was leather. Let's see, you are wood; lumber actually. How about Rona? That's a pretty good name and people would think you're Canadian. That's it, I christen you Rona!" She was now back in the clearing and heading for Manuel's shack.

"You stay out here and guard the place, Rona," and she went inside to look for food, matches, and utensils. She was hungry, having eaten nothing since her two oranges the day before, but most of all she wanted a fire. One night in the dark, on a mountain, in a jungle, was enough for a lifetime. She had decided to stay one more night. It made sense because it was now late, she was hungry and she didn't know exactly where she was. She also figured trying to walk down the hillside in the dark dragging Rona seemed like a bad idea. She'd stay another night and start fresh in the morning, but she'd stay with a fire.

Manuel's backpack lay near his hammock so she emptied the contents out onto the floor. There was a box of old style wooden matches which she set to one side, as she did a small Spanish bible and one other book, a well worn Spanish-English dictionary. Mixed in with these were shirts, underwear, socks, an extra pair of trousers, shorts and a bathing suit. At the bottom was a small zippered leather pouch. It was much like her grandfather's battered old tobacco pouch she remembered he carried when she was a little girl.

Unzipping it slowly, she held it to her nose. The faint scent of tobacco caused memories to flood back over her. She remembered the wonderful aroma of pipe tobacco when she sat on her Pompa's knee while he puffed away telling her stories of when he was young. It was a wonderful smell from the forever gone past because her grandfather had given up smoking many years ago.

Inside the pouch was a bundle of bills, in several different currencies. There were American and Canadian dollars, British pounds, a great many Euros, and a wad of Cuban CUC's. She didn't bother counting it, thinking it looked like several hundred dollars and of no real interest at the moment. What was far more interesting was a small blue booklet stuck in with the money, Manuel's passport.

"I'll be damned," she said out loud as she opened it for a close examination. "I thought he was Cuban," she muttered.

It was a Venezuelan Passport. Thumbing through it revealed a neat square stamp on one page dated just eight days before she was kidnapped. The stamp declared in block letters 'AIR' and was marked 'vacation', allowing the holder a one month stay. On another page was a Cuban Immigration stamp more than a month old. Turning back to the first page, Rachel took a closer look at the picture before stepping outside into the fading light. She studied the small photo for several minutes, and then spoke to the lump of wood in front of her.

"Rona, I know you won't believe this, but this is certainly not a picture of the man who kidnapped me. In fact, this guy here is quite a bit older, and although his name is Manuel, he is certainly not the guy who left here yesterday. I wonder what the heck is going on."

She re-entered the shack, refolded the clothing, and put everything except the box of matches carefully back into Manuel's bag. She picked up the pot and cooking pan and the bag of oatmeal and stepped out into the waning sunlight. "Come on Rona, we need some water for our much loved oatmeal, and then we'll start a nice fire and have a feast."

Placing everything next to the fire pit, she picked up the bucket and started dragging Rona toward the stream. She hated oatmeal but it could have been a bag of Brussels sprouts, which she really hated, and she would still have looked forward to the coming meal.

Chapter Twenty Three

Day Four: Ten P.M.

Nick and LJ groaned in unison at the sight ahead of them as they turned onto the drive leading up to the hotel's canopy.

Outside the lobby entrance, bright lights powered by a large noisy generator in the back of a pickup, lit up a young woman holding a large black microphone in her left hand and a sheet of paper in her right. She stood quietly as her makeup was attended to by a young man almost as pretty as her, while her hair was being fluffed and fussed over by a female aide. During all this, a cameraman stood beside his tripod, patiently waiting for the repairs to be finished. Nick and LJ glanced over at each other and grimaced. Both men knew their troubles might be just beginning.

"I think we'll park near the tennis courts," Nick pointed, and swung in beside the tennis courts before reaching the news crew. "We can slip across the lawn, behind those banana trees, and miss them."

"Good plan," was all LJ said.

The two men pulled some material from the backseat and slipped into the darkness near the trees, bypassing the commotion and making it to their rooms without incident. Nick knew he'd have to deal with the media soon, but this was not the time. Before entering his room he, turned to LJ, standing at his own door, key in hand.

"After your shower, call your list and I'll call mine and we'll have a meeting at eleven, after we eat. OK?"

"OK," LJ answered and stepped out of sight.

The eleven o'clock meeting started on time and all called were present. Seated around the table were the seven team leaders, hotel manager Sam Roy, Bella Brown, Nick, wife Ann, and a surprise guest, the Police Commissioner. He was at the hotel for a TV interview, and, hearing of the meeting from the manager, asked if he could sit in.

Anthony and Irene were also invited to join in and they sat together next to LJ. Nick counted heads and mistakenly thought there were thirteen around the table so he asked for someone else to join and Edith stepped in, claiming she would be the recording secretary. Nick wasn't superstitious, just cautious, and a bad counter.

The media had caught wind of the meeting and wanted in but were politely told to cool their jets by Bella Brown. She knew the press could be pushy, but seldom pushed too hard against a cute little ninety year old lady. The crews didn't go away, they just set up camp outside the meeting room door.

Nick called the gathering to order and introduced and welcomed the Police Commissioner who was a stranger to most at the table. He offered him the floor for any comments he may have but the police officer declined, asking if he might say a few words at the end, if something needed saying. Nick said of course, and moved on.

"I thought we'd go around the table and get comments or reports from each of the team leaders first. We'll start with Mr. Redhead of Team 1."

Raymond Redhead looked around as he squirmed in his seat, knowing all faces were turned his way. Taking a deep breath, he started by opening a small notebook and flipping through a few pages as he had seen a detective do on Law and Order, his favorite TV show. Ready, Mr. Redhead began.

"We had a very good day," he said in a broad island accent. "The people in Birch Grove were most co-operative and many volunteered to help in the search tomorrow. I knew they would and I assure you they will be a big help," he said proudly. These were his people in his town.

"The only comment we heard about strangers was from a shopkeeper who sold a shirt to a young man late yesterday morning. He only noticed because the young man asked what size would be right for a girl, and described her height and general dimensions, which basically match our subject. What was odd, he said, was that he wanted it large, after giving a smaller girl's shape. He didn't seem to care what color it was, or if it had anything on it, like 'Grenada' or some other 'touristy' slogan or flag. He was only interested in the size. He eventually purchased a white one with our flag on it." Raymond paused for a moment, rechecking his notebook.

"The shopkeeper wasn't sure how to describe his color. He said he wasn't black, like us, but he wasn't white like you. Very light brown was how he described it, but looking like a white man, you know, eyes, nose and hair. He was about thirty years old, spoke English without an accent but had very little to say. Oh, and another thing. He was on foot, walking, because the merchant went outside to speak with a couple of your people who had signs. He noticed the shopper heading south out of town with a poster under his arm." He closed his book and seemed quite pleased with his efforts.

"Good report, Mr. Redhead," said Nick. "Perhaps you could give all those details plus the name of the shop to the Police Commissioner at the end of the meeting." The young man beamed at the praise and the rare opportunity to work with the top policeman in his country; especially when that top cop was sitting down the table nodding his approval of the report.

For the next forty-five minutes the reports from each team were laid out for all to consider. Some were quite short, others longer, but all said the same thing. The terrain was hostile and would make the search difficult. Some areas had extensive farming underway and could be covered in a day by the crowds they now had available, but others would be a fight.

LJ suggested they direct the majority of their volunteer force into the easiest areas. He felt this would accomplish two things. One, it would get the farm areas done and out of the way, and two, it would give some valuable experience to the new searchers, making them more proficient for the tough sections when they moved into them. All agreed.

Once the reports were finished and the next day's program confirmed, Nick moved to the last item on his list. It was in capitals and simply said 'MEDIA'.

"You're all aware of the group of vultures huddled just outside this room. Are there any suggestions on the line we should follow dealing with them?" he asked.

"Nothing but the truth, the whole truth, and answer all questions honestly and crisply." This came from Bella Brown.

"I agree," said Harry. "We have nothing to gain and a lot to lose if we start beating around the bush or appear to be covering anything up. Besides, anyone watching will be sympathetic to Fred and Alice's plight and the feelings of Rachel's mother and father, so honest straight answers will do nothing but good. And Nick, you do it."

"Thanks for the confidence," said Nick.

"It's not confidence, my friend. No one else wants to do it and we all know you're too dumb to know what a rotten job it is," Harry shot back amid a round of laughter.

"Thanks a lot," was the only reply Nick could muster.

Police Commissioner Frank raised his hand as the group settled down, indicating a desire to say something. Nick, still shaking his head, waved him into the discussion.

"I have to say you people are certainly very well organized, equipped, and enthusiastic." His deep voice and formal, well-educated English accent taking command of the room.

"When Mr. Livingston first approached me regarding your intent, I had some grave misgivings. I knew he meant well but I wondered what good a bunch of senior citizens could be. Of course, I had not yet had the pleasure of meeting your Mrs. Bella Brown." This caused many smiles in the room.

"After some consideration, I decided you really could do no harm and although you might at times get in the way of our investigation, it would be a problem we could live with. Little did I know.

"Now, I believe it is we, the police, who may be getting in your way." This brought some outright chuckles from those around him.

"I am very impressed and I promise every resource and all the help the police force of Grenada can give. Tomorrow we are bringing in our entire auxiliary staff plus I have cancelled all leave and holidays. I pledge to you everything we have, to bring this young lady home and reunite her with her family." This last declaration brought a round of spontaneous applause from all those in the room.

"One thing I can offer right now," he continued "is to join your Mr. Archer as co-press representative, and meet the media beside him in a united front," and he pointed to Nick. "I believe there is strength in numbers and one can jump in when the other runs into problems," he smiled. "I might suggest as well, that the parents and grandparents slip away out the back door with the rest of you when we leave here to speak to our friends out front. They can talk to you later, after we've found the girl, and I suggest we do that right now."

"Good idea," LJ said, "you two go and conduct your press conference and we'll gather up all the papers and notes, go out the back and get the Lusinskis stowed away. If you're still at it when we're finished, some of us will come back for moral support." He took Irene by the arm and moved around to Fred's side, Anthony close behind. As far as he was concerned, the meeting was over and it was time for action.

Nick joined the Police Commissioner and they waited for the exodus out the rear to begin before heading for the front door, looking much like two men going to a hanging.

Chapter Twenty Four

Day Four: 12 Midnight

"Ever done this before?" Commissioner Frank asked just a moment before he turned the door handle and swung it open to the mass of media outside the meeting room.

"Never!"

"Well, relax; it's not as bad as some of your group would have you believe." And he motioned toward LJ and Harry as they headed out the back door with the others.

"Like most other people in this world, media types tend to be a little lazy and always look for the path of least resistance. Give them the truth in a way they can report to head office in a couple of minutes and they'll go away happy."

"I'll start with a short statement and introduce you. After that, I'll throw it open to the floor. I think they'll probably direct most of their questions towards me because I'm the obvious symbol of authority they can question. When they do get to you, stay calm, be honest, and don't let them rattle you."

Police Commissioner Frank confidently marched from the room into the glare of several floodlights, four cameras on tripods and a gaggle of reporters, photographers, curiosity seekers and hotel guests. Nick followed two steps behind, figuring the bright lights were a ploy to keep targets from running for cover, as any sensible person would, especially if they saw the mob behind the damned lights.

Commissioner Frank looked very smart and in complete command in his crisp, beautifully tailored uniform. Stepping forward to the battery of microphones, he calmly put on his officer's hat, took his time adjusting it perfectly, and looking out over the crowd in front of him, deliberately took a folded sheet of paper from his inside pocket. Nick glanced sideways and was surprised to see there was nothing on the paper in the officer's hand. It was blank, a prop.

"Ladies and gentlemen, my name is Winfred Frank and I am proud to hold the position of Commissioner of Police for Grenada, Carriacou, and Petit Martinique. We are an independent nation within the British Commonwealth of Nations and to any of you who have just arrived to cover this story, I welcome you to our wonderful island. I have a short statement and then I will answer any questions you may have.

"Five days ago a missing person report was submitted to one of our local police stations by the roommate of a young lady here in Grenada for study purposes. Although the woman had only been missing approximately ten hours, our staff took the report very seriously. The officers at the station opened a file and started to enact standard procedures for such a situation.

"The missing person's name is Rachel Lusinski, that's L,U,S,I,N,S,K,I. Miss Lusinski is twenty-one years old, white, with blonde hair, fair complexion, and stands about five feet two inches tall. She is approximately one hundred and twelve pounds in weight and is in excellent physical condition. We will make a fact sheet with these and several other pertinent facts available for your convenience at the end of this conference." Commissioner Frank noticed several reporters stopped writing these details, and knew he had scored a point.

He carried on. "If any of you have had a look at one of the large posters now placed throughout the island and around this hotel, you will have noticed she could easily be called very attractive as well." He allowed a slight smile at this point.

"Rachel is a Canadian citizen, a university student, and is doing post-graduate studies of marine life in the shallow waters of our island. These studies are important and much appreciated by our government. They could, in time, aid us in preserving our fishing and shellfish industry. She has been in Grenada approximately five weeks.

"When her grandfather, retired and living in Florida, learned of her disappearance, he immediately sought the help of his friends. Within two days, he, the girl's parents and a large group of his associates, who also are living in retirement in Florida, traveled here and are now, under the guidance of the Royal Grenadian Police Force, helping in the search for young Miss Lusinski," he paused, turning slightly toward Nick.

"Standing with me," he said "is Mr. Nicholas Archer, also a Canadian citizen, who will be acting as spokesman for the grandfather and his family and his group until such time as we have successfully completed our investigation. Now, if there are any questions, raise your hand and I'll try to get to all of them."

Typically, no one raised their hand because they were all too busy shouting out questions. Commissioner Frank stood quietly until some of the chaos subsided and then pointed to a man in front, "You sir," he said.

The reporter asked, "What's the chance she may have fallen in with a bad crowd and got herself into some mischief?"

"Nothing in our investigation would indicate that. All evidence indicates she should be considered a very serious student. Our investigation indicates absolutely no evidence of any involvement in drugs. No heavy drinking. We have nothing to suggest attendance at wild parties or even any very late nights. The young lady didn't frequent the late night club scene in St. George's or out around the university. There is no boyfriend, per se, but there have been occasional dates with fellow students. She would appear to be a daughter any parent would be very proud of". He pointed to the young lady Nick and LJ had seen earlier, "You're next," he said.

"Could this be a kidnapping?" she asked.

"We have received no demands from anyone. If it were a kidnapping, we think those responsible would have made contact by now."

A somewhat overweight scribe dripping sweat onto his notepad asked, "Does your island police force have the capability to conduct a proper investigation of this crime?"

The Commissioner glanced at Nick and answered, "First off, let's make it clear that at this moment, this is not a crime investigation. This is a search operation designed to find a missing person," and he waited for the note scribbling to end.

"Now, if you mean 'do we have the labs and equipment' to complete the search, the answer is both yes and no. We have some scientific equipment but not all those things we'd like to have available. However, we are capable of quickly sending items and materials off-island for forensic study and this has worked well for us in the past.

"If you mean are we trained to conduct this kind of investigation, the answer is a definite yes." He seemed to be enjoying himself.

"Several of our officers have attended the Royal Canadian Mounted Police training school, the Federal Bureau of Investigation Academy at Quantico, Virginia, just south of Washington, D.C. and the Scotland Yard Commonwealth Training program in London, England.

At least five of our officers have attended all three. I think there is enough expertise to do the job properly." The sweaty reporter appeared happy with the Commissioner's answer and asked nothing more.

The questions went on in the same manner until the rotund newsman jumped in again and asked, "Mr. Archer, what possible help can a gang of seventy and eighty year olds be in a situation such as this?"

Nick stepped toward the microphone but Commissioner Frank answered first.

"They have been a great deal of help in this matter."

The reporter wouldn't be put off. "It looks more like a public relations exercise as opposed to real physical help. I'm in my fifties and would have trouble trekking through these jungles. I doubt anyone thirty years older than me could do it. What say you, Mr. Archer?"

The Commissioner was going to speak again but Nick touched his arm, whispered he was OK, and stepped forward.

"I'm sorry to hear you're in such bad physical condition. You should take better care of yourself. Regular exercise, light stuff, much like most of the group from Florida do every day, can do wonders for a person's stamina, strength and general feeling of well-being. I would recommend you look into it." This answer caused some snickering amongst the crowd in front of Nick.

"As a direct answer to your question, I'll give you an idea of what these seniors are actually doing. You may be a little surprised to learn they have organized into seven groups of five and each group has its own territory to search. Each team has a leader and several support staff, usually the wives of the searchers, but not always. The support staff prepare provisions and refreshments for the searchers, run errands, finds or picks up needed items that may get lost, broken or worn out, and lastly, act as mobile communicators tying the searchers directly to myself, the Police Commissioner's men, and the other search teams." Nick stopped for a breath and glanced at Officer Frank. He had a small grin in place and nodded approval. Nick forged on.

"You must remember, these people are all retired and have unlimited time. Most have very good retirement incomes and many once owned businesses either sold or passed on to family members. They have adequate financial resources, and a deep desire to help their very good friend find his only granddaughter. There is little need for any additional motivation to get them out of bed each morning and into search mode. Even you sir, would do the same if it was your friend's child missing.

"They can and will trek through the hills of their search area and with God's help, and the able assistance of the Royal Grenada Police Force, they will find Rachel and bring her safely home." His tone left no doubt he would tolerate no more stupid questions.

The answer took the sting out of any nastiness the press may have harbored and Nick noticed a subtle change in the tone. Within fifteen minutes the questions ran out and the press conference broke up. Nick and the Commissioner walked back into the hotel.

"That seemed to go pretty well, don't you think?" he said to the policeman.

"Very well indeed, and I loved the way you handled that reporter." He said with a grin. "I had to force myself not to laugh out loud."

"He asked for it." Nick stopped and stuck out his hand. "I want to thank you for your assistance, support and understanding. You've been a big help."

"My pleasure, I just hope we can finish this all off tomorrow." And he took Nick's hand, held it firmly and said he would see him in the morning.

Chapter Twenty Five

Day Five: Six A.M.

Rachel rolled briskly out of Manuel's hammock and stretched like a cat. She felt great. She had slept soundly, peacefully, like she hadn't in days, dreaming of home and friends. It was the first time since walking down the road from the cottage, that she felt fully refreshed after a sleep. Rachel was very happy knowing this was the day she was getting out of her prison in the jungle and going back to civilization.

"Come on Rona," she said to her piece of wood, now doing double service as a jam, forced hard into a crack in the floor and up against the inside of the door of the shack. "It's time we started getting ourselves ready to leave this damn place."

She had wondered what might happen if Manuel did make his way back to show up unannounced during the night. She thought hard about it and finally decided she needed her sleep for the day ahead and she could only do that if she felt secure. Commandeering Manuel's sleeping shack because it was now the only one with a door, she used Rona as a makeshift door jam to keep unwanted intruders out. Her kidnapper would have needed a battering ram to get in and she would sure be waiting for him in the dark, cooking knife in one hand and raised frying pan in the other. Lucky for him, he didn't come around.

Taking the cooking utensils outside, she stood in the clearing, enjoying the freedom to consider her options and the luxury of deciding what to do next. Her first decision was not to restart the fire or bother with breakfast. All the food and fruit except for a small amount of oatmeal, was gone, and after her feast the night before, she sure couldn't stomach another spoonful of that wonderful Scottish staple. Not at least for the next hundred and twelve years, she thought, so she tossed the cookware aside.

Wanting to be on her way out, she busied herself gathering everything together on the floor of Manuel's shack, deciding what to shove into the Cuban or Venezuelan's backpack and what to leave behind. Rachel figured if he was gone, the things he left in his shack, like his passport, bible, dictionary and money, might be of some use to the police in their search for him. Tossing his extra jeans and underclothes onto the hammock, she kept his extra T shirt, swung the pack over her shoulder, and stepped from the shack.

Wandering about, she decided the water bucket and fry pan could stay by the fire pit with the small pot he used sometimes to make tea. Trying to imprint on her mind all the details of her home for the past several days before turning to go, she stood for a long moment looking around. Satisfied, she wound the tether up a bit on her hand to keep Rona close and started to move.

"Someday I should come back here and burn all of you to the ground," she shouted to the empty clearing. "Come on Rona, let's go and fill the water bottles and then get the heck out of here," she said to her lump of lumber and moved across the clearing and up the short path to the pool where the coolest and cleanest water splashed.

The silence of the surrounding forest engulfed her as she walked along the pathway, allowing her to hear the water of the stream bouncing over rocks and falling into tiny pools at the spot where she had bathed not many hours before. Only the rustle of the leaves of the waterside bamboo and the palms high overhead broke the spell of soundlessness. She couldn't help but think, under different circumstances, she could fall in love with the place.

Uncapping both water bottles, she stooped down to fill them, holding both underwater and watching the bubbles of air jump from the containers to the surface of the stream.

It was like one of those idyllic scenes in a Disney movie. There was a babbling brook, colorful birds flitting from tree to tree, and sunshine bathing the whole area as a beautiful young girl with long blonde tresses knelt to fill her water bottles. It was quite wonderful, but the spell lasted for less than the time it took to fill those water bottles.

It was broken when a rough male voice only a short distance away let out a roar like a bull, "what the bloody hell."

The voice was behind her and some distance away and the shock of it made her drop one of her bottles. Rachel spun in the dirt, looking in every direction to see who owned the voice, but no one was in sight. She heard the door of Manuel's shack bang as someone roughly slammed it open and she heard heavy boots pounding around on the plank floor inside.

Crawling toward some heavy underbrush between her and the clearing, she searched for a place to hide until she knew what was going on. A cold chill ran up her spine as she thought 'what next?'

Edging slowly on her stomach through the vegetation, Rachel managed to get an unobstructed sightline into the clearing. All seemed normal until a very large man with dreadlocks hanging haphazardly from a multicolored head covering stomped out of Manuel's shack with a pair of jeans in his hand, yelling at someone unseen while waving them over his head.

"Who the hell has been here?"

Only the silence of the jungle answered back.

"Damn," he yelled and kicked the pail near the fire pit as he lumbered across the clearing to Rachel's broken shack.

The huge man stood examining the broken doorway, reaching out to touch the upper part of the shattered jam still hanging in place. He scrutinized the somewhat askew beams with their ragged edges, perhaps hoping they could tell him what had happened. He clambered inside and Rachel could hear the thud of her faithful battering ram as the stranger banged it about in the room. In a moment, several pieces of the broken door flew from the shack out into the dust, kicked by the very angry man following them through the shattered doorway.

"Who the hell did this?" He shouted again to some unseen accomplice.

"Lester, Lester," he roared, turning to his left and right, stomping between the buildings, looking for someone Rachel couldn't see. "Where the hell are you?"

Again, only silence was his answer. Stopping his search beside the fire pit, he stood, large hands on huge hips, and again bellowed like a bull.

"Lester, you dumb bugger, you. Where the hell are you?" he bellowed.

"I'm right here Dumpy," the man called Lester yelled from three feet behind Rachel at the same time as he wrapped his rough hand around her ankle and started pulling her out of the underbrush. "I'm right here and I got me a fine prize."

Chapter Twenty Six

Day Five: Six A.M.

Manuel moaned softly as he shifted his left shoulder slightly in the dirt, trying to relieve a nagging cramp in his neck. It did no good.

He knew now there could be no doubt he would die where he lay and there was absolutely nothing he could do about it. Having reached this conclusion after much soul searching, he was at peace. An hour earlier, he had said his prayers and asked for absolution of his sins and although there was no priest about to give him the last rites, he knew all would be fine, God would understand.

The right side of his upper body was useless. He had given up trying to move his right arm or shoulder because each time he did, it caused him to almost faint. He also understood that even if the top half of him was good, which it wasn't, the bottom half was a mess.

Manuel knew he would never be able to move an inch from where he lay, certainly not under his own volition, and the possibility of anyone wandering past and finding him was extremely remote. He had picked the hiding spot for his venture all too well, and he would pay the ultimate price because of his diligence.

As he lay considering all this, his thoughts kept drifting back to his captive. He knew she was a bad-mannered, bad- tempered, spoiled brat, but she didn't deserve to die of starvation, chained to a ramshackle cabin in the middle of nowhere. He knew she had no food, her water would be all gone by now, and she couldn't make a fire or get near any firewood. She must be terrified. No matter how much she screamed or yelled, the chance of anyone hearing her was about as good as the chance of anyone stumbling on him.

He lay there thinking that maybe in another place, at some other time, and under some very different circumstances, they could have been friends; maybe even more; after all, she was very beautiful. Too beautiful, he thought as he closed his eyes and let his mind wander, only to have it wander back to a image of her, standing in the clearing in her white shorts holding a little towel in front of her, shyly asking for a shirt.

He had been a little embarrassed, thinking she could read his thoughts. She would have seen the look on his face of how he wanted the towel to just disappear before he turned to get her a shirt. He went into his shack to stand, out of sight, breathing hard, getting control of his mind, reminding himself of his mission.

Still he thought of her, now standing with her bare back to him, dropping the towel and pulling the T shirt over her head and her shoulders and finally over the smooth, unblemished satiny skin of her back. Even now, he had to force himself to stop wondering if her front was as perfect as her back.

Manuel sighed, thinking it was no wonder she hated him and yelled nasty things at him. She must have thought him not only a kidnapper, but a filthy lecher as well, scheming up ways to take advantage of her.

After many minutes, his thoughts wandered from his captive and turned to his family and his dear mother. This island, this Grenada, had taken another of hers. First, her husband, a brave man sent here by his leader, his hero, to help these poor downtrodden people. Now, her eldest son was being taken, slowly, painfully, in the same place. He felt great sadness for he feared she might never find out what had happened to him, or where he had died, or how. Mostly, she might never know why. Of all, this last fear weighed most heavy on him, it was possible she might never know why. His only hope was the letter.

Manuel had dropped a letter into the Post Office in Birch Grove the day before. He had worked for days, no, weeks, writing the letter, rewriting it, revising it, and editing every phrase, every word. The great Hemingway never worked so hard in his tiny hotel room in Havana on anything he wrote. The letter had to be perfect, and it was.

Addressed to the Prime Minister of Grenada, it was simple, forthright, and left no doubt he was serious and not to be taken lightly. If those who received it did take it lightly, grave consequences would befall his captive very quickly.

His letter, in English, was carefully composed. A young woman, a Canadian Embassy worker in Havana, moonlighting as an English teacher to earn a few extra pesos, taught him the rules on how to construct an English letter that was polite and to the point. He had learned well. The letter said:

Dear Mr. Prime Minister,

My father was murdered by the American gangster military forces when they invaded your beautiful island in 1983, while he was here helping to build an airport for your country. No one was ever punished for this crime.

Although my country treated my mother and my brother and sister with respect and honor, there has never been an apology from the mighty invaders for this crime against a humble road builder. That apology must come now.

I have in my custody a young lady, a student, who comes from one of America's most faithful allies.

I would ask you to please tell the President of the United States that he must apologize for the great

wrong his country did to Grenada in 1983 and, in particular, to my father, Louis Fernando Ruiz.

If he does not do this, I will kill the young lady and spill her blood into the soil of this island, as his people did to my father so long ago.

You have a newspaper, The Grenadian Voice, which seems to cover your island each week. Please ask them to print the President's apology on its front page. I will watch, and when I see the apology, I will release the girl. I will wait for the next two editions, but no longer.

I am sorry for any inconvenience this may be to you.

Manuel had purchased stamps in the Post Office and dropped the envelope into a mailbox just outside before he did his shopping. Hopefully his mother would someday learn of it.

Tired and sore, Manuel knew he must rest so he pushed thoughts of his home, family, and revenge from his head, closing his eyes to drift off into a light sleep. As he did, his last thoughts were not of his mother or family or his father. His last vision was of a young girl, shyly holding a towel in front of her and she wasn't yelling at him, she was smiling sweetly.

Chapter Twenty Seven

Day Five: Seven A.M.

"Get up," the man called Lester said roughly and stood back, holding Rona in one grubby hand and Rachel's tether in the other.

"Get yourself down there, my young sweetie and don't try anything funny or you'll get 'you know what'," and he grinned like a man who had just caught a delicious fish and was contemplating the supper he was about to have.

His toothless grin and the blatant lust in his eyes as he stared at her tight T shirt made Rachel shiver. If her captive knew, she wasn't thinking about trying anything funny, she was thinking about staying out of reach of the filthy hands of the piece of slime leering at her.

From below, the one called Dumpy let out another roar, "What the hell are you doing, Lester?"

Lester didn't answer. He just motioned Rachel to go ahead of him to join Dumpy, and when Dumpy turned his great bulk around and saw her, his mouth fell open.

"Where the hell did you find her?" he cried when he found his voice.

Lester was very proud of himself as he pranced like a peacock several feet behind his captive, holding her tether like a leash for a show dog at a competition. He excitedly moved toward Dumpy and handed him the cord.

"Here my friend," handing Dumpy the line. "I think we're going to have a very interesting night with this young beauty. Yes sir, she is one choice bit of female and we're going to have a very interesting night." His glee and lust sent chills down Rachel's spine as her mind whirled with plans and plots to get her out of this mess.

Dumpy moved slowly around Rachel, holding the tether like a string of pearls in his large hand. He looked her up and down, taking in her clothing, her messed hair and her scowling face. Finally, he stopped directly in front of her, dropped her tether to the ground and pointed to Lester to drop the chunk of wood he still held.

"Come and sit down," he said gently, surprising Rachel, and moved over to the stool that still sat in front of the shack with the broken doorway. "Come young lady, don't be afraid, come, sit and rest."

Cautiously Rachel moved across the clearing to the seat, still surprised by the tone of this huge man called Dumpy.

"You're the girl on the posters, aren't you?" he asked, squatting down on his haunches three feet in front of her.

"What posters?" She muttered.

"What posters she asks," and he laughed. "The ones stuck up on every bloody pole and building from here to Blue Bay; haven't you seen them?"

"No," was all Rachel could say, shaking her head.

"Well young lady, your pretty face is plastered all over this island and I don't know who's putting them up but they sure are getting them out there." Again he laughed, shaking his head at his good fortune. "You are one very popular girl and someone with a lot of money is trying hard to find you."

At this point, Lester jumped in with a leer and a laugh. "Hey Dumpy, that's an awful dirty shirt she's wearing. How 'bout she takes it off and we'll wash it so it's nice and clean."

"You keep your bloody hands off her. This lady is a missing person and there are some people out there who'll pay big money to get her back but they won't give a penny if we mishandle her. In fact they may try and throw us in jail, so just keep the hell away." It was obvious Dumpy was in charge.

Lester stepped back, unhappy with this turn of events and not sure he wanted to abide by his partner's wishes. Sulking, he moved away from Rachel, but couldn't hide his lust. She knew he was a problem that would have to be dealt with eventually.

Turning from his friend, Dumpy moved over to Rachel's old hut and lowered his bulk onto the step at the doorway. Rachel rotated on her stool to face him, all the while keeping an eye on Leering Lester, who was drooling by now as he watched her every move.

"What's your name?" Dumpy asked.

"Rachel, what's yours?" she shot back.

"Hudson, but everyone calls me Dumpy, have for years." The big man chuckled and jiggled all over, not seeming to mind a nickname gained because of his very bad appearance.

Hudson looked pretty dumpy. His T shirt was as dirty as the one Lester was wearing and was stained by sweat. There was a small tear from the collar running toward his right shoulder and a patch had been sewn on the front over his vast expanse of stomach. His trousers, incredibly far too large for even Hudson's great girth, looked like they hadn't been washed in a year. The bottom rear of each pant leg was torn to shreds from dragging along the ground behind his filthy sneakers. Hudson's nickname suited him perfectly, and Rachel wondered why anyone even bothered to put the 'Y' on the end.

Lester was going through Rachel's bag, pulling Manuel's spare T shirt and the books out one by one, tossing them aside in a pile. When he reached the small tobacco pouch he unzipped it and let out a shout.

171

"Lookee here Dumpy; we got ourselves a nice pile of funny money here," and he held up the wad of Manuel's stash. Laughing, he started to go slowly through the bundle, counting out the bills like a six year old. Before he got to ten the large bulk of Dumpy loomed over him, blocking the sunlight.

"Give it here," he thundered. "The pouch too, and put all that stuff back where it came from. Do it right now or it's the back of my hand you'll feel, you little twerp" and held out his huge hand.

He turned back to Rachel, stuffing the money into the pouch, not bothering to count it while a petulant Lester angrily jammed back into the bag all of the items he had just tossed out.

"What you doing with that cash, Dumpy? There's a lot of money there."

"Oh Lester, you simpleton, you're lucky you got me to take care of you. This is nothing compared with the reward this young lady's family will pay to get her back. We're going to be rich, my friend, rich, and this bit of mixed-up bills will mean nothing," and he flipped the pouch back into Manuel's bag

"Zip the bag up and give it back to, what's your name again, Rachel? Yes, give it back to Rachel. We want her to tell her rich family how nice we treated her, don't we." Turning to Rachel he said, "Remember how we're taking good care of you and make sure you tell them."

Dumpy stood, looking down at Rachel and then turned to Lester, who was still sulking.

"I'm going down to the village to try and contact her people. I also want to check out how big a reward there is for finding her. You stay here and keep an eye on her and your hands off. You understand?" he roared. Lester brightened at the prospect of being left alone with Rachel and happily shook his head up and down at the instructions.

"Don't you worry Dumpy; I'll take good care of her 'till you get back. You don't have to worry 'bout that," gleefully grabbing the tether the other man offered, while unsuccessfully trying to look innocent.

Rachel had a sick feeling in the pit of her stomach, figuring this was a major problem developing that would call for some very fast thinking. She casually glanced about the clearing, making note of where she sat and where every good sized rock lay around the place. She also memorized the location of the fry pan and pot near the fire pit. She didn't know what she could do or what kind of opportunity might suddenly present itself, but if and when one did, she wanted to be ready.

Dumpy reached deep into his trouser pocket and pulled out a scrap of paper and a stub of a pencil. Sitting back down on the shack's steps, he lifted a piece of broken door from near his feet and put it across his knees to form a writing table. He started to print something.

"You said your name was Rachel but I need to know your last name if I'm going to get help for you. What is it?" and he waited for her.

"Lusinski," noting his befuddled look. "L.U.S.I.N.S.K.I. It's an old Polish name." Dumpy laboriously marked down each letter on his scrap of paper as she spelled it out.

"Do you know who might be here in Grenada looking for you? I mean, could it be your father or brother out putting up all the signs and if so, what are their names so I can find them?" he asked.

"I don't have any brothers but I'm sure my dad is here and probably my mother and my grandparents too. So you better treat me well because my father has a terrible temper and would be very nasty to you two if he thought I had been mistreated while I was with you." She ran out of breath and had to stop.

173

"Oh don't worry about that young lady. We know how valuable you are and we don't mean to spoil our chances to reap a large reward for rescuing you from whatever problem you have," the shrewd, fat scoundrel said with a smile that was meant to assure and comfort her, but actually caused goose bumps on her arms instead.

"No, my dear, you're safe here with Lester while I go get your father and mother and talk to them about our reward. It won't take long and you should be out of here in no time. Now what are their names?" Dumpy said and raised his pencil to make more notes.

Rachel gave him everything he needed, suggesting if her family was on the island, they would be at one of the better hotels and Dumpy dutifully printed all the details. When he couldn't think of anything more to ask, he stood, folded his paper and stuffed it into his pocket.

Staring down at Lester as though wondering if he was doing the right thing and finally deciding he had no other option, he called Lester to come closer.

Threateningly, he shook his huge fist an inch from his partner's face and made it clear in no uncertain terms that Lester was a dead man if there were any problems, or any harm came to the girl. Then, saying he'd be back in two or three hours, he simply turned away from them and walked out of the clearing and down the path.

Chapter Twenty Eight

Day Five: Six A.M.

Harry Stanton slowly rolled out of bed feeling every single one of his seventy some years. He knew if Kitty was with him, she would bend his ear in no uncertain terms about how he was behaving like an old fool, tramping around in the jungle like some twenty year old. Then, shaking her head and muttering nonstop about how he should act his age, she would go into the washroom and start drawing a hot bath for him. Following that, she would rummage, still muttering, through their bags until she found the tube of Bengay she knew was always handy. The trouble today was that Kitty wasn't there. He had to get his own bath ready, and the place was too quiet, not enough muttering, and he didn't know where the Bengay was, but he sure needed it.

Harry knew the day before had just been a teaser. They hadn't arrived in the tiny village of Richmond until two in the afternoon and then spent a lot of time finding a good place to set up their base. After arranging the cars and making sure their supporters were alright, Harry had dug out his map of the area, made sure his different colored felt pens for marking it were in his pocket, then led his team into the bush to search out the high spots as LJ had suggested.

Team 5 was Harry's responsibility and he was serious about how it worked. Their search territory was a rough triangle with the north bordered by the twisting secondary road running from Birch Grove to Grenville, and on to the east by another secondary road running south from La Digue, to a village named Deblando. His easterly boundary was anything he could make it and he knew if he went too far, he could bump into John Hardy and his Team 2, or Raymond Redhead and the Team 1 hotel gang working southeast from Birch Grove.

It didn't matter. Their job was to search for a place in the hills where as few as two people or as many as five, could hide out for anywhere from a week to a month. Rachel's kidnappers could be using a cave, or set up in a clearing, but anything able to fill their living requirements would have to be substantial. There would have to be somewhere to sleep and some kind of privy, or outhouse nearby. It should also have some clean water close at hand and since the occupants would need to cook at least one meal a day, LJ said to keep an eye open for a wisp of smoke at mealtimes, or to try and sniff out a cooking fire.

LJ's training in the Marines, which went back almost fifty years, had been a big help. In discussions with the six other team leaders at a closed meeting the night before, LJ had told them some of the things he had been trained to look for when moving through areas thought to be hostile.

Water was an absolute necessity, particularly for drinking. They would also need it for cleaning, and cooking, so people tended to set up camp relatively close to some source of water. The further you had to trek for water, the greater your chance of being discovered.

Fire was another necessity, so one had to keep an eye open for any wood cutting in what would otherwise be an untouched area. Explaining exactly what to look for, LJ said if you come across a place in the bush with obvious firewood gathering activity, find a comfortable spot and sit down. He suggested they look for things like broken branches, freshly cut small tree trunks, or no loose pieces of wood on the ground. If what you saw wasn't far from a stream or river, you might be onto something.

He said 'sit and stay quiet' for anything from fifteen minutes to half an hour and you should time it with your watch, and make absolutely no sound. Listen very carefully.' Often you can hear what you can't see.

He also told of finding a high spot and sitting with a pair of binoculars for half an hour, just slowly going back and forth over the terrain below you, looking for smoke, running water and anything unnatural, like part of a roof, or a pathway.

LJ got a laugh with a short story of watching two very pretty, and very naked young ladies, bathing in a stream in Vietnam. They were laughing and splashing each other, having a grand old time, oblivious to the world around them, or the war that was ripping their country apart. LJ said it was the first time he'd ever seen his men fight over who did the usually boring job of searching and observing with the binoculars.

His crash course in search and destroy, as he called it, impressed a lot of the people involved in the search part of this operation. Many left the room thinking they wouldn't want to be hiding somewhere trying to stay out of the gun sights of an angry LJ Livingston.

The hot bath, combined with a liberal application of Bengay on all his many sore spots, put Harry in a better frame of mind as he headed to the restaurant for breakfast. He had told his team he wanted to be on the road by seven and in the bush by eight and was delighted to see all four other members halfway through their morning meal when he arrived.

"Hi guys," he cheerily called as he grabbed a coffee pot and headed to the table. "How's everyone feeling?"

"Oh shut up," said one while another lobbed a breakfast roll at him.

"None of us feel all that well," said Jim, a retired steelworker from Buffalo. "Hell Harry, it's been a long time since any of us had this much exercise in a month, let alone a day."

"Did any of you guys think to bring some Bengay?" Harry asked with a slightly superior tone.

All raised their hands, nodding yes in unison and everyone, including Harry, broke into loud, almost uncontrolled laughter, causing the wives, at another table, to cast very unapproving looks in their direction.

"Well, hell," said Harry. "We'll go out today, slog through paradise, find Rachel and feel much better tomorrow. We'll do it a little slower than the youngsters, but we'll do it better."

"Actually Harry, I think we should get the youngsters to do it and we just supervise," Jim said to a chorus of 'here here's'.

"Forget it. The youngsters wouldn't listen to you anyway. So if we want the job done, and we want it done right, we'll just have to do it ourselves."

To much good-natured belly aching, the group finished their coffee and prepared to leave for the hills. A couple went over to their wives because today they were rostered to operate the base camp. The other two headed out to the parking lot to get the cars. Harry just stood and missed Kitty.

Chapter Twenty Nine

Day Five: Ten A.M.

Dumpy waddled into the tiny village of Castaigne, looking much like a disheveled, Humpty Dumpty. Standing at the roadside, he mopped his brow with a decades-old piece of cloth, his sweat-stained clothes clearly showing the effects of his trek in the heat through the jungle. He needed a helper in his nefarious plan and he had just the right person in mind.

He had clambered down the hillsides, almost rolling like a giant beach ball at times, at others sliding on the seat of his pants, making his quickest exit out of the bush in the many years he had conducted business in the area. Now, after an hour looking for his first and second choice as co-conspirator, he moved slower, passing tiny houses along the roadway, seeking out one shack where he knew a friend who would surely help.

Arriving at the home he was searching for, he banged on the door with more force than necessary and danced a exited little jig as he waited for an answer.

Dumpy had thought a lot about the reward he would get while climbing down through the hills and knew he must find a way to limit Lester's share. They were partners, but after all, it was he who first recognized the girl, and he who had devised this plan to extract a fine reward for finding her. He worried about Lester and hoped he obeyed orders and left her alone. Lester's conduct was the only fly in the ointment and Dumpy would kill him if he harmed her or screwed things up.

Dumpy was set to bang on the door again when it swung open to reveal Alicia, the wife of his friend Horace, in a filthy rag of a dress with a babe on her hip and a sneering skeptical look in her always mean eyes.

"What you want Dumpy?" she asked suspiciously.

"Horace. I need Horace. Where is he Alicia? I need him right away." The big man sputtered in his excitement.

"What you up to Dumpy? What kind of trouble you trying to get my man Horace into this time?"

"No trouble, Alicia, no trouble at all. I just need a little help and I know he can give it and I'll pay cash, I promise. Now where the hell is he?"

"No need to talk to me like that, Dumpy. No need at all. If you want something, just watch your tongue and you might get it. No need to use foul language around me and the children". Alicia's preachy manner was always able to get under Dumpy's skin and make him a little crazy but he needed Horace so he took a deep breath and instead of giving her a punch like Horace would, he played the gentleman, or something as close to it as he could manage.

"Listen Alicia, I'm sorry I swore and I apologize. Now please, where is your fine husband on this fine day?" Dumpy said through clenched teeth, wanting to reach into the doorway and give her the smack on the side of her head he felt she so richly deserved. Of course, if he did that he would never find Horace so he just smiled sweetly, or what he hoped was sweetly, and waited for her umbrage to die down.

"That's better Dumpy," she said, taking command. "Now, let me think," and she took several seconds, enjoying the moment, knowing Dumpy might explode in a screaming, swearing fit at any minute. "Oh yes, he's out in da bush with a bunch of white guys trying to find some stupid little rich girl who went and wandered off and got herself lost. Some people came around and he said he would help them but he ain't getting paid."

Dumpy wouldn't believe that for a moment. Horace never offered to do anything for anyone without getting paid, ever. He wouldn't save a child from a burning building or push a little old lady from the path of a speeding bus without first negotiating his fee. Dumpy figured Horace must have been lying to his wife to keep her hands off the money. It wouldn't be the first time.

"Did he take his phone?" Dumpy asked.

"No. The battery's low, and besides, the searchers had phones and radios and so did the police so he wouldn't need his." Alicia was getting ready to close the door.

"Can I use it? He won't mind and I'll pay him. In fact, listen, I'll give you a couple of dollars right now just to use it," and he whipped out a few bills from his pocket knowing she'd never pass up this opportunity.

"OK," Alicia said, making a five dollar bill disappear from Dumpy's hand with the speed of a frog catching a fly. She turned to get the phone.

"Here, give it back when you're finished," she said and slammed the door closed. Dumpy didn't even notice the door crashing shut in his face; he was already dialing the number of a friend in St. George's who could tell him where the real money was.

Dumpy's plan was to find the family of the girl as quickly as possible and arrange the reward he was sure was being offered. He would let the family know he had an idea where the girl could be found and as soon as the reward was determined, he would lead them to her.

He had to be careful. He didn't want them to think him a kidnapper, having anything to do with the girl's disappearance. He was a rescuer, a civic minded citizen of Grenada, doing his duty in this time of a visitor's needs. The fact he got paid was beside the point.

Dumpy grinned happily as he moved away from the front door of the house while dialing his friend. As he stood waiting for an answer, he considered the possible colors for his new pickup his reward money would buy. Red seemed best.

Chapter Thirty

Day Five: Eight A.M.

For long minutes after Dumpy disappeared down the trail in search of his precious reward, Rachel and Lester 'the leering lecher' as Rachel mentally named him, sat quietly fifteen feet apart acting as though neither knew the other was there.

He casually glanced in every direction, looking up at tree tops, around the clearing and over toward the cabin behind her, constantly trying not to be caught staring too long at the front of her red T shirt. She just sat very still, one eye on her keeper, and the other watching the open spot in the underbrush where Dumpy and Manuel before him, had vanished. Sitting there, she wondered if she would ever be able to walk out that way.

Finally, after what seemed a very long time, Lester stood, stretched and as casually as someone with his limited degree of intelligence and sophistication could muster, tried to start a little friendly conversation.

"What the hell you do to get all them people out there lookin' for you?" he asked with what he considered a sympathetic smile.

Turning toward him, Rachel was set to let rip with a long string of nasty comments, but seeing him standing there, toothless, unwashed, unshaven, in badly fitting, mended clothing, she thought better of it. This was an ugly man at least a foot taller than her, probably seventy five to a hundred pounds heavier, and he held her leash in his filthy hand. She had no idea what he could or would do but she knew blatant lust when she saw it and she saw it in Lester. She took a different tact.

"Some crazy man kidnapped me five or six days ago and brought me here. He kept me here, tied to that shack," and pointed toward the near hut with the broken door. "I'm so glad and grateful you guys came along to rescue me." She looked up at him and gave what she hoped was a genuine 'you're my hero' look. She hoped God would forgive her for telling such a lie.

"It was nothing," Lester declared. "We saw your picture and felt bad for you so we set out to find you, knowing these hills as good as we do. Like the back of me hand I knows them, I do." Lester waved his arm toward the jungle around them, trying to impress.

"What kind of work do you do in this forest that makes you know it so well?" she asked, being nice and prim and interested.

"Oh, we grow a little stuff up here, over there a little bit," pointing to the hills on his left, into an area above the small stream and pond where he had caught her earlier. "You know what I mean, a cash crop sort of thing. This here clear spot is where we stay when we're working our crops, you know."

Rachel knew exactly what kind of crop it was. It had very long narrow leaves on the end of it's stems. Lester's plants were the kind grown back home indoors; usually in rented houses, ruined by the high humidity it took to develop one of those cash crops. Police were always cleaning out some grow-op in the Toronto area but two more always sprung up for each one closed.

"It must be hard work," she offered.

"Not really, we take our time and haul our product out for market. It's worth all the effort and we're both strong boys you know."

She almost answered 'yes, but smell isn't everything', but caught herself. She figured she could laugh later and knew she had to keep him chatting. He was one of those people who didn't think well about two things at the same time, and as long as she kept him bragging about how good his marijuana business was, he might have difficulty making other, more intimate plans for their time together.

"Is this the time you start getting your crop ready for market?" she asked, trying to keep the conversation going.

Lester paused. He wasn't so completely stupid not to reason that this young lady had very little interest in his agricultural efforts. He had no idea why she was asking all these questions but he was getting a little tired of this chatter about plants and work. His train of thought pulled back onto the main line from the spur of his work project, and he wanted to change the subject.

"Boy, it's getting hot isn't it?" was his subtle way of making the change.

Rachel looked up, noting his altered demeanor and the different tone of his voice and felt a chill run up her spine.

"Yes, it really is. Do you have a bottle of water handy?"

Lester thought for a minute and looked up the trail toward the stream.

"No, but I think there's a couple up by the stream. Maybe we should go up and get them. Let's walk up to the river and get some nice cool, fresh water. That's a good idea." And he turned to lead her up the path.

"While we're there, you might want to wash some of the dirt and grime off, you know, clean up a bit for your family and everyone." Now he was almost panting.

"Well I don't know, my kidnapper let me wash once a few days ago behind my shack, but he promised not to look and I know he didn't."

"Oh, I wouldn't look, I promise you that. Not me. Not one little peek. I have to hold this cord you understand and I'll just sit with my back to you and watch the jungle. You can be sure, not one little peek from me, no, you can bet your last dollar on that." He was not only panting, he was drooling, too.

"Okay, I guess it'll be all right, lets go," and they started across the clearing past the fire pit, Lester leading the way, almost doing a joyous jig.

"Maybe we should take the bucket so I can rinse myself off when I'm finished," she suggested, pointing to the pail lying just ahead of them, resting where Dumpy had kicked it earlier.

"Good idea, good idea," panted Lester as he rushed past the fry pan and coffee pot to reach down and grab the bucket.

'It's now or never' thought Rachel in terror as she bent low, grabbed the heavy frying pan lying at her feet, and swung it in one movement up and over her head, swinging it over her and down toward the back of Lester's head. He sensed something happening because he turned and looked up and back at her just as it connected with his temple and forehead.

With a hoarse scream of pain, Lester dropped the pail and the cord to grab the side of his head, blood blasting out from the huge cut across his brow and back toward his left ear. He staggered across the dirt, stumbling, yelling and cursing, as Rachel just stood there frozen in wonder. She just couldn't believe he hadn't fallen down unconscious like everyone did on TV, or in the movies when bashed on the head. He wasn't out cold; he was staggering around the clearing, reaching for her, screaming obscenities at her and threatening things she could never repeat to her mother. The terror she felt before she hit him was nothing compared to what she felt now. If she had eaten any kind of breakfast that morning, she would have thrown up.

Lester was regaining some semblance of stability and was plodding in her direction. Blood was still spurting from his head and his left eye was closed but he managed to lurch toward her, Frankenstein like, bloody left hand holding his wound and right hand straight out in front of him, reaching like a claw for his assailant.

Rachel panicked and started backing up, only to trip, falling backward as Lester unknowingly stepped on her tether, causing it to pull her foot out from under her. Now on her back stretched out on the ground, she looked up to see Lester hovering above her, blood dripping down on her and into the dirt.

"You just stay there like that you little witch, 'cause I've got something for you, I have. You're going to pay dearly for this," and he stepped closer, reaching down toward her T shirt.

Still holding her weapon, Rachel silently called for strength from places she had never called to before, and swung the frying pan one more time. She couldn't get the heavy utensil very far off the ground, but she raised it as high as she could. Swinging it in an arc from it's resting spot in the dirt above her head, it swept like a scythe, raising to about a foot off the ground to crash into his left shin. The cracking sound of the bone shattering was as loud and clear as a gunshot.

It seemed like minutes passed as Lester rolled on the ground, his ear-splitting screams slowly reducing to a whimper. Rachel didn't speak to him and tried not to look at him, lying in the dirt with his bloody head and a leg oddly out of shape. He was crying, once or twice begging her not to hit him again, but she really didn't hear and she wasn't interested in inflicting any more pain. She just wanted to get away.

Without hesitation, she jumped up, grabbed her tether and raced across the clearing, dragging the lump of wood behind her toward the pathway out of her prison. Crying hysterically she ran, and all she could think of was her mother and father and how she wished they were here to put their arms around her.

Chapter Thirty One

Day Five: Eight Thirty A.M.

The search was well underway in all seven areas. The crews left the hotel around seven in a long convoy that worked its way through the streets of St. George's, and out onto the main road north to Grenville. In what seemed to be no time at all, the line of vehicles started getting shorter as three dropped out at Birch Grove, and another three as the convoy passed through Adelphi.

Peter Baxter tooted his horn and waved as he dropped out at Lower Capital, followed by his wife Anne and another car. By eight o'clock, all were in place, out of their cars, and organizing into packs of searchers made up of at least two of the Florida group and a handful of local volunteers.

The police had positioned one officer at each of the seven spots, drawn from the Birch Grove Station, the St. George's main station and the Grenville Station to the north. To augment this force were at least a half dozen more Constables available from these and other stations throughout the island ready to jump in if needed. All were connected by radio, either hand-held or in their cars, and each carried very specific instructions from their superiors to do whatever was needed to help.

Nick drove from one base camp to another, meeting the volunteers and thanking them, checking each camp's set-up and making notes of what might be needed, or what was surplus and eligible for lending out, if needed somewhere else.

Everything was ticking along as planned with no problems, until he got to the Team 6 base in the tiny collection of homes called Plaisance, a couple of miles south of La Digue. Unlike the other operations where a general buzz of activity involving searchers and support workers was the norm, this location was quiet and still with everyone standing in a tight group in one spot, none moving. He knew something was wrong before he stopped rolling and turned off his motor.

"What's happening," he said as he shoved through the group gathered beside a parked car.

"The man no too well," said a local search volunteer in his heavy accent.

Now through, Nick looked down where he could see who it was and he thought, 'oh my God'. Alice Lusinski was on her knees, tears on her cheeks, holding her husband's hand. Fred, very pale, was stretched out on the grassy area beside the parked vehicle, head cushioned by a bundle of hotel towels. He opened his eyes and turned slightly when he heard Nick ask what was going on.

"Hi, old buddy," he all but whispered, looking up with a wane smile, "I guess I'm not as young as I thought I was. Seems as though me old ticker has finally given up the ghost." Alice was now in full crying mode.

"Oh Nick, what can we do?" she asked.

"Don't worry Alice," he said as cheerily as he could, "only the good die young," and he turned to those gathered around.

"Has anyone called for a doctor? Has anyone called for an ambulance or called the nearest hospital?" He looked around and spotted the young police officer assigned to this team.

"Have you contacted anyone?" he called to him.

"Yes sir. I called immediately he went down, and the ambulance is on the way. The nearest hospital is in Grenville, and I think they plan on taking him there sir." He seemed calm and capable, giving off an air of authority and having everything under control.

188

"How about a doctor?" Nick asked.

"I called. One is on his way, sir," answered the policeman.

"Is the General Hospital in St. George's better equipped for this sort of thing, you know, heart trouble?" Nick wanted to know.

"Well sir, it is the biggest and best equipped hospital on our island. I would think it may be better, it does have much more staff and equipment, but it is a lot further from here. We have several fairly new and well fitted out ambulances but it would take much more time to get him there." The policeman was trying hard to be helpful.

Nick bent down on one knee and took Fred's other hand and asked, "Are you comfortable?"

Fred grinned and said, "Well, I have my pensions, a nice home in Florida, a small cottage on Lake Erie up in Canada and some savings in bonds and Registered Retirement Plans. Yes, I'd say I was comfortable," and he started to laugh, coughing lightly.

"I'll bet you've been waiting years to use that joke," Nick said, laughing along with him and gave Alice a wink. "If you can make fun of having a heart attack and falling down on the ground, you can't be all that bad. I should make you get up and get to work in the bush. Seriously, how are you feeling, my friend?"

"Oh, not too bad, considering, but please, do me a favor and get these guys out in the bush looking for Rachel." Fred stopped for a minute, as though trying to catch his breath, and then continued, his voice not quite as strong as before.

"Nick, they're just standing around gawking at me and taking up space and wasting time. They can't do anything for me and I'd feel much better if I knew that they were out looking for my granddaughter. Find Larry, he's part of the team and he knows what we're doing.

Ask him to try and get things moving, please." He slumped a little bit and Nick thought he had fainted, but Fred waved him away and Nick got up.

"OK everyone, over here please" and he moved about fifteen feet away from the prostrate man and his comforting wife.

"Now all of you listen up please. Fred is having some heart problems and help is on the way. We have a doctor coming, an ambulance is on the road, and the hospital has received a heads up that we're coming. We also have the police officer here with his radio." He stopped and noticed everyone was listening, including Fred and Alice over on the grass.

"I tell you this because there is something you can do to help Fred feel better. If you do it he will probably relax and his problem will at least not be aggravated. It will surely calm him down if he knows his team, you group of good people, were out beating the bushes, looking for his little girl.

"Larry is up to speed on the search procedures. He knows what must be done so listen to him and let's get this show on the road." Nick waved Larry into the circle from the side lines and stepped aside with a whispered 'get them moving' order.

Within five minutes, the first subgroup of searchers was moving into the bush northwards toward Deblando and the second group was set to head out straight up a hill westward. Five minutes later, all searchers were gone and a peace enveloped the area around Fred.

Nick again knelt beside his friend looking to see how he was.

"I'm so sorry Nick," Fred muttered. "This is such a damned nuisance and just when she needed me most."

"Don't be silly. You've done all the legwork on this up untill now and all Larry and I have to do is point everyone in the right direction and give them a gentle shove. Don't you worry, if she's in this section, that gang will find her." Nick could see Fred was breathing easier and looked a little more relaxed.

Alice Lusinski joined in, "Thanks Nick, you handled that well and I'm sure they'll do a great job. Now, tell me, where is that ambulance?"

Her timing couldn't have been better. As she uttered the last word, a large white and orange ambulance swung into their clearing and ground to a halt. Before the dust settled, two young Emergency Response attendants were out, each with a large briefcase-like pack, sprinting toward Fred. These guys looked serious.

Nick and Alice stepped back out of the way, and within seconds, Fred had an oxygen mask over his nose and mouth, with the bottle turned on. The other attendant wrapped a blood pressure device around Fred's upper arm and was squeezing a rubber ball, filling it with air. They had not looked at Alice or Nick, or even said hello.

Alice had a viselike grip on Nick's arm, watching every move the men made when one of them suddenly turned, looked up, and said to her in a clipped British accent, "Excuse me madam, you are the wife, I presume." Alice nodded yes.

"Jolly good," he continued. "Could you tell me if he has any allergies, reacts adversely to any drugs, or is taking any medication at the moment?" He waited, still on his knees, for an answer.

"Fred has no allergies, and I don't recall him ever reacting adversely to anything other than a bad putt he made. He's not a big one on drugs or pills of any kind. As for medication, the only thing he takes are these, and has for several years," and she fished a small bottle of pills from her purse and handed them to the attendant.

"His doctor prescribed them. I carry the bottle to make sure he takes them when he should, otherwise he never would."

The young paramedic read the label on the bottle, referred to a small book in his kit, put both down and picked up a hypodermic needle. Swiping Fred's left arm with some alcohol, he stuck it in Fred's as quickly as Nick had ever seen it done.

"That should take care of him," he said as he stood and turned to Nick and Alice. "I should think he has had a little problem with the regularity of his heartbeat. You know, a valve opens slowly or stays open a little too long, that sort of thing. I've given him something to relax, slow him down somewhat, he should be alright now. Tell me, has he been under any stress lately?"

Alice looked at Nick, and Nick looked at Alice, and both almost burst out laughing in relief.

Nick recovered first and answered the surprised medical man. "He has been under a great deal of stress in the last several days. In fact, far more stress than anyone should ever be forced to endure."

"Are you staying in this area?"

"No," Nick said, and told the man of their mission and where they were staying.

"Well, he should be fine, but he needs some rest and quiet. Since you're staying at Grand Anse, I think we'll take him down to the General Hospital. It will be closer to you and much easier to visit. The longer trip will do him no harm. Would you like to come along?"

Within minutes, the peacefully breathing Fred was on a gurney, pushed into the ambulance, and ready for the ride south to hospital. The driver helped Alice in through the side door, closed everything up and got in behind the wheel. The attendant came over to Nick before getting in.

"Are you in charge of the old gang that I heard had come down here to help?"

"I'm one of their organizers," was all Nick said.

"Well, everyone on the island wants you to find that girl safe and sound, so I just wanted to wish you good luck and good hunting," and with a quick shake of Nick's hand, he was in his ambulance and they were on their way.

Nick stood for several seconds, watching the ambulance disappear and just shook his head. Turning to go, he approached the waiting policeman and thanked him for his help, suggesting he explain what happened to the doctor when he arrived, and to thank him.

Climbing into his car, he hoped there were no more problems like this.

Chapter Thirty Two

Day Five: Ten A.M.

LJ sat quietly, legs crossed, almost motionless. His perch was a flat rock near the top of the tallest hill in his team's target section. He could see down on approximately a quarter of that section and he had been slowly sweeping the hillsides and valleys for half an hour with his binoculars. He was calmly looking for anything that might give him some help.

He chuckled at the irony of it all when he found his look-out and started the systematic examination of the terrain below. He was using the same binoculars he had carried for thirty years as a Marine, and looking over the same hills he had the last time he saw combat. That was more than a quarter century ago. The big difference now was there was no gunfire, no roar of helicopters, and no sixty pound load of assorted equipment strapped to every possible spot on his body. He also didn't have black greasepaint smeared on his face.

With him now were his faithful old binoculars, a small two-way radio, a cell phone, and a one liter plastic bottle filled with water. He was thankful there was no need for a rifle, pistol or grenades.

LJ's first visit to the island nation had been in the twilight of his long and varied military career, when he was in his late forties. He was, by far, the oldest member of a unit of youngsters, inserted into Pearls Airport early on the morning of October 25th, 1983. They arrived in large twin rotor choppers from the Fort Snelling, one of five ships in a battle group tasked with delivering and supporting forces ordered to seize the airport and all the surrounding territory.

All went well, with only erratic anti-aircraft bursts from a lone battery of Russian-made guns positioned north of the runway. They couldn't shoot straight, but seemed determined to test the nerves of everyone sitting on the incoming aircraft. This nuisance was quickly addressed by a couple of Cobra gun ships who raked the battery with 20-mm cannons and 2.75 inch rockets. This display of testiness had ended the irritation.

Once on the ground, LJ's unit also ran into sporadic rifle fire from the airport's terminal building. This ended when the two platoons of Marines returned the fire and the Cobras came in and laid down a short burst or two. Wisely, the men inside dropped their weapons, scurried out the back doors and ran for the bushes. By seven-thirty a.m., the shooting was over, the airport secure, and neither side had lost anyone. LJ, who treated his young charges like a hen treats her chicks, thought it was a hell of a great way to run a war.

Over the next twelve hours LJ and his unit were joined by many more men and they moved from the airport into the city of Grenville. They took it slowly, securing major intersections, setting up check points, and anticipating major opposition with every step. There was none.

The citizens greeted them with smiles, flowers and open arms. They were happy to lend the Marines trucks, show them where several large caches of weapons had been hidden, and lead them to the hiding places of some of those on the most wanted list. The island was being liberated from a brutal and oppressive regime and the citizens were grateful. They knew those responsible for the death of their Prime Minister would soon face justice.

After securing Grenville and the surrounding area, LJ and his men were ordered into the hills to the west and south, charged with finding the insurgents who ran when they saw the Marines coming. The Americans search was made easy by the extensive help from the locals, some who passed on the word that the Marines were coming, thereby eliminating much shooting as they tracked down their quarry.

It was those few days of action in the hills of Grenada which convinced LJ it was finally time to retire from the Marines he loved so much. He went on to Lebanon for a short tour after Grenada, but had decided, high in the same jungle where he now quietly sat, that it was time to call it a day. Running around in the bush, laden down with backpack, rifle, pistol, grenades, plus all the other things a soldier had to carry, was not the life for a man fast approaching his fiftieth birthday. It was a job for those with fire in their belly, a job for younger men.

LJ never regretted his decision to retire. He joined the Marines when he was eighteen, saw a large part of the world, and left thirty years later, much healthier, and much wiser. When he got out, he purchased a failing printing company in Patterson, New Jersey, where he had been born, and worked hard to bring it back to life. He passed it on to his sons when it got too big for one man.

He had a good life, a good wife, and was enjoying his retirement, but he had never dreamt he'd ever return to any of those places where he had waged war. It was a strange feeling.

"LJ, are you there?" crackled his radio. It was Anthony Lusinski, down the hill and about five hundred yards behind with the group of searchers.

"LJ here," was all he said, keeping it short out of habit.

"See anything up there?"

"Nothing. No smoke. No buildings. Keep coming, I'll keep looking."

"Roger," and Anthony switched off.

LJ had thought it a good idea to keep Anthony away from his old man while they were searching. They didn't need the distraction of a father and son battle out here in the bush. This search was going to be tough enough.

One of the locals had spent some time the day before drawing a rough pattern of all the streams and brooks that were too small to be marked on their maps. The area was laced by waterways, fed by the almost constant rains in the high hills. Some rivers were substantial with large picturesque waterfalls and tumbling rapids down the hillsides. Seven Falls, Fontainbleu, and Concord Falls, were all within a few miles of where he sat and all were touted as tourist attractions. LJ thought this important, deciding to leave any area where there was no fresh running water to the end of the search. That represented about twenty-five percent of their area.

LJ's cell phone started ringing and it took him five of those rings to fish the damn thing out of his pocket.

"Hello," he growled, sounding a little on the grumpy side.

"Nick here, and a good day to you as well. Is Anthony with you?"

"No, he's in the bush with the rest. I'm up a hill having a look see. Why?"

"Fred had a heart attack of some kind. He's on his way to the hospital with Alice."

"Which hospital?"

"The big one in St. George's," Nick said.

"Then he can't be too bad."

"Why would you say that?" Nick shot back, thinking that talking to LJ was like conversing with an answering machine.

"Because, if he was bad, they would have taken him to the hospital in Grenville. It's about four times closer, he'd be in hospital faster, and the ride would be smoother." LJ said. It was like he was talking to a simpleton.

"You're right. Man, you are sharp. Now, if you're not too busy, could you get hold of Anthony and let him know what's happening?"

LJ thought for a moment before answering.

"No. What's the use? He'll be with me in an hour so I'll tell him then. There's nothing he can do for Fred right now, and we have a job to finish. If you like, I'll give him my phone so he can call you and you can give him all the gory details. OK?"

"You're right," Nick admitted. "Let him call me when he meets up with you. I may have a little more information by then. I'll call Ann and ask her to get Irene and go up to the hospital to meet Alice when they come in. She'll take care of everything. I'll get her to call back if there's any more news. Talk to you later," and Nick hung up.

LJ put the phone away and shifted his position, thought for a moment, then put his binoculars up to his eyes, starting his slow, methodical sweep of the hills and valleys far below.

An hour later, the team of searchers met up with LJ and he laid out the map so he could mark the area just covered. He then pointed out two hills just west of them he wanted searched next. One had a stream LJ had spotted minutes ago as the sun climbed high enough to reflect off it. The stream had been shaded by trees up to that time. The other hill, slightly to the right of the one with water, looked like a good prospect as well.

"We'll start for those two now," he ordered, pointing to the targets. "Since we have twelve bodies, Anthony can take five and go for the one on the right. I'll take five and hit the other. Any questions?" and he waited for a response. None came.

"OK, now we'll take ten for a breather, and then be on our way. Anthony, can I talk to you?" he asked, motioning for the younger Lusinski to separate from the others and follow him to a spot some twenty feet away.

It only took LJ a few minutes to explain all he knew about Fred. Pulling his phone out and hitting the dial back button, he silently handed the phone over and walked away. Within seconds, Anthony was talking to Nick, getting all the details.

Five minutes later he rejoined the group, handed the phone to LJ and suggested they get started. All he said was, "Let's get a move on, my daughter is out there somewhere and she's waiting."

Chapter Thirty Three

Day Five: Twelve Noon

Rona was fast becoming a major pain in the backside, thought Rachel as she came to a halt once again to jerk and tug on her tether, trying to dislodge the chunk of lumber from a tangle of tree roots. She'd been moving as fast as she could to put as much distance between her and the clearing, but Rona had other ideas.

She didn't know where she was going, but figured the island was pretty small, so if she just kept moving, preferably in a straight line, and downhill, she'd bump into something, or someone, civilized. Her problem was the damned doorframe.

Once the panic of getting away subsided, she settled down and kicked her brain back into gear. She started by coiling the tether up, holding it in her hand, so she could tug it along the ground, keeping it a little closer. This soon became a nuisance and she found it easier to leave the thing where it sat and forge ahead the full length of the tether so she could locate the best route down through the undergrowth. Rachel would then stop, pull Rona toward her, and then move ahead.

The problem was Rona. One would think the hunk of wood had a mind of it's own, intent on searching out every rock snag, every exposed root, and every entanglement she could find in her effort to stop Rachel dead in her tracks. By the tenth time it jammed, snapping her arm with a jerk and forcing her to go back and yank it free, she was no longer calling it 'Rona' in an affectionate manner. She was calling it things like 'bastard' and 'bugger' and a few names that were actually nasty. She was also threatening dire consequences involving fire, if this crap didn't stop.

When Rachel started her panicked escape that morning, leaving the moaning Lester in the dirt of the clearing, she took the same path out both Manuel and Dumpy had taken when they left. Clearly defined, it followed a winding downhill slope for twenty-five yards past the privy, generally paralleling the small stream from above the clearing. Beyond the little outhouse, the trail was not clearly marked and by the time the privy was out of sight behind her, the path didn't exist in front of her. From that point it would just be guess work and blind luck.

Rachel had a logical mind and was able to calmly assess most situations when and if a solution was required. She read with a passion, not only school books, but anything else handy. Fiction, mystery, self help, history, corn flakes boxes, it didn't matter. She'd read anything she could get her hands on and was able to retain a lot of what she read. Like all people who possessed an inquisitive mind, she absorbed facts, knowledge and miscellaneous tidbits of useless information one would never need, or so one thought.

Now that her panic had subsided and she was back in control of her mind, she knew if it was morning, which it was, and if the sun was on her right, which it was, she was facing north. Knowing she was pointed north, all she had to do was keep the sun on her right as she moved through the bush and she would generally be heading north and not going in circles. Of course, she was smart enough to know that after mid-day, to keep heading north, the sun had better be on her left, and she was very close to mid-day.

She also knew people tended to be noisy. Very little was done that was quiet, so if she stopped often and just listened for several minutes, it not only gave her a rest, but she might hear someone banging on a piece of machinery with a hammer or nailing shingles on a roof while listening to a blaring radio.

There was no doubt in her mind that sooner or later she would find someone who could help get the tether off, and eliminate her anchor.

She also hoped whoever she found could give her something to eat. It had been a long time since her last real meal and her stomach told her it was sure she was starving to death. Lastly, she would ask them to point her in the proper direction for her trek back to St. George's Town.

The slope was getting much steeper and more slippery as she made her way down through the trees. She began to worry that Rona might have taken offense at being called so many bad names and took it into its blockhead mind to tumble down and give her a sharp smack in the back of the head. To make sure this possibility was eliminated, she started to roll the three foot chunk of lumber, with its jagged edge on one end, down the hill ahead of her. She held onto the tether, and then followed when the thing came to rest. It worked, and Rona seemed less inclined to get snagged.

The next hundred yards down the hill was a steady advance of twenty feet at a time. First, she'd give Rona a shove with her foot to start her rolling down the hill; then she'd watch it bounce to a stop or grab the tether with both hands to slow it down or bring it to a halt. It was a slow and tiring process.

As her angle of descent increased and the footing less sure and the effort to keep from falling took more out of her, Rachel looked around for a spot to sit and rest. She hadn't realized dragging and pushing Rona through the jungle would be so difficult and found she needed frequent breaks for a breather. She needed one of those breaks now.

The chunk of wood had stopped its bouncing through the bush and lay quietly against the base of a tree. Rachel slid on her butt down to it and using it as a seat, plunked down and stretched her long legs out in front of her. Slowly, her pulse rate came down as she lay back against the tree, relaxing. It was during this moment of tranquility, eyes closed and breathing slowly, when she heard a sound that made the hairs on the back of her neck stand straight up. It was the bark of a dog. Not a big dog, a small dog, yapping at someone or something way off in the distance. Rachel knew if there was a dog, there were probably people close by.

Sitting bolt upright and straining to determine the direction of the sound, she heard the barking again. This time it wasn't one short burst, it was a series of yelps and barks and they were drifting up through the bush from far below and way to the left of where she sat.

On her feet instantly, she shoved Rona from her resting place and kicked her down the hill, literally running with the tumbling piece of wood as it bounced down the steep slope through the brush. Rachel was happy, excited; knowing someone was out there with their pet and they were making enough noise to lead her out of the undergrowth.

Suddenly, in this rush to find the animal, Rona bounced up off a large rock and flew out into space, disappearing from Rachel's view. The silence was deafening and, just as she started to move forward, the tether snapped tight, ripping her foot out from under her and knocking her to the ground on her back. Sliding down through the dirt and brush on the hillside, she knew she was heading for some kind of edge where Rona had disappeared seconds before, and she was being pulled down the soft wet slope by her damned four by six wooden tormentor.

Five feet from the edge, her hand passed over a tree root and she grabbed it and hung on for dear life. The root held, stopping her slide into oblivion while almost jerking her arm out of its socket. She lay there gasping, feeling the tug of Rona on her leg, swinging in space fifteen feet below her, like an anchor holding her in place.

Seconds turned into minutes as Rachel forced herself to calm down, think through what had happened, and figure out how to solve the problem. She was alive and still in reasonably good physical shape. She was lying on her side in the dirt, hanging onto a tree root a couple of feet from the edge of a precipice of some kind. She had no idea how high the cliff was or how far she would drop if she went over. She also knew she was held in place by a cord attached to a three foot long piece of doubled two by sixes. She almost laughed when she thought of it and how it should be a 'piece of cake' getting out of this fix.

Her anchor stopped swinging in the wind below as she thought about her predicament and tentatively bent her knee to scratch it. She found when she did, the rope came with her and the anchor moved up as well. Although heavy, it was not too difficult to haul the chunk of wood up so Rachel adjusted her body a little, dug in her heels and slid up the hill a half dozen inches further away from the edge. If she could do the same over and over she may be out of here in no time. She moved her leg up again and the maneuver worked again.

For the next hour, Rachel slowly pulled her foot toward her, bending her knee, then digging her foot into the ground. Next, she would bring her other leg into the same position, dig that heel in, and push her body back up the hill, while her tethered leg slowly straightened out. It was exhausting and scary because she knew one bad move, or one slip could send her hurtling back down toward the cliff's edge. Slowly, she worked her way up into a sitting position against a tree trunk about eight feet from that edge. She had noticed much more resistance to her efforts during her last two attempts and figured the wood was getting caught in some brush or against a rock outcrop. On the last try, she had to jerk her leg up and down several times quite violently before her anchor broke loose and let her pull herself up to the tree. She needed a rest. Now no longer afraid she would go flying out into space following Rona, she could relax and think a little more about her predicament.

Rachel knew she had to get the chunk of wood up the cliff side and back next to her or she'd be going nowhere. There was no way of sliding the loop off her ankle and short of banging away at it for a week, no way of cutting it free. The only answer was to get it up and that required some real ingenuity.

Looking around her, she noted the large number and varied sizes of vines hanging from the trees above her, so she reached out and grabbed one. It was stiff, not very flexible, like a rope left unused for years in the back of a barn.

She played with it, working it back and forth, attempting to soften it a bit so she could use it. She found she could flex it somewhat, causing the fibers to soften a little, making it easier to work with. She also discovered that the one she was playing with held firm in its upper attachment and she could use it as a safety line if need be. That was a step in the right direction.

Sitting comfortably, confident she was going nowhere she didn't want to, she took a long time to look around her to evaluate the terrain and the large trees and underbrush that ran to the edge of the cliff over which she had almost fallen.

The brink ran both to her left and right but in different ways. On her left, it rose as though heading up to the top of the hill. The steep slope of the land running toward the edge diminished until there was no slope at all, just level ground seemingly cut by a knife eons ago to form the cliff.

On her right, the cliff stretched downward, disappearing around a curve amid dense undergrowth. The hill itself ran to the edge in an ever increasing angle until at one point, Rachel knew a human hiking in the woods couldn't get through without falling, let alone a girl in sandals dragging her friend along behind. It was obvious if she intended to move, it would have to be to her left.

Rachel decided that if she moved carefully to her left and got Rona to swing along with her, she could make it to the level section. Then she'd crawl to the edge and look over without fear of rolling down and out into space. After considering all other alternatives, she decided the plan was sound.

The vine she had been toying with hung from a spot slightly to her left, so Rachel figured it would be her safety line for at least the first twenty feet of her sideways trek. Gripping it with one hand, she carefully bounced her bum along the ground for about a foot and stopped. She was now away from the safety of her tree trunk, sitting on a steeply sloping hillside, only eight or ten feet from the cliff's edge. Her tether now stretched on an angle from her foot to disappear over that edge about a foot and a half to her right. Now she had to get the wood block free and swinging so she could move it along with her. This would prove easier said than done.

For more than an hour, Rachel fought with her tether and the door jam, as she slowly bounced along the ground, then manipulated the block of wood along with her. Occasionally, the rope just swung free and the block would move as though under its own volition. The rest of the time it seemed determined to test all of Rachel's patience, stamina, and temper. It was well over an hour by the time she reached the next tree and she was soaked in sweat. She was also very sore across the bottom from the sharp stones she had bounced onto more than once, but she was getting there.

Again it was time to rest, so Rachel found a comfortable spot, pulled the cord up a little, twisting it around an exposed tree root to relieve the tension on her leg. She then spent some time nestling into a nook between the roots of the tree, intending to relax for a little while and catch her breath. Almost instantly, she was sound asleep.

Chapter Thirty Four

Day Five: Four P.M.

Nick was stuck in traffic just north of St. George's when he got the news. LJ had found a hideout high in the mountains with every indication of recent occupation by two people, one of them possibly a female. There was one major twist. In the middle of the hideout, on the ground near a fire pit, was a local man with a badly broken leg and a very large wound on his head. What he was doing there or what happened was still a mystery, but the police were on their way with medical help.

He asked Nick if he had his maps with him and when assured they were in the car, LJ asked him to turn around and head back north. "We may have to pull everyone from the other areas and concentrate the search up here." he said.

"OK, I'll be at your base camp in half an hour and I'll call the Police Commissioner. He may have someone who knows the area and we'll check if it was a grow op you found, or some other thing used by the locals."

"Good idea," LJ agreed. "Another thing. Get hold of that Redhead fellow from the hotel, the one you have working Birch Grove. He grew up in this section so he might be able to help as well."

"Will do," Nick said, asking "what are you up to now?"

"I have two taking care of the injured guy. He's conscious but he isn't saying much, just moaning about his head and his leg. I've got everyone else doing a close search of this immediate area. You know, on hands and knees, sifting through garbage and the ashes in the fire pit. The pit's cold but even with a rain last night, the ashes are still dry down into the center so it's only a couple of days old. There's also a few cooking utensils, some clothing, and a couple of towels." LJ stopped for a minute and spoke to someone who had interrupted the phone call.

"Nick," he said, "one of the guys just found a woman's bathing suit in one of the shacks, a one piece, looks kind of small. I've got it here. He's gone to get Anthony. I sent him up the trail to check that out. He'll be here in a moment. I'll call you back," and he cut off.

Nick put his foot down a little harder on the accelerator, holding his breath as he roared through the curves of the winding mountain road. As he hit a straight stretch, his phone rang again.

"Nick here," he said.

It was LJ again. "It's Rachel's bathing suit. Anthony says she bought it a week before coming down here. Her mother helped her to pick it out. Rachel showed it to him. There's absolutely no doubt, it's hers." He paused for a breath and carried on.

"Another thing Nick. There seems to have been some kind of trouble here in the past day or two. The doorway to one of the huts has been smashed up pretty bad and the guy here with the bad leg says he has no idea about it because it happened before he got here. Looks like someone took a sledge hammer to the building. Two of my men went over it carefully, checking for blood, but everything's clean. I can't explain what could possibly have happened." He stopped, waiting for a response.

Nick's mind was racing, trying to work out an alternate plan, literally on the fly. This changed a whole lot of things and the focus of the search would have to be altered drastically.

"OK, here's what we do for now," Nick said. "See if you can mark the place so it can be seen easily from the air by a helicopter. Send someone down to the village to see if they can get a colored canvas, or tarpaulin, you know, like the blue ones they use in Florida after a hurricane. Get a couple and have them stretched over the roofs. Either that or have someone splash red paint on them.

"I haven't called the Commissioner yet but I will now and find out if he knows where we can get hold of a chopper. That way, we can bring in some of his experts and take out that injured fellow. Also, they might have some idea about the doorway you say is wrecked, so I'll ask him to get a crew up there." Things were starting to fall into place in his head.

"It's getting late and it will be dark in a couple of hours. We can't do much more today, but we have time to set up a major effort for tomorrow," he continued.

"I'll still meet you at your base camp. I'll start shutting down the other search groups and chase those closest to you over to your base." He stopped and thought for a moment.

"Work out the best route from where you are to your base, and look around for possible exit routes for Rachel and whoever she's with. I'll get back to you." And he hung up without another word. He had a lot to do and he hoped Grenada didn't have one of those stupid laws against driving and phoning at the same time.

The first person he called was Harry Stanton over near the tiny village of Richmond with Team Five. They were only a few miles from Birch Grove and Nick knew he could probably get over to LJ's area before him. After several rings, a panting Harry answered.

"Yes," he roared.

"Excuse me," Nick said, "I thought I was calling the nice, even-tempered and incredibly polite Harry Stanton. I must have dialed the wrong number, I'm so sorry to have bothered you sir." Nick was grinning as he said all this.

"Smart ass," was the reply, "I'll bet you are not crawling around in a bloody bug infested jungle that's hotter than hell. Have you any idea what this does to my bursitis? Not only that, I'll bet right now your fat backside is plunked in a nice air conditioned car."

Nick was laughing so hard he had trouble keeping the car on the road. He could just see Harry, soaked in sweat stumbling through the bush, wild mop of snowy hair stuck out every which way.

"As a matter of fact, I have been working like a slave and have some very important news for you, if you will just stop your bloody grumbling and listen," Nick responded.

"OK, shoot".

"That's better. First, I am sitting in a nice air conditioned car hurtling north toward Birch Grove. Let's face it Harry, it's a tough job, but someone has to do it."

"Oh shut up about the air conditioning. What's the news?"

"LJ has found the camp where Rachel was being held. It's just west of Birch Grove, high in the hills, mountains, actually, from what LJ says."

"How does he know it's the right spot?" Harry asked, very serious now.

"A bunch of things but the main item is her bathing suit. They found it at the site and Anthony has confirmed it's hers. And by the way, there is a guy there with some injuries and the cops are on their way.

"What I need from you, my dear old friend, is to gather your crew together, get back to your base camp, shut it down and head over to LJ's base. We've still got a couple of hours of day light and you can help organize what may be a complete change of strategy. On the way over, stop at St. James and pass the info on to Vince Strong and have someone run up to Lower Capital and alert that guy on his anniversary, Peter something. Get them all to move over to LJ's area.

"By the way, if you can find the fellow from the hotel, get him and his gang up there too." Nick stopped to think.

"We're on our way. See you at LJ's". Harry said and rang off.

Passing through Birch Grove, Nick marveled at the number of posters tacked to everything stationary. Ed's crew had done a super job in a very short time. It was an impressive display.

LJ's base camp was like an anthill. There were cars and vans everywhere, small groups standing about and support women at open trunks handing out bottles of water and cans of pop. As Nick looked around, another three cars pulled up with Peter Baxter, his wife Anne, and all their searchers and support people.

"Hey Nick," Harry called from the other side of the mob and moved over to join him. "Everyone knows about LJ's discovery. We met two of his crew heading for a shop in Birch Grove, so I sent two of ours with them to help. They should be back soon."

"Good work. When they get back, send half a dozen into the hills with them so we have a strong group that knows the route and the easiest way to get up there and back. Have the police and medical people gone through yet?"

"Yes, and I sent that hotel fellow to lead them up. He said he knows where the place is. Claims he's been there before, a long time ago. I offered help for their stretcher but they said they had enough." Harry was pleased with himself.

Nick was also pleased. The discovery of the bathing suit in the shack certainly reduced the search area into a much more manageable size, and Nick had a few ideas on how to cover it.

"Harry, we need two things. First, find out who has lights. Flashlights, lanterns, Colemans, you know what

I mean. It will be dark in an hour or so and we'll need some light. Secondly, I would like to set up a highway patrol on this road," and he waved his hand toward the pavement running past their parking area.

"It has to go as far as Belvidere to the west and south down the road to the police station just above Adelphi. If Rachel's captors are bringing her out, these are the only roads they can use so let's set something up and start it going as soon as possible. We might even think about running it all night." Nick's phone rang and Harry waved as he moved away to start rounding up volunteers for the road patrol.

"Nick," it was LJ. "There's something odd going on up here."

"Like what?"

"Well, this injured guy says he hurt himself falling down but I think there's a hell of a lot more to it than that. I'm curious to know where he fell and how he got back here to this clearing. If you saw his leg, man, he sure didn't walk back and I don't think he could even crawl.

"The cut on his head is another thing. He looks like someone tried to take the top of his head off with a samurai sword. This guy is telling us a fairy tale." LJ stopped for a second to talk to someone with him.

"Are the cops and medicos on their way up?" he asked.

"They've been gone awhile and should be there soon. The young lad from the hotel knows where you are and he's leading them."

"Good. I'll keep working on this guy. I'm sure he knows more than he's letting on. It could be the kidnappers laid a beating on him before they left and threatened him with a bigger one if he talked. Leave him to me. I learned a couple of tricks over the years on getting information out of a jerk who thinks he can stonewall me." And he hung up.

Harry now had a list of volunteers ready to drive slowly back and forth on the designated roads to keep an eye open for anything unusual. He came over to Nick with a big grin.

"Is there any chance of widening the road search by a couple of hundred miles? I've got enough drivers ready to work all night to cover every square inch of this island and a few left over for Barbados, Jamaica and the southern half of Florida."

"Don't knock enthusiasm," Nick said. "Without this gang, we'd be lost." And he threw his arm over Harry's old shoulders. "By the way, I got a surprise for you."

"Like what?" Harry growled.

"Well, I noticed what a grouch you've been lately so I called Florida and told Kitty she better get down here and try to cheer you up. She's probably hanging her clothes up and cleaning up that wreck of a room of yours right now."

Harry brightened up like a kid who had just been told he was going to Disney World. His grin was truly ear to ear.

"Bless you my son. I knew there was some reason I never fed you to the sharks back in Florida." And Harry went back to his drivers whistling a very happy tune as Nick made a mental note to remember to thank his wife, Ann, for the suggestion.

Nick's phone rang again. It was LJ.

"The cops and medicos are here and getting ready to lug this bum out. Man does he ever smell. I doubt this guy has ever been immersed in water since he was baptized as an infant."

"Just don't smell him then," laughed Nick.

"Can't help it. You would smell this guy coming from thirty paces. He sure wouldn't do well sneaking up on someone unless he was down wind.

"Anyway, here's what we're doing," and he laid out the plans for the next hour. The sun was low and twilight was moving in and they wanted to break into small groups and come out from several directions; just in case someone was between them and the road. He figured it would be dark in about an hour so if Nick could hold on, he would see him then, and he hung up.

Nick felt good. They were getting closer.

Chapter Thirty Five

Day Five: Six P.M.

"Let's take a break for a minute," one of LJ's fellow searchers said, as he scrambled over some tree roots and found a rock to sit on. "I'm just about ready to fall over."

LJ agreed and called loudly to his left and right for everyone to take ten. He knew they couldn't look much longer because the sun was beyond the hilltops and it was getting very gloomy down in the valleys and gullies they were crawling through. All were beginning to believe they were close to quitting time and should be thinking of heading for the cars.

Anthony found a smooth section under a tree and stretched out, looking every bit as though he was getting ready to drop off into a deep sleep.

"Do you think it's time for us to get out of here?" he asked LJ who found a spot to sit next to him.

"I think so. The police say we've covered half the hill and, if we swing to our right, we should be back at the base in twenty minutes. The light's fading fast and we could hurt ourselves stumbling around these hills in the dark." He stretched back to ease the pain in his knee, looking up at the quickly darkening sky.

"Damn plastic bags," LJ muttered, half to himself, looking at a spot way above their heads. "You see them everywhere. Hell, Edith and I saw them in China flapping in the breeze high in the trees when we drove up from Beijing to Badaling visit the Great Wall. They're a bloody abomination."

LJ obviously didn't like the universal white grocery bags hanging in this tree or anywhere else. "Look up there. See, look at that damn thing. You can't even grab some rest on a tropical island without seeing them. Damn, the bloody things are everywhere" and he pointed to a spot high above their heads where a white plastic bag was hanging lifeless, caught in a limb. The two men lay back quietly staring at the offending intruder into what was otherwise a pristine natural paradise.

"Notice anything funny about that bag you don't like so much?" Anthony casually asked.

LJ stared at it again, studied it for a moment, and said no. It was just a piece of garbage and whoever threw it there should be horsewhipped.

Anthony was still relaxing, trying to make small talk until they started down again.

"Tell me, how come the leaves in that tree are moving so much from the breeze up there, but that very light plastic bag is rock solid hanging straight down? Another thing, how the hell did it get there in the first place? Take a look. It's surrounded by branches and leaves and other trees. How could it blow through them, getting to an inside branch, and then just hang there like a lump?" He yawned and took another swig of water from his bottle.

LJ studied the bag for a long time, rolling Anthony's words around in his head and then quickly stood up. "You know, Mr. Lusinski, I think you're right; there is something funny about that bag. The damn thing is wrong and I think we should try to find out why." He started moving toward the large tree as he spoke.

"Hang on a minute. What you going to do, climb up there and yank it down?" Anthony said as he got up and followed.

"Not a chance. I'm going to delegate," and he strode over to Raymond Redhead, and asked how they could get the bag down. As Anthony came close, he heard Raymond laughing and saying 'no problem, Mon.'

"What are you doing?" Anthony asked.

"Well, I figure one of these young bucks might want to impress us, but it turns out this is actually no challenge at all. He says this is the Spice Island. As soon as a boy can walk, he learns how to climb a tree so he can pick nutmeg and help his family. He figures they'll have the bag down in a minute or two," and he gave Anthony a smile. "It was pretty bright of you to notice how it was hanging and not moving," and the two watched the young man make his way up the tree and into the branches far overhead.

LJ held his breath as he watched the climber get close to the bag as the rapidly thinning branch started to bend downward. Slowly now, the young man stretched out to his full length, moving very carefully until his fingers crept around the bag handle, and started inching it toward him. His tiny movements were so careful and slow it was hard to see them at all.

Suddenly, he shifted backwards on the branch, slid to the tree's trunk and stood up, waving the bag with a large grin of bright white teeth. In less than two minutes, he proudly handed the bag to LJ.

"Thank you very much," he said with a slight bow to the young man. "Mr. Redhead said you were the best climber he knew and I must tell you, I will never doubt his word when he tells me something." The climber beamed at the praise.

"Let's see what we have here," LJ said as he knelt and dumped the contents of the bag on the ground. All strained forward to have a look. Out fell two cans of chicken noodle soup, a can of Irish stew, and a can of pork and beans.

"Pork and beans," quipped one onlooker. "Well, I guess we can safely say the stuff didn't belong to a hiker from an Israeli tour group."

"You're probably right, but whoever these belonged too, they must have been above this spot at some time, 'cause you couldn't throw this load from down here all the way up there. It had to come from above us, up there on those rocks, and you have to wonder why someone would throw perfectly good food over the edge?"

"Whoever it was may have fallen," offered Anthony, looking up beyond the top of the trees. "If they did though, they must have hit the ground with one hell of a thud."

"You may be right but fall or not, there could be other things around here and we should take a quick look." He turned to the group now all standing around them and said, "Fan out from the bottom of that tree. Look for anything on the ground, a plastic bag like this one, a backpack, anything. Be sure to check under the bushes. Let's go, we're losing light," and he started looking with the rest.

Soon they were all crashing around in the underbrush, pushing branches aside, lifting giant leaves of wildly growing tropical plants, and peering into crevasses and holes.

Suddenly one of the hotel workers, a shy fellow in his late teens or early twenties, screeched out in terror as though he had seen a spirit, or ghost. He had stumbled on a body.

LJ and several others rushed over toward the hollering and found the lad standing back in horror, pointing at the body of a man stretched out on his back, with ants and other crawly creatures moving all over him. It was likely he was looking at his first dead person, and he was terrified.

Anthony arrived and stood quietly looking down.

"Poor bastard," LJ said. "It looks like he was still alive for a while after he fell. Look at his left hand. He was moving it, pushing the dirt around."

LJ asked that the boy who made the discovery be taken to the edge of the area while they prepared the body for removal.

Kneeling down, he moved the left arm closer to the victim to make it easier to wrap a shroud around him for carrying out. The police officer kneeling beside him stood and started a radio call to his supervisor down at the base camp. He was interrupted by another yell, this time it was LJ. He startled everyone with it. While shoving the dead man's outstretched arm closer to the body, the dead man groaned.

"Good Lord, he's still alive," he yelled, shaking off his surprise and taking charge of the situation immediately. "Bring that light over," he called to the police officer still on his radio. "Quick, shine it here."

In seconds, he had banged out a half dozen orders and was directing people all over the place.

The policeman was relieved of his lantern and asked to get the other cops and their flashlights. It was growing very dark and LJ knew it would be pitch black within minutes.

Next, he tossed Anthony his phone to let the Commissioner know, and to tell him to send another doctor and another ambulance if possible. He also told Anthony to call Nick.

He then got two of the hotel crew to start making a large fire about twenty-five feet away, just out from under the canopy of trees so it could be seen from the air. He sent two more down the trail about three hundred yards to dig another fire pit and start a second fire to guide people up the trail to the victim. He then sent five more down the same trail with instructions to spread out all the way down to the road, but to keep at least within voice contact. He wanted a doctor brought up quickly, and these guys could pass him from one to another, all the way up to the fires.

Two seniors standing near were summoned, given the one light they had, and asked to start carefully cleaning him. LJ told them to lightly brush off the ants and other nasty things crawling on his face, hands and arms. He warned them to be careful touching any part of him because they had no idea what was broken, bent or ruptured and they already knew he groaned when his left arm was moved.

Asking around for a fresh clean unused handkerchief, he showed the two how to twist it into a rope, stick it into a water bottle, and then hold it over the mans lip's so a little water could drip onto them, and seep into his mouth without causing him to choke or gag. They were to keep doing this as long as he could take it. Within seconds, several of the searchers nearby hauled out their half empty water bottles and contributed them to the effort.

LJ was like the commander of a force involved in a battle. He was calm, almost too calm, and decisive. He gave clear, simple orders directly to the ones from whom he wanted action, and tolerated no hesitation or arguments. If someone started to comment on an order, LJ's voice dropped an octave, and he would stare at his target and say "please, do as I ask." That was enough to get everyone to do what they'd been told.

As the minutes passed, quiet spread across the area as each man did the job requested of him. Several had seen military service in their youth, and had even fought in different areas of the world including Korea and Vietnam, but none had spent thirty years in the Marines, and all respected LJ's uncanny ability to instantly assess a situation and see that a solution was implemented quickly and properly. It was easy to take directions from him, and they all knew they were being guided by a quality leader.

The fire was now roaring in its pit, and the two hotel workers were off gathering more wood to keep it big enough to cast a great red glow over the scene. The other fire, down the trail, was visible from LJ's vantage point, and he could see a third fire much further beyond that. He was pleased at the initiative someone had shown.

Walking over to where the injured man lay, Anthony joined him and both stooped down to check their patient.

"How's he doing?" Anthony asked.

Vince Strong, who had arrived on the scene behind the police with their lights, looked up and shrugged. "He seems to be breathing a little easier, and we've managed to get about a quarter of a pint through his lips. Because of the angle he's on, if we give him too much he'll choke, but what we're giving him isn't coming up, so I think it's doing some good; that drip works really well." Vince got up and motioned to LJ and Anthony to move away from the patient.

"There's another thing LJ. Stan cut open the trouser legs on this guy's pants. The left leg seems alright but his right is black, and it smells pretty bad. Just let the medical people know when they get here.

"Also, we used some pieces of flat rock to scrape out everything beside him and smoothed out the ground so they can get a body board under him when it's time for the move. I don't know though, from what I can see, his whole right side is one hell of a mess." Vince stood quietly for a few more seconds, and then moved back to take the plastic bottle and cloth drip from Stan. None had any idea who the unconscious man was, and the police were reluctant to start rummaging around in his pockets for fear of hurting him more. His ID could wait until later. Right now, they were going to do everything possible to keep this stranger alive, no matter how hopeless it seemed.

It reminded LJ of a hopeless effort in Vietnam after a late afternoon fire fight. Ten minutes earlier a patrol of Vietcong had done everything they could with small arms and mortars to kill LJ and his buddies. The Marines, a close, experienced and very capable unit, had successfully fought them off, doing much damage to the attackers.

After the skirmish, one enemy soldier lay on the ground near LJ, bleeding badly. With the action over and the battlefield quiet, it was just LJ, on his knees, desperately searching for a vein in the small yellow arm for the plasma IV needle. The injured man was no longer an enemy. He was just a man, wounded, needing help.

The IV did no good. The man's life was gurgling away through a gaping hole in his chest and there was nothing LJ could do. At the end, as the choppers came in to take him and his fellow Marines out of the rice paddy, the little man opened his eyes and smiled sadly up at his helper. Straining, he twice whispered 'ban phuroc cho ban' as the spark of life fled from his eyes.

The simple phrase and the man's smile were burned into his mind, and for many days, he asked everyone he met what the words meant. Finally, a busy Army Chaplin gave him the answer.

Most of the Vietnamese people were Buddhists, he told LJ. 'Ban phuroc cho ban' was a personal phrase that people offered to someone special. It translated into something roughly akin to 'Bless You.'

A commotion in their area brought him sharply back to all the present problems. A large group of people, mostly policemen, were staking out the area, while several medical personnel followed, passing through the

223

police line, following directions to the unconscious man on the ground. There was a stretcher, body board, IV holders and several black medical cases carried by aides and nurses. This was a serious effort by a large contingent of Grenada's medical profession.

The senior Police Officer approached LJ and asked if he was in charge. LJ said he was directing affairs until the proper authorities arrived, and now that they were present, he was happy to stand back out of the way.

The officer was very polite, and thanked him profusely. He assured him the man would get the best possible care and they would have him out of there very quickly. An ambulance was waiting at the end of the trail and there were enough police to get him safely down to it. LJ thanked him and turned to those in his group who were near.

"Anthony, Vince, the rest of you, I think our job here is over. Let's start packing up and head back to the hotel. Four of you should stay and douse the fire when the removal is complete and then go down and snuff the other fires as well. The rest can head back. I think we could all use a good bath and a strong drink, although not necessarily in that order," and the job of closing down began while the doctors and medics did their work. The idea of a bath and a drink after a very long day was enough to make everyone move a little faster than usual.

Chapter Thirty Six

Day Five: Seven P.M.

Rachel felt as though she wouldn't be able to sit in a chair for a week. It had taken hours to move the fifty or sixty feet along the edge of the cliff and it had been a fight with Rona, and her tether, every inch of the way. Now she was on an almost level piece of ground, and it felt good to be lying on her stomach, instead of sitting on her very sore backside.

To keep from sliding down the incline and falling over the cliff, she had to sit with her heels dug in, and slowly bounce herself sideways in the direction of more level ground. Her plan was to get on the level area, slide on her belly to the edge, look over and down without falling, and figure out a way to get her damned piece of wood up the side of the cliff and back into her arms. It was a great plan but she never thought it would take as long as it had, and she never counted on sharp stones and pointed sticks laying in wait for her approaching, bouncing, bum.

Rachel had always been afraid of heights, and standing on the edge of a building or near a precipice made her nauseous. She had refused to go up the CN Tower in Toronto on a school trip one time, standing outside at the base instead, smarting from the comments of her classmates. They all boarded the elevators to head to the top but they would have had to hogtie her to get her up there. Now she had to go to the edge of a cliff and look down. This could be difficult.

Gritting her teeth and thinking, 'well, a girl's got to do what a girl's got to do,' she started slowly crawling toward the abyss. Holding her tether in one hand, she could feel the tension on it as the wood slid down the cliff-side. She looked up, noting the failing light and picked up the pace of her crawl. She didn't want to be trying this in the dark.

Rachel slid out enough to give herself a clear sightline over the edge and down the rock face. It was straight down, and rough, with pieces of stone and wayward roots jutting out every which way as far as she could see. It seemed to be a very long way to the bottom.

Moving her tether well out in front of her, with her arm stretched into space, she could see Rona ten or twelve feet below her, gently swinging on the line of cord. It was a clear path up but the cord passed between two jutting pieces of rock and Rachel could see if she pulled the line up, Rona would not be able avoid those rocks. She had to devise a way to hold the rope a foot from the wall, so Rona could pass beyond the reach of the obstruction. If she could do that, Rona would carry on up to the top. A piece of cake, she thought.

Sliding back, she rolled over to see what was available nearby. She spotted just what she needed, but it was a good ten feet away and back the way she had just come. Looking at the darkening sky, she thought, 'what the hell', stood up, yanked the tether to bring Rona up against the rocks, and simply walked back toward the long broken branch of a tree lying nearby. She pulled it from the underbrush and stood, stripping off some of the small branches and twigs from its length. When satisfied it would do the job, she turned and walked back to the edge.

Now on the ground again, Rachel jammed the cord into a split at the thin end of the branch and placed the thick end on the ground and plunked her stomach on it. Slowly easing the branch forward from beneath her, she slid it out over the edge and slightly downward. With a huge sigh of relief, she saw it was working. As she pushed the branch outward, the tether went with it, and the chunk of wood on the end begrudgingly followed, slowly swinging out from the face of the cliff beyond the blocking pieces of stone.

Now with both hands free, Rachel slowly hauled on the cord. Inch by inch, the block of wood moved up toward the girl at the cliffs edge, passing, by just a quarter of an inch, the rocks jutting out from the cliff side. She held her breath, squinting into the darkness, trying to see what her anchor was doing. It was doing just fine. When the block of wood finally cleared the edge of the rock face, the ecstatic girl just wrapped her arms around it and gave it a kiss. She was free again.

It was late; almost pitch black where Rachel lay with her lump of wood safely in her arms. She knew, just like the night before that she could never walk out in the dark. She figured if she could get as far as she had, another night in the woods wouldn't kill her, so she started sliding back to a safe spot next to a tree about thirty feet from where she lay. She crawled into the sheltered area on the upper side of the tree's base, curled up with her log and wiggled and worked her way into a comfortable position. In moments she was off, dreaming of mothers, fathers, grandparents and school friends, enjoying the sleep of the innocent.

Chapter Thirty Seven

Day Five: Eleven P.M.

A dozen weary people sat around a table in the bar area close to the pool, rehashing all the day's happenings. Not all were privy to the information and changes racing about the island during the day, and Nick, LJ and anyone else who could add something, tried to bring everyone up to date.

The injured man LJ and Anthony found in the hills was lying in the main hospital in St. George's, and the last report simply said, although not yet conscious, he was stable. He was badly battered having a broken hip, a shattered pelvis, smashed upper and lower right leg and a smashed right knee. He also suffered a broken collarbone, a ruptured disk in his spine and a severe concussion. His right arm was also broken. On top of all this were cuts, bruises, lacerations, abrasions and bug bites. Smiling, LJ said he hadn't seen any railroad tracks up there in the hills, and couldn't understand how he'd been run over by a train. They all agreed he must be one tough hombre to survive all he did.

The doctors were trying to save his right leg as they spoke, and they wouldn't know how that would go until the next day. Along with all his other ailments, the guy was badly dehydrated and they had been pumping liquids into him ever since the medical team had come on the scene.

LJ and Nick spent an hour with the Commissioner at nine o'clock and found out a lot of things going on in the background.

"You know that skinny guy we found up in the clearing, the one with the leg that looked like a cow stepped on it," LJ told the group. "Well, he is, as the

228

expression goes, 'known to police.' His name is Lester Adams and he's had scrapes with the law for the past twenty years. Right now, he has a partner; a huge fat guy named Henry Hudson who is also 'known to police.' This partner is known to everyone, including the police, as Dumpy. The cops are all looking for Dumpy while they keep Lester under lock and key in the hospital."

"Do they think he's involved in Rachel's disappearance?" asked Anthony.

"Not with her disappearance," LJ replied. "According to police, these guys couldn't organize a two car funeral on a one way street. They're petty crooks, too lazy to work and too stupid to be good at the profession they've chosen. The cops are going to give this Lester a real grilling now that his leg is set and his head stitched up."

"What about the other one? Do they think he's involved? It's damned funny we find this pair right where the girl was being held," someone asked.

"He's a different matter. The police have no idea who he is, where he's from, or what he was doing in the hills," Nick offered. "They think he may be the fellow who was seen in Birch Grove buying groceries and a T shirt. Commissioner Frank had pictures taken of him after he was cleaned up and a team will go into Birch Grove first light tomorrow. They also hope to question him in the morning.

"The other thing the Commissioner told me makes no sense at all. He said the Prime Minister of Grenada received a very strange letter late today which he sent over to Police HQ with instructions to check it out. The PM thinks it may relate to the disappearance of Rachel. Commissioner Frank says it very well could be." Nick sucked on his beer.

"What did the letter say?" Anthony asked.

229

"It was from someone who claims his father died during the American invasion here in October 1983 after the communist coup. The dead man's name was Louis Fernando Ruiz. He was a road builder working on the new airport at Point Salines, so these details and the name would make it almost certain he was a Cuban." Nick checked his notes and continued.

"The letter writer claims he has a student girl from an American ally, which certainly could be Canada, and he wants an apology. He demands no money, no safe conduct off the island, nothing but an apology from none other, now get this, the President of the United States. If it wasn't so damn serious it would be funny."

Quietly Anthony asked, "And what if he doesn't get his apology?"

"He said he would kill her in two weeks."

An audible gasp could be heard from the group.

"Two weeks?" one called from the back, "why the hell would he give them two weeks?"

"He wants the apology from the President to be published on the front page of the Grenadian Voice, a weekly, and he gives them two editions to get it done," Nick explained.

"And they think the broken-up guy we found unconscious in the bush could be the letter writer?" again Anthony spoke softly.

"He could be but no one is sure. We should know tomorrow."

"Do they think the kidnapper was alone or are there others?" Anthony was persistent in his quiet questioning, making notes on a small pad on the table in front of him.

Nick had an uneasy feeling and caught a dark glance from LJ. He knew from his friend's expression, the old Marine had the same bad feeling and was thinking the same thing he was. LJ answered Anthony but tossed in a little extra information just in case the Rachel's dad had any plans for a late-night visit to the hospital.

"The police feel the wording of the letter suggests there is only one person involved, but they wonder; if he was alone and holding Rachel up in the hills, and he is now lying in hospital and the girl is not in the hideout, where in hell is she?" Nick held up his hands in exasperation.

"They want to talk to this guy, and they have several police guarding him at the hospital and he's heavily sedated. The other one, Lester, is across the hall and he too is under guard, so I don't think either one of them will be doing any chatting tonight." Nick hoped Anthony got the message.

LJ stepped into the conversation at this point with his thinking for the next day.

"There are only two conclusions possible at this moment. Either some villain still has Rachel and has moved her to a new spot, or, she has managed to get away and is on her own in the bush. Either way, we have to get back out there and look harder than we did today." Many heads around their tables nodded in agreement.

"I suggest we call it a day and get some sleep. Lets say a six a.m. wake up, we'll aim for a seven A.M. departure, and a before eight a.m. search start. How does that sound to all of you?"

Everyone seemed in agreement, even Anthony. Partial drinks were finished, chairs shoved back and papers collected. LJ nodded to Nick in the breakup confusion, indicating he wanted a private chat. Nick understood and moved away from the crowd, stepping toward the front desk area of the hotel. He glanced back to see LJ casually following. There was no sign of Anthony anywhere.

"I think we have a problem with Anthony," LJ said when the two met near the hotel's guest computer room.

"I think you're right, but I don't know what we can do to stop him short of tying him up."

"Can't do that," LJ shook his head. "What we can do is disable his rental car and then ask the security guard at the front gate to let us know if he leaves the property and hails a cab. If he does, we'll know for sure where he's going, and maybe we can stop him from making a big mistake."

"Good plan my friend, proving once again that you're not just another pretty face." They were both chuckling as they set out to get things in place. Because Nick was in the car business, it was his job to steal the high tension distributor connector from the engine of Anthony's car. LJ's task was to find the security chief to arrange the reporting system, and the appropriate reward for doing so.

Chapter Thirty Eight

Day Six: One Thirty A.M.

Nick was dozing when the quiet tap caused him to gently roll out of bed and whisper to Ann to go back to sleep. Slipping into his shoes, he opened the door, knowing it was LJ. Still putting his shirt on, he slid from the room and the two men walked wordlessly down the walkway to the stairs and out onto the grass.

"The security guard told me Anthony tried to start his car and it wouldn't go. He checked under the hood but couldn't do anything so he stood around, looked into several cars, I guess for keys, then headed down the driveway to the street." LJ was whispering as they hurried across the lawn to their car.

He had their car started and shooting down the driveway before Nick's door was closed, braking suddenly where the guard operating the security gate was ready for them with information on Anthony's movements.

They learned that because taxis were scarce this late at night it had taken Anthony a while to hail one. He had disappeared around a far corner only a minute before in a white Honda, and the last three digits of the license was '27J'. LJ thanked him before slipping him a sizable bill, then bolted through a red light and roared off down the road toward St. George's.

By the time they swung onto Lagoon Road and passed the Fire Station, LJ had his quarry in his sights. The only car on the road was a small white one with an unlit taxi unit on the roof, meaning it was busy. LJ took his foot off the gas and slowed down to a point where Nick's heart started going again.

"Where the hell did you learn to drive like that?" he said when he could finally speak.

"The Marines," he said with a grin. "My first assignment was in the motor pool and they had me driving officers and VIP's all the time. You had to know what to do if hostiles were after your hide. You can imagine driving a big sedan in Lebanon or Saigon with a gang of insurgents taking shots at you and your high-ranking passengers from the tops of buildings. Man, they taught us how to drive in ways you couldn't imagine."

"Well you sure didn't forget your training," Nick allowed.

LJ laughed as he kept a safe distance behind the taxi, keeping him well in sight but not close enough to be recognized by someone inside.

They followed the same route LJ had taken several days before, when he went for his first chat with the Commissioner. Staying well back, they drove around the Lagoon to the Carenage, passed the still busy docks to the library, then swung to their right and went through the tunnel well after Anthony's taxi had passed through. Nick suggested they fall way back as they neared the hospital, so as not to arouse any suspicion of being followed. They could make it up on foot when Anthony got out of the cab. LJ nodded and kept silent.

Pulling onto a grassy spot with Fort George between them and the hospital, LJ cut the engine and motioned Nick to hop out and follow him.

They stood under the great bulk of the ancient fort. Originally built by the French in 1705, it was still in use as the home of several police services from head office all the way to a boot repair shop for the island's entire police force. Over the years, it had seen many strange things including shoot outs, executions, assassinations and the occasional name change, but it still stood, dominant and solid. On this night it just sat silently before them, large and foreboding.

"We'll walk from here," LJ said in the darkness.

Nick followed, aware of the dark hulking fortress above on his right, and the glittering lights of the vibrant city below, on his left. Under any other circumstances, it would have been a delightful place to take his wife for a walk, but tonight, they were out to keep a friend out of trouble.

"There he is," whispered LJ, pointing to the front of the hospital where a man was casually standing and looking around.

"Can we get to him before he enters?" Nick asked.

"I think so," putting his hand on Nick's shoulder. "You go to the right and I'll come in from the left. If it looks like we might lose him, shout his name. Believe me, he'll stop and look around. It works every time." He gave Nick a shove to his right and disappeared silently into the night.

Nick ran in a crouched manner across the road and along a low stone wall running toward the front entrance of the hospital. He was surprised at how silent he could be and figured some of LJ's training was rubbing off. He stopped for a moment, but LJ was nowhere to be seen and the whole area was enveloped in a late-night hospital-like silence. It was spooky.

Running again, Nick was almost within spitting range of Anthony who was approaching the entrance doors when he heard him shout, "what the hell are you doing here?" and a return of "Trying to keep you out of prison," by LJ who had appeared out of nowhere, standing ten feet away from Rachel's indignant father. For several seconds the two men stood frozen, staring at each other.

"I don't need you to tell me what to do. Why don't you just buzz off and leave me alone."

LJ, as big as Anthony, stepped closer and put his hand on the distraught parent's arm, more as a comfort than a seizure.

"My friend, don't do this. I'd hate like hell to have to bring your daughter up to Richmond Hill Prison to visit her father. By the time we find her, she will have been through enough and won't need that. Besides, she shouldn't be exposed to all those killers and assassins I helped put in there and who still have the best view on the island, and neither should you. Please, my friend. Let the police do their job in the morning and give up this plan of yours. Come on back to the hotel with us, Anthony."

The distressed father stood silently staring at the ground. He knew LJ was right and he knew he was being a fool but he was desperate and had to do something. It was a stupid idea to think he could sneak into a hospital, find the already injured mystery man and beat some answers out of him with his bare fists. He knew what he was up to could not end well, but he hated to admit it. The only thing that kept his act of stupidity from being unbearable was the fact that the old man with his hand on his arm was a good man. He somehow understood, and he truly wished only the best for him and all his family.

Gently guided by LJ's hand on his elbow, Anthony turned from the hospital's doors, and slowly started back to the car. Nick followed several steps behind, not wanting to break the spell.

Chapter Thirty Nine

Day Six: Six Thirty A.M.

It took Rachel several minutes just to stand upright. She had slept a long time and was so stiff and sore she could hardly move without moaning. It took her long, agonizing minutes rubbing her knees, elbows and neck, trying to work some life back into her joints. As she massaged each spot, she thought how she would never again believe those movies where people slept on the ground, then jumped up at sunrise to bounce around like they had spent the night on a five-star hotel mattress.

It was getting light by the time she could move without crying in pain so she brushed the leaves, twigs and dirt from her clothing as best she could and looked around, ready to go. She was now able to see far enough ahead to start moving downhill without bumping into trees or falling over cliffs. This time she was going to damn well get off this hill and find something to eat. Man, was she hungry.

She spent some time tying the tether around the nails jutting from the end of Rona, so she could hold one end of the piece slightly off the ground as she made her way through the bush. The chunk of wood was too heavy to carry for long, but keeping one end up while the other end dragged kept it a lot closer and sure made the going a lot easier. She felt better as she started down the slope.

The sun was up now and the jungle had come to life as she slowly wended her way through the pathless undergrowth. Several times she had to stop, check all around her, and retreat back the way she came in an effort to find a suitable route. It was difficult but she knew she was winning, moving down and getting closer to a way out.

Once, while quietly resting, she heard the tinkle of running water, and found a small spring gurgling out a trickle that ran down the hill and disappeared into the soil. Rachel spent a good half hour catching the tiny stream in her hands, sipping the cool fresh water with glee. She couldn't remember when plain water had ever tasted so good.

When she had enough and finished splashing a little on her face, she told herself it was time to get moving. Now knowing there were posters out there gave her a real boost. It meant people were actually looking for her.

I don't care how long it takes, she thought, I'll get out of here. When I do, I'll get cleaned up and then I'll find me a great huge steak to sink my teeth into. And with it I want a baked potato with lots of butter and sour cream; and fried onions too. She wanted lots of fried onions.

From deep down inside came a grumbling sound. It was her stomach answering her back, telling her to hurry up.

Chapter Forty

Day Six: Four A.M.

It was after three when Nick and LJ finally shoved Anthony back into his room, and threatened him with death if he set one foot out before six-thirty. None of the search leaders had realized how great the strain was on him, and how much effort it had been to keep up appearances during this whole escapade. His daughter was missing and everyone just expected him to act normal and go about searching for her, the same as all the other searchers.

Anthony was not like any of the other searchers though. Neither Nick nor LJ had given any thought to how he would feel. Each day the man crawled out of bed, joined the other searchers and went out to thrash about in the bushes. It never occurred to anyone that during all this, he must have been thinking he could, at any moment, stumble on the ugly remains of a once beautiful young lady, his only daughter. Nick could have kicked himself for not considering this fact right from the start.

LJ had slipped into his room when they got back from the hospital to grab a bottle of Bourbon and half a dozen cans of soda. Nick and Anthony were waiting for him at the now closed bar by the deserted pool. It would take an hour of tough conversation and several strong drinks to bring Anthony around to agreeing to let the police do their job, for now.

Once Anthony was safely in his room, LJ agreed he wouldn't be able to sleep just yet so they left the Bourbon on the table to age a little more and returned to their respective rooms to collect their maps and notebooks. There was still a lot of work to be done.

239

When Nick got back, LJ was fumbling around behind the pool bar searching for a light switch. Within seconds they were bathed in bright light with maps spread all over the bar, their bottle of older Bourbon beside them and at least three security guards approaching to see what the heck was going on.

"Excuse me," a voice called from the shadows.

"You're excused," answered LJ with a grin.

"What's going on here?" the same voice demanded.

"Come over here into the light, for heaven's sake. I hate talking to a person I can't see," LJ called back.

A tall black clad security guard emerged from the shadows, holding his baton as though to beat off some aggressive monster.

"Oh, it's you Mr. Livingston. I'm sorry to have bothered you. I thought it might be a young guest or a staff member looking for free drinks. I was just checking," the security guard said.

"It's alright son. Glad to see you guys are on your toes. In fact, maybe you can help us. Could you come over here please?" and LJ waved to the fellow and pointed to his map. "Do you know this area?"

The guard approached, waving off the other two, and spent several minutes studying the map, running his finger from one spot to another.

"I know this area well, sir. I lived up here for a long time. What do you need?"

LJ laid out what they were doing, where they found the two men, and asked how the guard would search the area if he had to. Over the next half hour, he gave a detailed synopsis of the good and bad areas in the search zone, giving them much good information before returning to his rounds.

When their plans for the day's hunt were finished, the two friends sat back and considered the lightening sky above them.

"How do you like the place?" asked LJ.

"I love it. I always thought Florida was the place to be but this island sure gives it a run for its money." Nick answered.

"I know. It doesn't take long to get to you. It was the same the first time I was here. The greenery and wildflowers were gorgeous, the people friendly, and it has one of the best climates I've ever come across. A guy could come down here and happily never go home."

"Has it changed much since the last time?"

"Oh hell yes, it's changed an awful lot. It was poorer then, and I'd have to say dirtier. There were far fewer cars, more carts and horses and more junk and scrap lying about. Now, well I could hardly believe it. The place is so much cleaner and well cared for. The painted buildings and homes, clean cars and busses, no garbage on the streets, it's just plain wonderful.

"It also has the feel of being more prosperous. Not only are the cars clean, they're newer and there's a hell of a lot more of them. The shops have more products available. In fact, there's little difference from Florida. The variety of food seems greater, and above all, the people appear much happier. You hear more laughter in an hour now than you would hear in a month back then." LJ stopped and splashed in a bit more Bourbon into their glasses.

After a long sip, he continued. "You have to remember the place had been under a corrupt dictatorship of one kind or another for twenty years before we arrived. Coard, a commie psychopath, was only the last of a long line of tyrants. Bishop, the Communist PM who Coard had ordered shot, came to power in 1979 in a coup and was arming the island to the teeth with the help of Cuba, the Czechs, and Russia. Bishop ousted an idiot named Eric Gairy who bankrupted the country. He was

241

overthrown while he was away at a United Nations conference on UFO's." LJ took another sip.

"These were the people who organized the notorious Mongoose Gang and who had the country under heavy manners for years."

"Heavy manners? What the hell are heavy manners?" Nick asked, dropping ice cubes into their glasses.

"These Mongoose thugs, under orders of the so-called government of the day, would say people had to be taught 'manners', you know, discipline them. They'd go around in gangs of five or six, beating anyone they thought needed teaching, which was just about everyone. 'Heavy manners' was just them being more vicious to more people. From what I understand, they would wreck newspapers and beat the publisher and his staff half to death if they printed something the government didn't like. Things like that.

"In '79, when Gairy left for New York, Bishop led a coup and took over. It was a popular change of government here on the island. Bishop was charismatic and a much loved leader, so the new regime had the majority backing of the people.

"Bishop's problem was that it was at the height of the cold war and he was an avowed, open communist. This meant no one in the western block acknowledged his legitimacy and since he was leading a country completely bankrupted by the previous leaders, he took help from where he could get it. He connected with Cuba, Russia, and China and, before long the island was turned into an armed camp full of weapons and run by half-wits."

LJ sat quietly, sipping his drink, before continuing.

"There was one big problem. Bishop liked to be liked. He was a populist. He was not a hard-line, old style, Stalinist like a large segment of his party, including several members who had been to Russia for training.

"This anti-Bishop group of crazies was led by the psychopath Bernard Coard, who, by the way, lived for a long time in a prison high above St. George's. These hardliners decided Bishop had to go, and since he was idolized by the people, the only way was to kill him. So they did. They killed him and seven others, up in that old fort by the hospital.

"That's where we came in. You know that part of the story but I must say, I fell in love with the place." LJ was finished what, for him, was a very long speech.

"I can see why. It's as close to paradise as you can get" Nick said as he finished his drink and stood up. "We have a big day ahead of us so I think I'll have a long shower and spend some time making myself beautiful."

"Hell, don't do that," laughed LJ. "It's almost five. We should be on the road by seven and if you try to make yourself presentable, we won't see you for a week."

Nick scooped up his maps and papers and said something rude as he walked back to his room, laughing quietly at his friend's comment.

Chapter Forty One

Day Six: Seven Thirty A.M.

Commissioner Frank stepped from his office and told the duty officer his destination, telling her to call the front desk of the hospital if anything urgent came up.

Winfred Frank had been promoted to Commissioner only seven months ago. This Rachel girl's disappearance could be called his first big test in his job and could well determine the direction his future would take.

He was pleased at how the press conference had gone. The stories he had seen or read were all positive, giving the impression his police force was on top of things. One commentator said the police appeared to know what they were doing and that their liaison with the group from Florida had been a stroke of genius. For once, he thought, the press had got things right.

Striding across Bottom Square past several parked cars, he started down the only roadway access into, and out of, Fort George. On reaching the end of the short road, he turned left to walk along the pathway to the hospital. Above him jutted a row of ancient black cannons, benignly pointing out toward a glistening new cruise ship berthed far below on his right. He stopped for a moment, thinking of how important these two incredibly different images were to his country, and how much both were needed in these difficult times. Both the cannons, silent for almost two centuries in a fortress four hundred years old, and the cruise ship, part of the twenty-first century and full of strangers from around the world, made the Grenada he loved what it was, a country of tradition looking forward.

Continuing on, he nodded to respectful hellos from those passing by as he considered the problem of the men lying in the hospital. One of those men he knew well, and he guessed that one would spill out all he knew, with only a little persuasion. Commissioner Frank hoped he knew a lot.

The other was a mystery. Though he was sure the man was from Cuba, how he got into Grenada was another mystery. He was also sure he was the man who wrote the letter and that his last name was Ruiz. At the moment, one of his friends in Canada was quietly checking out this thread with some people in Havana. One way or another, he would know what was going on before this day was over.

At the front doors of the hospital, a uniformed officer smartly saluted his superior and held open the door. Once inside the medical centre, another officer, this one of higher rank, saluted and directed him down the hall, where another officer led him to a small section with two rooms opposite each other. His guide told him Lester Adams was in the room on his left, the other, unknown man, on his right. Commissioner Frank turned to his left, indicated to the officer to open the door and stand outside and guard the room. The Commissioner wanted to be alone with the patient.

Lester was lying in bed with his plaster encased leg held high in traction by a confusing series of ropes and pulleys. It looked terribly uncomfortable.

"How do you feel Lester?" the Commissioner asked.

"How the hell do you think I feel? I feel bloody awful. My leg hurts, my head hurts, there's police all over the place, and I'm treated like a prisoner when I haven't done nothing wrong. I have no idea how long I'm going to be in here. You're damn right I feel bloody awful."

"Now, now, Lester. The doctors are doing the best they can, and your injuries are pretty severe. I'm told you fell down; that's how you hurt yourself."

"You're bloody well right, I fell down," snorted Lester, full of bravado and umbrage at his great misfortune.

"Where did you fall down Lester?" the Commissioner asked quietly.

"Over a small cliff, I did. Over a small cliff and hit some rocks."

"Then how did you get back to the clearing?" again quietly, almost casually.

"I crawled, you fool, crawled on me hands and knees."

The Commissioner moved in close to Lester and leaned forward to within a foot of his face, smiling so wickedly, Lester shivered.

"You're not telling me the truth Lester. I know you're not, and you know you're not. You didn't fall over any cliff, and you certainly didn't crawl back to the clearing. We have found no evidence of crawl marks in the ground. There's no blood splatters anywhere on rocks, except within ten feet of where you were found and no one, not me, or Dumpy, or you, could crawl an inch with a leg busted as badly as this one." And he reached back and gave the cast a good sharp rap with his knuckles. "Now please Lester, tell me the truth."

Lester let out a yowl at the blow to his leg and gasped "Don't do that, don't hit my leg. They told me the slightest problem with it and I would never walk again. Please don't touch it." Lester's bravado was all gone. He looked like he would start crying.

"I promise not to touch your leg if you promise to stop telling me your stupid lies. Now Lester, lets start again. What the hell happened to you and where is the girl?"

"What girl?" Lester stammered and when he saw the Commissioner look at his leg again and raise his hand, he almost shouted "Oh that girl. The one on the posters. Yes, now I remember. Sorry, it just slipped my mind. What do you want to know?" The short, lopsided battle was over. Lester was ready to tell everything.

Half an hour later, Commissioner Frank stepped from Lester's room and before going into the stranger's, he took out his phone.

"Nick? It's Winfred Frank, I'm at the hospital" and moved down the hall so no one could hear him. "I've just had a little chat with Lester Adams, the man LJ found at the camp up in the hills. Can you spare a moment?" When assured Nick was all ears, the Commissioner filled him in.

He told Nick how Lester and Dumpy had stumbled on Rachel less than twenty-four hours ago. He told him how they thought they might get a reward and how Dumpy planned to cash in. Commissioner Frank suggested Nick or LJ should expect a call soon.

He got his biggest reaction from Nick when he told him how Rachel had belted the guy over the head with a frying pan and when that didn't stop him, she smashed his leg with the same pan, shattering his shin bone.

"I'm telling you my friend, old Lester is going to walk with a limp the rest of his life." Commissioner Frank sounded like he was enjoying this whole exercise.

"Nick, we know she was with Lester about eight-thirty yesterday, and we know she was well enough to inflict major damage to a man much larger than her. Lester says she's out there someplace, he doesn't know where, attached to a piece of wood by a cord, and she's in fine shape. He also says he never wants to see her again. Now, all we have to do is find her."

"Thanks Winfred. We have almost two hundred people here, and we'll find her, believe me, we'll find her." As he put away his phone, he turned to the group of searchers in front of him.

At the same time, Winfred Frank turned to the guard on the mystery man's room, indicating his desire to enter. He didn't know this man but he was sure he would when he was finished.

Chapter Forty Two

Day Six: Seven A.M.

LJ's cell rang just as he was climbing into his car for the drive up to the search area. It was Police Commissioner Frank calling.

"Hello LJ, where are you now?" he asked without preliminary small talk.

"Just starting up for the search zone. Actually, you just caught me with my hand on the car door."

"Can they live without you for a short while, and meet me at the hospital? I think there's something you can do here, to help us all. I'll tell you about it when you get here. At the front door, half an hour, possibly?" There was no doubt he wanted LJ to come.

"I'll be there. See you then," LJ said, and rang off.

The first thing LJ did was call Nick, who was fifteen minutes ahead on the road north, to let him know of the call from Frank. He said they should just get on with the search and not wait for him. He would catch up later, he said as he pulled onto the busy street and headed for the hospital for the second time in eight hours.

Traffic hadn't reached the rush hour level and the drive up through the city was an easy one. Parking proved to be no problem at the hospital so LJ found himself several minutes early and took the time to wander about the grounds below the fortress walls. There was a lot of new construction underway at the island's main medical facility and from the looks of the activity, they were well on their way to doubling the size of the place.

When his short tour of the outside ended, the old Marine entered through the hospital's front door just as

Commissioner Frank stepped from an office across the foyer.

Waving LJ over, he held the door and ushered his guest into a well appointed executive office. The room was large with floor to ceiling bookcases covering two walls filled with important looking leather bound books. The floor sported a thick carpet, a large antique desk and an assortment of plush armchairs scattered haphazardly throughout.

"Nice place," LJ smiled, as he ran his hand over some books on the shelves, noting most were medical or health oriented.

"Victor Saunders is the administrator here and an old friend of mine. He offered this so we'd be comfortable, and yes, you're right, it is very nice." The two men sat opposite each other in a pair of fine wing-backed chairs.

"I'll get right to the point, LJ. The little thug you found in the camp with the bashed in head and broken leg has been very helpful in providing details of his run-in with Rachel. His name is Lester and I don't think he has yet recovered from his encounter with your young Canadian buzz saw.

"We know she was alive twenty-four hours ago when she was laying that beating on old Lester. When done, she ran from the clearing dragging some piece of wood on a long line. We're not sure what that's all about. We figured this all happened two or three hours before you found him.

"Since she's on her own, there's no reason to believe she's not alive now. We think she's out somewhere in the bush, frightened, wandering lost around the jungle, hauling some kind of wooden anchor behind her. It could be very dangerous. Look at the other fellow you found. He slipped near the edge of a cliff, and fell about seventy feet through the trees, to where you found him. How he didn't kill himself is beyond me."

"How is he doing, by the way?" interrupted LJ.

"He's doing quite well, actually, considering his fall, and the time he lay out there unable to move. His injuries are extensive, no longer life-threatening, but extensive. He may lose his right leg, we're not sure, but I think he'll be here some considerable time. Then there will be charges, a public trial and most probably, a very long stay in our prison." He sat there, looking across at LJ, letting his words sink in before he continued.

"Actually, I invited you here to ask if you could help me with him. He is a very difficult person, and won't answer any of our questions. He's polite and thankful for the care he's getting, but beyond that, he just looks at me or anyone else questioning him and says nothing. It has nothing to do with language, because he speaks English very well. He's tough and won't even verify who he is.

"His only real response to any of our questions has been to ask to talk to the man who found him. Said he would like to thank the person responsible. I thought about that and was wondering if you could go in and visit him. I won't ask you to play policeman and I wouldn't want you doing anything you feel uncomfortable about. All I would ask is perhaps you could poke about a bit and see what you can come up with."

LJ thought a long moment before answering. He was an upfront kind of guy, not the subtle or devious type who could do this sort of thing easily.

"Why don't I just ask him straight up who he is, where he's from, and what the hell he thought he was doing?" he asked the policeman.

"You could do it that way. Who knows, it just might work." Commissioner Frank shrugged his shoulders.

"Play it by ear and if you think that's best, try it. You never know, if he is from Cuba, as I'm sure he is, he may not feel too happy having policemen questioning him, so a civilian may get through. Give it a try. If it works, good. If not, you'll have my thanks for giving it a go." The policeman stood as LJ slowly rose from his chair.

"OK, let's get at it," and the two men left the plush office and walked down the hall towards the hospital room and the mystery man.

LJ closed the door quietly behind him after gently knocking. He hadn't expected an answer when he rapped out his arrival, knowing the knock was a courtesy everyone gave a patient before entering their room. Without any hesitation, he strode across to the bed, stopped, and looked down.

In it lay a man who, other than having his right arm held off the bed in a white shoulder to finger cast, and a right leg under what looked like a tent held up by a metal frame, seemed surprisingly well. He was newly shaven, scrubbed clean and without bugs and grubs crawlihg across him. His hair was brushed to one side and LJ was surprised at how good looking this young man was.

"Hi," LJ said "other than all this," and he waved at the traction holding his arm up, "how are you feeling?"

The man smiled and said, "I feel a little groggy, but other than some soreness, quite good, thank you."

"You'll probably feel one hell of a lot worse tomorrow. I've had a few injuries in my past and it takes a day or two before your body starts to punish you for treating it so badly." And he smiled back at the patient.

LJ walked around the bed, pulled a chair close and sat down next to the man's good arm.

"My name is Louis John Livingston, what's yours?"

"Manuel, Manuel Fernando Ruiz," said the patient.

"Well it's nice to meet you again Mr. Ruiz. That sounds like a Cuban name, or Puerto Rican, or some other Spanish area."

"I'm Cuban," the injured man said.

"Well, whatever, one would never know it from your English. I'm here because I'm the guy who led the team that found you out there in the bush and you were in no condition for any introductions or idle chit-chat then."

"I'm glad you could come to see me. The police told me about you earlier, and I asked to see you so I could thank you. It was good of you to come so quickly."

The old warrior told the young Cuban he was welcome and to think nothing of it, but felt a little uncomfortable knowing this pleasant exchange between rescued and rescuer was a little more than it appeared. LJ knew it wasn't the only reason he visited and figured it was now or never, so he told Manuel the other reason.

"Well Mr. Ruiz, saying hello and getting your thanks are not the only reasons I'm here. I don't know if you thought about it, or even had the chance to wonder what I was doing when we found you. Did you give that any consideration?" LJ sat quietly watching the patient, and then continued.

"We were out looking for a missing Canadian student who we believe was kidnapped, quite possibly by you, about a week ago. Her name is Rachel Lusinski. Do you know who I'm talking about?" LJ waited for some comment, but the injured man said nothing.

"I'm a good friend of her grandfather, who is very worried about her, and I'm here with about thirty other retired friends of his, as a search party." LJ watched Manuel's face as he spoke, trying to determine his mood.

"So you have found her then," he sighed and looked away from his visitor. "Good, I was concerned she would starve to death up there, while I lay in the mud thinking I would die there."

LJ sat silently for several seconds, wondering if he should tell the man they hadn't found Rachel yet, then decided honesty was the best policy.

"No, we haven't found her. We found your camp but she wasn't there."

"That's impossible," he almost shouted, agitated. "She was fastened to the building she slept in. She had a line running from her ankle to a bolt at the door. She could never undo it. I don't understand." Manuel was shaken by the news.

LJ waited while Manuel calmed down and thought about what lay ahead for the young man. He probably faced a few more rough operations and many months of pain and rehabilitation. Then he was sure to face a long trial and probably years in prison. What surprised LJ was what he was worrying about: the young girl he had kidnapped. He was upset by the whereabouts and well-being of his victim. LJ figured the guy couldn't be all bad so he might as well tell him the whole story.

"The doorway of one of the huts was badly broken. We wondered what had happened, and I think she may have devised a way to smash it to pieces.

"She was last seen yesterday morning around eight-thirty as she ran from the camp. She had fought off a very nasty fellow who must have tried to assault her but she left him bleeding and in pain in the dust. Right now, we have about two hundred police and volunteers combing the bush below your hideout, looking for her. We'll find her, and soon. Don't worry about that." And he patted the young man's hand.

"Did you and all of the friends of her grandfather fly all the way here from Canada?"

"Canada? Oh no, we all flew in from Florida. Only a couple of our group came from Canada. The rest of us live on the west coast of Florida. The girl's grandfather is from Canada originally, but he now lives year-round near us. The rest of us are from all over the United States. I'm originally from New Jersey."

"Then you're an American?" the Cuban asked quietly.

"Born and raised. Yes sir. My family goes back several hundred years in the New Jersey and New York areas," LJ said with a tinge of pride.

Manuel lay quietly for a long time just staring up at LJ, obviously deep in thought. Finally he spoke.

"The police officer told me if it was not for you and the way you took charge when you found me, I would probably be dead. Your action saved my life. He said you took control and organized everyone. Why would you do that for an enemy?"

"Enemy, what do you mean, enemy?" LJ was genuinely surprised. "Why would you call me an enemy? We're not enemies."

"I'm from Cuba," he spoke loudly now. "You're from the United States. We are enemies." Manuel's voice had risen from its quiet conversational level. His good hand was shaking and he was very agitated. LJ was worried he might have to leave and let him settle down.

"Son," LJ said softly, "you and I are not enemies. I was in the Marines for thirty years and I even fought on this very island, but I am not your enemy. I know the government of your country does not like the government of my country and the feeling is mutual but it does not mean you and I are enemies. These things happen all the time, but it never lasts.

"A long time ago, during the reign of Queen Victoria, an English Prime Minister named Lord Palmerston said nations have no permanent friends or allies, they only have permanent interests. At the moment, it is in the best interests of both our countries to maintain their present positions. But mark my words, things will

254

change in time and this will be all forgotten." LJ let this sink in.

"Don't worry, someday, our relationship with Cuba will change. Look at Germany and Japan, they're our best friends now. Look at Vietnam, American tourists visit every day.

"Mr. Ruiz, individual people are not enemies. They just love their homeland, believe in their governments, and serve when their country calls upon them to do so. That's what your father did here, and so did I.

"Believe me, we are not enemies. We are just people from two different lands. Other than there being over forty years difference in our ages, and the language we call our native tongue, there is very little difference between you and me."

Manuel was silent as he digested these words. He had never really met a real live American other than as a waiter, let alone chat with one in an intelligent talk about politics and life and all the things that matter. He thought Americans were different; people easy to hate, people fitting the image his uncle had painted so long ago in the tiny house where his mother had cried.

He found it hard to believe this gentle grey-haired old man sitting next to him was one of the hated monsters who lived only a hundred miles from his homeland.

He was nothing like the gangsters his uncle had raged on about; nothing like the crooked rich men who exploited the masses. He was not wearing a flowered shirt and there was no camera hanging from his neck. He had no sunglasses and there was no cigarette jutting from his lips. He was a normal person, one who actually sounded very sensible. Manuel had been with this man only a short time but he liked him and his calm quiet manner.

"But you may have killed my father."

"Yes, that's true. But he, or one of his fellow workers, may very well have killed me. If that had happened, I would not want my boys in New Jersey spending all their years hating your father for something he may or may not have done. Son, you and I, and your father, are the people who make the world turn. Without us, nothing happens. We do what we have to do, then march into the future, getting on with life." The old Marine now stood quietly, looking down at the young man, hoping he understood.

"I have to go now," he said. "I want to join the search teams in the hills so I must be leaving. Before I go, I would ask one thing of you please."

"What would you like?"

"I would like you to co-operate with the police. There is nothing to be gained by not answering their questions, and it may make it easier for you. They will find out everything they want to know eventually, so you might as well make sure they get your side of the story first." LJ reached down and took Manuel's left hand firmly in his and shook it, Boy Scout style.

"It has been very nice to meet you Mr. Ruiz. I hope your injuries heal quickly and properly."

"It has been nice to meet you Mr. Livingston, and very informative. I believe you to be a wise man, and you make me think I may have been mistaken. I will think about the things you have told me. Will you come to visit again?"

"I would be glad to. Now if you'll excuse me, I must go find that lost girl and get her back to her parents," and he turned and left the room, leaving the injured man with much to think about.

Chapter Forty Three

Day Six: Nine Thirty A.M.

As LJ drove, he thought hard about the young Cuban stretched out in the hospital, and was unable to shake the sadness he felt for him. Commissioner Frank had shown him the letter Manuel sent to the Prime Minister, and he now could understand a little of what must have been going on in the boy's head for so many years. What a bloody waste, he thought.

The policeman said he had contacted the Cuban Embassy and informed them that they may have a Cuban National in custody, and they would be informed officially, when it was confirmed. He also promised he would keep LJ up to date on the situation.

His thoughts were jarred back to the present and the road he was on to the search area by the jangle of his cell phone. He looked at it with distaste and thought it was time for a new ring tone, if he could figure out how to change it. He guessed he'd have to wait for a visit from one of his grandchildren and get them to change it, like the last time.

'Hello," he said.

"Is this Mr. Livingston, Mr. LJ Livingston," a voice asked.

"Yes it is," he answered.

"Well LJ, my name is Hud," and LJ cut him off in mid-sentence.

"My name is Mr. Livingston. You will address me as Mr. Livingston until I give you permission to call me anything else. If you don't understand that, this call is over," and he waited for a moment and on hearing no reply, hung up.

A few minutes later, the phone rang again and LJ smiled as he picked it up and answered.

"Mr. Livingston, please forgive me. It was presumptuous of me to be so informal, please forgive me." The voice groveled.

"What would you like?" LJ asked abruptly.

"I'm calling in regard to the pretty young girl pictured on posters all over the island. I and some of my associates may be able to help you and your colleagues find her."

"Do you have her?"

"To the best of my knowledge, right at the moment, she's with a friend of mine, and he's taking very good care of her. I'm just calling to arrange the reward I'm sure is offered, so we can set up a meeting to arrange bringing the girl to you."

"I see," LJ replied "well there is a sizable reward, the family has offered twenty-five thousand dollars, American dollars, not EC, and it would be available to anyone who rescued the girl and turned her over to us." LJ felt he was fishing off the pier in Tampa Bay, the way he was reeling this one in. "Yes, I think we can arrange a meeting, if you have indeed found the girl." He thought he heard a gasp at the mention of the amount.

"Oh indeed, we have found her. Yes, yes, we have found her. We would have brought her straight out but she was quite disoriented, and hungry, very hungry and quite honestly, in an almost hysterical state. We thought it best to make her comfortable, prepare some food and drink for her, and let her rest while I came out of the hills and contacted you.

"I instructed my partner, a Mr. Adams, to prepare a good meal for her and stand guard while she rested. He's a fine man, one of the best, and you can rest assured the young lady is fine and well cared for.

"Are you sure she's alright?"

"Indeed she is," said the caller. "My assistant, Mr. Adams is taking good care of her as we speak. We're in the horticultural business you know, and were up in the hills checking on some new plantings, you know. We grow flowers, things like orchids, anthuriums, alpinin purpuratas, that kind of thing. All the while we've been tending our plantings we've been keeping a sharp eye open for the girl. My partner and I've been following the news you know, and like every citizen of Grenada, we wanted her found. So you see, the posters and the news played a big part in how we found her,"

"Well Mister, I don't think I got your name. What is it?"

"Hudson, just Hudson. That's what everyone knows me by so just call me Hudson," the voice said.

"OK Hudson; lets meet someplace where there's a bank nearby, and we'll have a coffee and work out the details. There's a hotel on Wharf Road near the Christ of The Deep statue, you probably know it. It's the one with a large open air restaurant across the front, painted red and white, I think. How about I meet you there in half an hour? I'm fairly slim, six foot three and I'm a senior with white hair, how will I know you?" LJ could almost hear him panting.

"Mr. Livingston, I know the restaurant you've suggested, an excellent choice I must say, and you will recognize me by simply looking for the largest man in the place. I'm somewhat rotund."

"Great, I'll see you in half an hour". And he hung up but he didn't put the phone down. He had someone to call.

"Commissioner," he said, when the call was answered, "LJ here. I just got a call from that Dumpy guy, the big one. Yes, he wants a reward, and says Rachel was hungry so Lester was making her something to eat and she's safe with Lester at this moment." There was a pause for a few seconds and then LJ laughed. "You say she wasn't in the room when you questioned Lester. My God Winfred, that means Dumpy, or Hudson, was lying to me. I'm shocked, shocked." The two men had a good laugh over this.

"I've set up a meeting with him, in half an hour," and he gave the Commissioner the location and the details of the amount of the imaginary reward Dumpy was trying to extort. Winfred assured LJ several of the islands finest would pick up Dumpy, and bring him into the Fort for some serious discussions about his role in this kidnapping.

The Commissioner also said Manuel had become far more co-operative than he had been during his first two interrogations. He had willingly offered them a great deal more information on how he got out of Cuba and into Grenada. He thanked LJ profusely for whatever it was he did to cause the change.

LJ just passed it off as an old man giving a young man some advice, and the young man being smart enough to take it.

They talked a little more about Dumpy and Lester and their agriculture business and the Commissioner had a great laugh, saying he had never seen anyone smoke an orchid and he knew those two half-wits only grew stuff for smoking. He said one had to admire the nerve of that fat crook and his stupid side-kick before they rang off.

With the conversation ended and LJ carrying on with his driving, both men moved on with their respective duties, laughing at how strange life and the world around them could be.

Chapter Forty Four

Day Six: Ten A.M.

Rachel had been slowly making her way down the hill for most of the past couple of hours, and needed a rest. There was no more barking dog, so she just had to trust her instincts and keep moving and listening. You never know when someone's dog might start yapping for food or water.

She was hungry, her backside was very sore, and all the rest of her was still stiff from the night between the roots of the tree. Rachel had slept in a few strange places in her life, but she was sure that was about the strangest. She hadn't meant to sleep so long but she was so worn out from the fight with Rona, she just couldn't stop from dozing off and sleeping soundly for hours.

Resting her head back against a tree, she closed her eyes and contemplated the past seven unbelievable days. She had been kidnapped, duct taped, stuffed in a car, led through the jungle, and chained to a ramshackle hut, where she was fed oatmeal day and night. After that, she was left alone, managed to break out and then was captured again by 'dumb and dumber', the Laurel and Hardy of the Caribbean. Finally, she had to bash one on the head, run through the bushes and almost fell over a cliff. She felt like she was the star of a modern day 'Perils of Pauline' movie. Now that all seemed in the past and she could rest, take it easy and listen to the rhythm of someone banging on a piece of metal.

Rachel sat bolt upright and thought to herself, 'What the heck are you doing? That's someone telling you the way out, and you're sitting here like a klutz'. She jumped up, no longer tired.

"Come on Rona," she yelled "we're being paged and we're going home" and she started down and to her right where the sound seemed to be coming from.

It was surprising how fast Rachel now moved, dodging around trees and barging straight through bushes, yanking Rona behind her with a strength even she didn't know she had. Fresh scratches on her arms and legs from branches and bushes caused not a moment's hesitation as she worked her way toward the rhythmic sound, still coming through the undergrowth like the very slow beat of a drum.

Bursting through huge philodendrons, she screeched to a halt before a small watery ditch between her and the most beautiful paved road she had ever seen. She pulled Rona out beside her and reached down, picking her up.

"Look Rona, look. It's a beautiful, lovely, wonderful road. We made it." And she gleefully tossed the lump of wood across the ditch to land with a loud clunk on the pavement. Finally she was out.

Following Rona, she stood beside her on the road, looking both ways for the steel banger she had heard. She was alone, but the sound was still on her right, so she started down the pavement in search of her beacon, happy to be back in the real world again.

"Come on Rona, let's go find our noisemaker and give him a big kiss," and she grabbed up the tether to more easily drag her companion along behind her.

The road twisted and turned, winding its way through the steep hills running sharply upward on both sides. It was in good condition with a well-maintained surface, making the chore of dragging the three foot chunk of lumber much easier than on the hillside.

She laughed as she thought how strange she would look to anyone seeing her for the first time. She wore sandals, a pair of very muddy white shorts and sported a body-hugging red T shirt glued to her well-developed, but very sweaty upper body. Her long blonde hair had not been washed in a week, a world record, and was all over the place looking as filthy as could be. To cap off this picture was the odd fact that she was being followed by a piece of wood on a cord. She must have been a sight.

The intermittent banging was much closer now, and as she approached the next curve in the road, she could hear local music between each clang. The noisemaker had a radio playing somewhere near. Rachel was getting excited as she rounded the corner, and came to a sudden stop at the sight before her.

Parked at the side of the narrow winding road was a large old dump truck with one of its back wheels lying on the pavement near the rear of the rig. Standing over the wheel was a tall, thin, shirtless man with an unruly mop of white hair. In his hands was a long, heavy-looking sledge hammer that would fly up over his head, then come crashing down onto the rim of the wheel. Each blow made the heavy wheel bounce on the road. She had absolutely no idea why he was beating a tire.

Rachel stood watching the man effortlessly swing the hammer as though it weighed only ounces. She was surprised at how easily he swung the tool, and how hard it hit the rim. She thought this guy has sure done this more than a few times before.

The sight of the old man whacking the tire kept her from moving for several seconds or from noticing something very strange about the truck. Along the side and on the back of the old, dented and dirty dump box were taped large posters of a girl. It took her a second to realize it was her. The smiling face looking down was hers. She had heard of the posters but the first sight of one stunned her.

Moving slowly forward with Rona in tow, she tried to make enough noise between blows of the hammer to catch the man's attention. He heard and stopped his labors, slowly turning to see what was going on behind him, holding his hammer in a defensive manner. Rachel had stopped when he turned and he looked at her for several seconds before slowly turning back to his truck and up at the posters duct taped to the box. Not moving any faster, he turned back and his gleaming old dark face broke into a wonderful great grin.

"Come, young lady," he said gently and beckoned as he would to a frightened kitten. "You look like you could use a drink of cool water and a place to rest. Come, don't be afraid."

Rachel didn't move, instead, she burst into tears.

The hammer swinger was Clinton Cranston, a truck driver of something more than sixty years who had been hauling every imaginable commodity through the hills of Grenada for more than forty of them. A happily married man, grandfather of two girls about the same age as Rachel, he had stopped one of the sign crews he had seen along the road and asked for a couple of posters for his truck. The crew not only handed over three posters, they pulled out a small ladder and taped them into place. Clinton was determined to help in the search, and now the object of everyone's attention was standing in front of him, crying her eyes out.

"Now, now child, everything is going to be just fine. You're not to worry anymore, everything will be fine," and he put his arm gently around her shoulders and guided her to the running board of his truck so she could sit down.

"What have we here?" Clinton asked when he saw the tether strung out behind her. Reaching down, he grabbed the cord and pulled, growling when he saw the large piece of wood attached, and then noting the lacerations on Rachel's ankle. "What bloody devil did this terrible thing to you, child?" he demanded. "What type of beast would do this?" Clinton Cranston was very angry.

Mr. Cranston turned to the toolbox bolted to the frame of his truck and rattled about looking for something. When he finally found what he wanted, he let out a quiet exclamation of satisfaction and returned to Rachel's perch on the running board. He held what looked like giant pliers as he stepped toward her.

"Hang on young lady, I'll have this awful thing off you in a minute," and he knelt down and took hold of the tether. With a great deal of effort and much huffing and puffing, he managed, with some help from Rachel, to get his bolt cutters through the cord without cutting off the poor girl's foot. At long last, Rachel was free, truly free.

"Come on now child, I'll help you up," and he took her around to the passenger side of the great truck and reaching up, opened the door and offered his arm. "Clamber up there and give me a few seconds to gather up my tools and get my shirt on and then I'll try to get you home. There's a small cooler on the floor with cold water in it. Help yourself."

Clinton moved to the rear and rolled the flat tire into the ditch. He knew it would be safe there, and he could retrieve it the next day. Next, he let off the jack holding the rear axle off the ground, pulled it from under the truck and tossed it into the jack box attached to the frame. He knew if he took his time with his empty truck, the single inside tire could carry him a long way on its own. Looking around to make sure all was in order, he climbed up into the cab.

Rachel had finally stopped crying, and was much more in control of her emotions as she sipped from a bottle of water. As Clinton settled into the driver's seat, she reached over and placed her hand on his sturdy black arm.

"You've been so kind. I hate to ask anymore of you, but there is one more little thing," she hurried on, fearing he'd stop her before her request came out. "Could you do me a favor? Could you get me my piece of wood, please?"

"You mean that thing on the cord I cut you from a few minutes ago?"

Rachel, wide-eyed and serious, nodded her head up and down.

The old man smiled the way a grandfather would smile at his favorite little girl. The one he would do anything for.

"No problem," he smiled, and climbed back down onto the road.

Rachel waited, finally hearing the clunk of Rona hitting the floor of the empty dump box behind her. The driver's door swung open and Clinton climbed back in behind the wheel.

Rachel smiled the way a granddaughter would smile at a special old friend in her life, then leaned over and kissed his cheek.

"Thank you," she whispered.

Beaming, Clinton turned the key to get the old engine going. Shifting into gear, the great noisy truck started down the road, the two people sitting in the cab wearing wide and happy smiles.

Chapter Forty Five

Day Six: Two P.M.

Clinton Cranston, Rachel's intrepid chauffer, drove her from the back road spot where he found her, to the main highway connecting St. George's to Grenville, then turned south on that road to a police station a short distance south of Birch Grove. There he discovered the station locked up tight. An old lady passing told him the police were all out in the hills looking for the lost girl, and pointed to a poster on the station wall.

He stood for a moment considering his options, then, with a shrug, climbed back into the truck and smiled at his passenger.

"It appears they're all out looking for you, and we're here looking for them. I guess we'll just have to go down to the main station, so you can be safe. I know there's a bunch of people from the United States and Canada looking for you with the police, they were on television, so the guys down there will know what to do. Just hang on little lady, and don't worry. I'm staying with you, 'till I know you're safe."

"I'm not worried anymore. In fact, this is the safest I've felt in a long time," and again she gave him a heart-melting smile.

Clinton drove her in as far as he could with his truck, but it was much too big for the busy city streets, and would never make it up the hill to the fort. So once in town, he parked and hailed a taxi. The cab driver gave Rachel's disheveled appearance a curious look then suddenly twisted his mirror to see her better. He recognized his passenger, and started into a spirited exchange with Clinton in the local patios, leaving

Rachel unable to understand more than a couple of words.

When they arrived at the station, the beaming and excited driver jumped from the car, opened Rachel's door and offered his hand in assistance. When Clinton pulled out a handful of bills to pay, the cabby got quite agitated and shoved the money away. Clinton told Rachel, as they walked across Bottom Square, that the driver's story of his part in her rescue would grow as the days passed and the drinks flowed. He said it with a grin so big he made her laugh.

The young receptionist casually looked up from papers on her desk and fairly jumped from her chair when she saw who had walked into the office. With no hesitation, she scurried down the hall without saying a word. Shoving a door open without knocking, she called out the person inside. "Come quickly, come quickly."

The Commissioner came out looking stern but his demeanor changed to a look of sheer joy. He was truly happy, ushering the object of so much concern, and her protector, into his office while the receptionist was chased to the lunchroom to make tea.

The next hour passed in a blur for Rachel. The Commissioner and two female officers whisked her and Clinton out of Fort George, around the short curvy road and in through the front doors of the hospital. While one officer and a nurse guided her to a suite and assisted in preparing her bath, the other police woman went to the kitchen to arrange food for the new guest. All the while, Commissioner Frank stood in the foyer giving one of the several policemen still assigned to the place, a long list of instructions. The officer stood quietly scribbling notes.

Finished with his scribbling subordinate, Commissioner Frank turned to Clinton, saying he would like to ask him some questions, and wondered if he minded waiting a few minutes. The old man agreed, found a nearby chair and sat down to watch and marvel at a man completely in control of the situation.

Nick and LJ were called and told the good news and asked to let the girl's father know. An officer was sent up to Rachel's grandfather's room in the hospital where he was actually getting ready to check out. His heart problem had been stabilized and the news would probably be more beneficial than any of the pills he had been given. LJ's wife, Edith, now a recognized expert at driving on the wrong side of the road, was bringing Fred's wife to the hospital to pick up her husband so she could also get Rachel's mother, Irene, and bring her along.

The police in the field were being called out of the bush as the search was now officially over, and the media was informed there would be a press conference at the hospital at six p.m.

Finally, an officer was dispatched to Rachel's residence where Sylvia, her roommate, would help gather up some clean clothes and personal items from their still sealed room.

Commissioner Frank discussed the situation with the hospital's Chief of Staff and a complete examination of Rachel was to begin after she had had a long bath and a good meal.

When all seemed in place, the Commissioner sat down beside Clinton to ask about his part in the rescue. He was a little surprised when told of the size of the chunk of wood and said he'd have a police car to take him back to his truck to collect it. He also suggested sending someone from Birch Grove to pick up his flat tire, but Clinton waved the offer aside with a laugh. "Don't worry about it Sir. No one would steal that old piece of junk. I'll get it in the morning."

Satisfied with the details Clinton provided, Commissioner Frank stood and held his hand out to the older man.

"Thank you Mr. Cranston. You bring honor to your country and your quick and proper service is much appreciated. This Officer," and he waved a smart looking young man over, "will take you back to your truck. Please drive carefully and remember, everyone in Grenada thanks you." One look at Clinton as he left with the uniformed policeman would make a person think the man had just been knighted.

Commissioner Frank looked slowly around the hospital foyer and decided everything was under control, so he walked out the door and strode up the pathway to his office. His big problem, as he saw it, was what to do with the young Cuban still lying in traction in the hospital.

No charges had been laid as yet, and he wanted to talk to Rachel about that before the press conference. He also had to decide how to handle the Cuban Embassy and whether to tell them about the Venezuelan passport found in the kidnapper's bag that now sat on his desk. Having the distinct feeling he may be treading through a field of broken glass, he decided the most prudent thing to do was to wait and see how the situation unfolded.

For her part, Rachel was having a great time. Her two attendants were the funniest pair she had ever met and they kept her laughing from the moment she arrived at the hospital.

She reveled in her long soak in the tub, and in taking her time washing her hair under the shower. When finally she stepped from the bathroom, she felt, and looked, like a princess.

While in the tub scrubbing off days of dirt, her two new friends arranged a mountain of food delivered from the hospital's kitchen so the three of them could have a feast.

The pretty young nurse, designated as Rachel's attendant, seemed a twin sister of the police officer assigned to assist her. Within minutes, the girls discovered the nurse was on duty when Manuel arrived in emergency from the jungle, and she was one of the staff who helped prep him for the O.R., including stripping and washing him. She had no qualms about describing in great detail all she saw and because her wide-eyed observations were less than clinical, they resulted in much hilarity. It was the most fun Rachel had in a long time, and all three made a solemn pact between giggles, they would never reveal what was discussed in the room.

When the bath, the meal, and fun with friends ended, the family arrived in a cacophony of squeals, crying and laughing. Her mother, the always calm and ever beautiful Irene, wanted to know every detail and demanded to know at least three times if her kidnapper touched her in any way. She told Rachel her father was coming in from the search and would see her soon.

Her grandmother only seemed interested in her health and well-being, checking her hands and arms, and inspecting her face and head, looking deep into her eyes, softly asking if she was sure she was alright.

Her grandfather simply hugged her, kissed her on the cheek and then quickly turned away, so she wouldn't see the tears in his eyes that she saw anyway.

Her father arrived and shed much of his stern exterior, simply holding his daughter close, saying little before stepping back, giving the attention back to her mother and grandmother.

As the visit progressed, she found herself increasingly defending Manuel, explaining how well he had treated her and how he appeared to be a nice man who had made a few wrong decisions. It was an odd feeling, sticking up for the guy who had kidnapped her.

An hour passed, and a bottle of wine emptied when the Chief of Staff arrived and announced it was time for her medical examination. He carefully explained everything to the four of them, and since time was marching on, suggested since it would be early evening when all was done, Rachel might just want to sleep when it was over so they should say their goodbyes now. He did say they had the hotel's phone number and would call if anything came up.

The next fifteen minutes were spent in tearfully happy goodbyes.

While all this was going on, weary searchers were straggling back into the hotel, wives going directly to their rooms to freshen up and the husbands going directly to the pool bar. Soon the bar was so crowded and noisy, two additional bartenders had to be drafted into service, and the poor swimmers had trouble getting anything to drink.

LJ and Nick held court sitting on tall barstools, at a high table set some distance from the bar. They had a clear view of all those coming and going and, of course, their drinks had to be delivered to them. It was one happy get-together with all the earmarks of it developing into a very noisy party. During the revelry, LJ nudged Nick and pointed toward Fred, leaning on the hotel's low white fence separating the grass from the wide white beach.

Fred was watching a couple walking slowly in the sand at waters edge. It was Anthony and Irene. She was probably filling him in on the details of her visit with Rachel, but she must have been talking softly because they were very close. With the late afternoon sun, the soft sand, and the warm Caribbean waters gently washing their feet, Fred, perhaps, was dreaming of them getting back together, and wondering if his stupid son had the sense to make it so.

At nine o'clock, the hotel manager cornered LJ and Nick and said he had consulted with the hotel's owners and they agreed to cover all expenses for a large 'welcome back' party the next evening. The owner suggested it include the media, politicians, police officials, and anyone involved in the search and rescue project. Of course, it would feature the center of that effort, Rachel, who was expected to be released from hospital by noon.

Nick thought it was a great idea, until Ann and Edith claimed they had nothing to wear and would have to go into St. George's the next morning to shop for dresses. Within minutes, a shopping expedition as large as the search effort was being put together by all the wives. The men just groaned and ordered more drinks.

All the while a happy, well-fed and content young lady slept much like a baby sleeps, safely bundled between crisp, clean white sheets with a small smile on her face. The only difference between her and a real baby was the chunk of lumber wrapped in cord at the foot of her bed, and a small alarm clock near her head, set to go off at eleven p.m.

Chapter Forty Six

Day Six: Eleven Ten P.M.

Rachel was awake before the alarm sounded, shutting it off in its first seconds of ringing. She'd awakened feeling wonderful after four hours of heavenly sleep on a mattress, in a room, and between wonderfully smelling clean sheets. Silently, she slipped on some of the clean clothes delivered by Sylvia, picked up the handwritten instructions sneaked to her by the funny young nurse, and gently turned the handle of her door, slowly opening it half an inch. The halls were silent, with no one in sight.

Taking a quick glance at her instructions, she slipped from the room, quietly closed the door and carefully moved to her right, heading for the door with the red exit sign above it.

Once through it and into the stairwell, Rachel quickly skipped down the steps two at a time, stopping on the next floor. Again, half an inch of a slowly opened door revealed an empty corridor and the all enveloping silence. The hospital appeared to be asleep.

Across the hall and two doors to her left was her target, room 211. A chair stood outside with a crumpled newspaper on the floor beside it, but whoever had been sitting there, presumably a guard, was gone. Without hesitation, she stepped from the stairwell, scurried across the hallway, and slipped into the semi-darkness of room 211.

Rachel had to do this because she knew it would be her only chance to talk privately with her kidnapper. She would be leaving the hospital in the morning, and he was being held by the police, under almost constant questioning. From what her nurse friend had said, he would need several more surgical procedures over the next few weeks and she would be gone from the island by then. She just couldn't walk away to another life without seeing him and getting some answers.

She moved quietly across the room in case he was sleeping, and if he was, would probably just look at him, and then leave to figure out something else. She need not have worried. As she approached the bed with all its wires and pulleys, the patient turned his head, looked into the dim light at his visitor, and broke into a smile. Rachel simply said 'hi'.

"How are you?" he asked.

"I'm fine. How about you?"

"Oh, I'm doing well. They have some work to do on my leg in the morning, but considering the distance they tell me I fell, I guess I'm lucky to be alive." He shifted a bit to get a better look at her. "I'm glad you came."

"Are you?" she said without smiling.

"I was worried about you. I have thought much about you."

"Why did you lie to me?" she demanded.

"What lie? I never lied to you. I always told you the truth. How did I lie to you?" Manuel was agitated.

"You said you were Cuban and told me stories about Cuba but you're actually a Venezuelan national."

"Oh, the passport," Manuel quickly calmed down. "I'm sorry, I understand. I am truly from Cuba. I was born there, as was my father, and his father before him. I am a Cuban.

"I found that passport lying on the floor of the hotel where I worked in Havana. The picture looked a little like me and I knew it was my way off the island. Cubans can't leave Cuba without permission from the government, and I would never be granted permission, so I pretended to be from Venezuela, bought a ticket and flew to Caracas. Several officials at the airport looked at the passport and waved me through. It was easy to go from Caracas to Barbados to here."

"You can't leave Cuba, why not? What kind of law is that? What about vacations? How about schooling? How stupid," Rachel spit out.

"It's the rules we must live by, even if we don't agree with them. I will have to pay a price some day for breaking them."

"What have the police said to you?"

"They have asked a lot of questions. They wanted all the details about my father, what kind of work he did in Cuba, how he died, how I was able to learn English so well, how I got here, why I picked you. They have asked many questions and I'm very tired of them". He wasn't smiling now but his mood changed a little when he mentioned her escape.

"The senior policeman, I think he's called Commissioner, told me how you were able to break the doorway and make your escape. It was a good way to do it. You are very smart." They looked at each other in silence, separated by much more than a few feet of hospital room.

"I'm going back to Canada with my mother and father in a couple of days, and I wanted to see you, talk to you, before I left." Rachel quietly said.

"I cannot understand why. You must hate me. The last time you spoke to me, you shouted with anger and demanded better food."

"I don't hate you but I did grow to hate oatmeal. I feel bad for you. I never thought you would just walk away and leave me to die on that mountain. I knew there was some problem. I'm sorry you fell. I'm sorry you're so badly hurt and need more operations. I was told about your injuries and I wanted to wish you well and tell you I will think of you often in Canada."

"Thank you" he said with great solemnity, "I will think of you always."

The conversation came to a halt and again the silence of the vast cultural gulf between them enveloped the room. There was not much more either could say, or needed to be said. They would both go in different directions, and live their different lives, always wondering about the marks left by the other in the short time they were together. The room seemed filled with a sense of great sadness.

During this silence, Rachel considered asking if he really meant his threat in the letter to the Prime Minister but pushed the thought aside. Deep inside her she knew it would be better through the years to believe he hadn't meant it.

"Thank you for coming. It was very kind of you."

Rachel stood for several more moments in silence then moved closer and bent down to kiss his cheek.

"You're welcome Manuel, I know you would never harm me," she said softly. "Take good care of yourself and have a good and long life." And she turned, disappearing from the room as quietly as she arrived.

Chapter Forty Seven

Day Eight: Two P.M.

Commissioner Frank, LJ, Harry, and Nick sat by the pool in the shade of a large umbrella emblazoned with the emblems of the many great beers of Grenada. Nick had suggested it would look good on his patio back home, but LJ didn't think they could get it on the plane, so he tossed the idea.

They were all in a good mood, probably a holdover from the party the night before, and they were basking in what was an advertising agent's idea of a travel promoter's perfect dream day. It was hot but the breeze refreshed and the soft sound of the surf backed up the rustle of the palms overhead. It was a time for relaxing and discussing all the little items that required attention. Nick and LJ both had their local beers and Harry, his ever present soda and ice. The policeman, in uniform, stuck to a bottle of Ting, a local citrus soft drink.

"How is our Cuban patient?" LJ asked.

"I'm afraid not as good as we might have hoped. I'm sorry to say they had to amputate his right leg several inches above the knee very late last night, actually, early this morning. It was either that, or he would have been gone in a week". From the look on the Commissioner's face, he was as upset about this as his three companions.

"Damn" was all LJ said.

"What are you going to do with him?" this from Nick.

"I'm not sure yet, but I have a few ideas, and since we have been through this thing together up to this point, and you are aware of all the details, I'd like an opinion or two from you, before I take any action." His companions agreed and all four made themselves even more comfortable, ordered another round and prepared to discuss, and solve, these major items.

"I understand you went and talked to the young man," the Commissioner said to Nick.

"Yes, LJ took me up to see him yesterday morning. In fact, we met Rachel as she left the hospital with her mom and dad. Pleasant girl. It's the first time I've met her and she seemed quite charming. Good looking too," Nick grinned.

"She is both those things but she also seems to have a stubborn streak, and certainly a mind of her own," suggested the Commissioner.

"At my request, her mother and father brought her up to my office immediately after you saw them. There were a few things I wanted to get clear." The Commissioner took a sip of his soft drink and carried on.

"Before you or her parents arrived at the hospital yesterday morning, this headstrong young lady managed to slip away from the officer assigned to watch her, and sneaked through the hospital to find the Cuban's room. Don't ask me how. I suspect her young nurse attendant had something to do with it, but we'll never know. She was in with him for about ten minutes, and I have no idea what they talked about. She wouldn't say, but he knew at that time his leg was going to have to come off. I don't know if he told her, but somehow, I doubt it."

"How did you find out she had seen him?" LJ asked.

"She told me when she and her parents were in my office."

"I'll be damned," said Nick.

"The other thing she said may surprise you as well. She told me flat out that she would not help me, or my country, prosecute Mr. Ruiz in any way, shape, or form. She thought he was naïve, unworldly and the product of

279

a massive propaganda machine, but she didn't think he was a bad man. She told me she was going home with her parents and she would not be back, for any reason."

Nick said, "I'll be damned," again.

The Commissioner nodded in agreement and continued. Neither he nor Nick noticed the grin on LJ's face.

"I received the report from the hospital on her medical exam. It was very thorough and clearly states absolutely no indication Rachel had been touched, or sexually interfered with in any manner. He could have easily done just about anything he wanted, but he didn't. So it would seem she's right, he's not a bad man. Mr. Ruiz may be stupid, but I'm with her. I, too, don't think he's really bad either."

"You seem to have a little bit of a dilemma here, my police officer friend," LJ mused.

"How do you figure that?" the Commissioner asked with a smile.

"Well, if she won't testify, or even swear out a complaint or whatever you call it, how do you tie him to her? We found him lying in the jungle a long way from the encampment where she was held. You have no fingerprints from the stolen car, so it would be hard to tie him to that. No one saw him take her or saw him with her. It might be hard to make a case without her." LJ stared straight at the policeman, looking for an answer.

"If we, or should I say I, wanted to make a case, I could. But you're right. It would be difficult, very expensive, and very time consuming. We know she was at the camp because her bathing suit was found there. We also found some of his clothes that were in his backpack along with his passport and some money. Off shore DNA testing would prove they were his so that puts him in the clearing. We also have his letter to the

Prime Minister admitting to what he was doing and demanding a form of ransom. He gives his father's name in that letter and he most likely licked the envelope to seal it so the DNA test would help there. You are correct my friend. It would be difficult, but definitely doable." The Commissioner sat back.

"Are you going to proceed?" LJ asked quietly.

"I haven't made up my mind yet," he said. "There are other considerations and I have to weigh each one, aside from the kidnapping itself."

"You mean the problem of him being a Cuban and how it could look like Grenada was trying to hurt, or shame, a Cuban national, and therefore, his homeland for their role twenty-five years ago. It would mean a big public trial, covered by the world's media; a trial that the alleged victim refused to testify or get involved in.

"It could even look like you may be acting for the American government as their lackey or surrogate, in the constant efforts to discredit Cuba and the Castro brothers. A big trial could be construed as payback for the foreign aid your country receives from the U.S. Yes, my good Mr. Franks, I do believe you do have a few other considerations here." LJ had a sad smile as he said this.

"You are a very astute man, Mr. Livingston. You should be in politics."

"Not me, Mr. Commissioner, I'm a soldier. It's a whole lot easier to shoot your enemies than try to talk them out office. I wouldn't make a very good politician because I'd probably have my gun out too often." And they all shared a laugh of relief over this exchange.

Nick had a question here and jumped in. "How would you explain away what has gone on over the last eight or ten days, if you don't prosecute the man in the hospital?

"We've put up a ton of posters and you've held a couple of news conferences, complete with international TV crews covering the story. These are things you'll not be able to walk away from and ignore. Everyone will want some form of closure on this event."

"I've thought about these things as well." The Commissioner said. "One saving feature is we do have two villains in custody who are involved in this affair up to their ears. Believe me my friends, these unsavory halfwits have been an ongoing minor crime wave on this island, and both have a long history of proving they are bad men. One tried to extort money from you for the safe return of the girl, while the other, supposedly guarding her in the hills, was set about doing some very nasty things to her. Lester Adams is still in hospital recovering from his well-deserved beating, and Dumpy, the world's dumbest extortionist, is safely tucked away in a jail cell." He paused as the waitress brought another round of drinks.

"I think Rachel will sign a statement saying she was assaulted by Lester and she had to beat him off, causing his severe injuries. She will sign it because it's the truth. I would also hope to convince you, LJ, to sign a statement describing how 'Dumpy' attempted his telephone extortion. With these in hand, I believe we can convince them to plead guilty to some lesser charges than kidnapping, put them away for a while, and give this island a rest from their mischief. They really are a damned nuisance you know.

"As for the Cuban, he's paid a big price already for being so stupid. The doctors say he will never be the same. With his leg gone, problems with healed bones never being perfect, scar tissue, he will be paying a price for a long time. I think he should just go home and spend the rest of his life thinking about that," and he sat back and watched his three companions.

"I guess it's my turn to say, I'll be damned," grinned LJ. "You've got this worked out pretty well, haven't you? You're a very intelligent and thoughtful man. I must say congratulations Commissioner. I think you've done a great job thinking this through." And he laughed as he sat back in his chair.

"One thing though". The Commissioner asked, turning to Harry. "Do you think the rest of your people will go along with the program?"

"I would think so. They're a pretty astute group with many years of watching a world run by fools. I would think that most, if not all, would appreciate the good sense in your suggestions, but there is one last thing. How do you handle the Cuban? He can't stay in the hospital forever. Can you just send him home?" Harry was playing Devil's Advocate.

"I had a quiet chat with the Cuban Ambassador very late last night, after the leg came off, and asked how he felt about ending this problem the way I've suggested. I told him I would need assurances the man would be decently treated if sent home. I also pointed out we would have some Canadians who could visit Cuba to check up on Mr. Ruiz, if need be.

"I believe he talked to Havana last night because he called me very early this morning and said he had a green light to arrange everything. Mr. Ruiz will be quietly flown home when he is well enough to travel and there will be no repercussions or disciplinary activity. He will be treated decently.

"The internal story will be that the Government of Cuba allowed him to visit the site of his heroic father's death which occurred long ago when he was caught in the crossfire of an American military action. His injuries were the result of an unfortunate accident. They've toned down the rhetoric somewhat and won't mention capitalist dogs or blood-thirsty, invading, baby killers in any statements. I think the times, as you Americans say, are a-changing."

"Can we be sure of that?" Nick asked.

"Mr. Archer, your countrymen represent Cuba's largest source of tourist dollars. If not for Canadians, Varadero would be close to a ghost town. How would it look if your Toronto and Montreal newspapers and your national TV featured the story of a Cuban thug kidnapping a pretty young Canadian girl, and chaining her to a hut with no running water or toilet facilities? I can see the front pages now.

"No, the Castro brothers may be Communists but they are not stupid Communists. This one little man is of no value to them. He comes from a tiny village in a rural area and he will go back there. He has no connections and will soon be forgotten. He is not worth the impact his story could have on their tourist industry. They would very much like to see the whole thing just quietly disappear."

"And you have convinced them it won't disappear if they don't agree with your proposal." LJ said with great respect.

"Let's just say they understand how things work in this world," Commissioner Frank said with a smile.

Nick looked at LJ and Harry and both looked relieved. LJ had been worried about Manuel ever since he first met him. He, too, believed him not to be a bad man, just badly misguided but LJ knew Manuel had done a bad thing and there must be some punishment.

Nick felt the same way. What Manuel started was now drawing to a close, and the young man would pay the price for his bad decisions the rest of his life. With the news of him losing his leg, Nick figured it may be enough punishment for his sins. He felt the commissioner was subtly asking the three men if they felt justice had been done. He was looking for approval from some valued friends.

Looking over at LJ, he could see how he felt. They could now influence the flow of events by simply agreeing with the plan, and convincing the rest of the Florida group to do the same.

"It's a done deal, Mr. Commissioner," he said and reached over to shake his hand. LJ followed and simply said "Ditto". Harry said nothing but his broad grin showed his feelings as he firmly shook the Commissioner's hand.

Epilogue

The Twelfth Day: Ten A.M.

LJ and Edith Livingston were the last of the Florida group to leave the island. LJ had wanted to stay a couple of extra days and visit some of the places he hadn't had a chance to see while involved in the search, and Edith wanted to rest and relax and soak up some sun and a few Rum Punches.

For two days after the grand 'welcome back' party, LJ and Edith took turns shuttling fellow searchers to the airport before they finally found some time for themselves. It was only then they were able to take a leisurely drive north from St. George's to Grenville and slowly work their way through its busy streets. Once out of that city, they moved a few miles further north past the village of Paradise, to Pearls Airport, now sitting abandoned on a back road. This was where LJ had first landed in Grenada those many years ago and though unused and abused, it sure seemed the same.

A local man, relaxing in the shade of a tree near the old apron area, told LJ the runway now occasionally hosted unofficial Sunday afternoon drag racing competitions by local car enthusiasts. LJ marveled at the excellent condition of the single strip as he walked across it and down to the eastern end where it abruptly ended at the water's edge.

Edith waited in the car, happy to watch as her man wandered about the small airfield, remembering his time running around the place with his men while being shot at. She had brought a magazine but it lay in her lap ignored. She was content, watching her husband of fifty years visit his past and she couldn't help but reminisce herself on how difficult and wonderful and exciting those fifty years had been. Life with LJ had been a lot of things but it surely had never been dull.

LJ seemed to enjoy climbing in and out of two junk Russian- built turboprop aircraft, sitting forlornly in long grass beside the pot-holed entrance road. Stripped of anything worthwhile or valuable many years ago, the decaying wrecks, one with wings drooping like a mortally wounded bird, were sad remnants of the planes LJ and his men had seized in a brief battle a quarter century before. He had been surprised when he drove in to see them still sitting there, and wondered of the fate of the twelve crewmembers. They were captured when LJ and his fellow Marines took the airport and those twelve became the first prisoners taken by U.S. forces that day.

Finally, after respectfully listening to the ghosts of friends and foes alike, LJ climbed back into the car.

"Ready to go?" Edith asked with a warm smile.

"Yea, it was interesting to come back but I've seen enough. It's the first time for me. I've never visited a place where I soldiered to see what it was like or how things worked out. It's different, but it's the same in many ways. It was like walking through a movie set where a bunch of actors had played parts in a war movie. It wasn't like I was the one who had done it." He stopped talking, took one last look around the place, and started the car.

Edith reached over and took his hand. "Are you sorry you came?"

"Oh hell no, not in the least. It was fascinating to see how little it had changed and how well I remembered it. It seems like it is exactly the same place, just in a different time and on a different planet populated by different people." He sat for a moment in the running car then turned around on the grass and without a backward glance, headed south.

On the relaxed drive back to St. George's, they talked about the huge party at the hotel to celebrate Rachel's return, and how it had been such a smashing success. They had met the Governor General, several ambassadors, and a flock of local politicians, all trying to get some face time with the local media.

Rachel, of course, was the star, and handled herself quite well, moving about the ensemble smiling, shaking hands and occasionally giving someone a friendly hug. You would never have known she had just lived through a difficult and frightening week as a hostage in a mountain hideaway.

During the speeches and introductions, one of the loudest bursts of applause from the crowd was for the modest truck driver standing quietly on the peripheral of the gathering, content to watch and be a small part of the celebrations. He seemed genuinely surprised at the response of those present when Commissioner Frank introduced him and asked him to step forward so everyone could see him. Clinton Cranston was the second most popular person at the party.

Edith and her husband laughed about Fred's demands to have his drinks delivered to him because, he said, he was a 'sick man, you know'. It was all great fun, but now it was time to head home.

In fact, for some, it was well beyond time to go home. Anne and Peter Baxter, the young couple celebrating their twenty-fifth anniversary, had extended their vacation to stay and help. They left to get back to work the day after the party. The rest straggled out until there was just LJ and Edith left. Now it was time for them as well.

Their flight left at three-thirty and it was only eleven a.m., so they planned to check out early, drive down to Blue Bay for lunch, and then return their rental car just before their flight. They had lots of time so neither was moving very quickly.

"You just about ready?" he hollered from the washroom.

"Yes, if you come here and help me close this bag," she called and he came out and sat on it for her.

"I knew you were good for something but I'm sure you couldn't have done this twenty-five years ago," she laughed as he squished the suitcase shut.

"I'm still as trim as I ever was. It's the damn suitcases that are getting fatter". And he slung it next to his for delivery to their car. "OK, let's go," and he looked once more around the room to make sure nothing was left before they set out for the front desk.

"It seems awfully quiet," Edith commented as they walked along the pathway pulling their bags behind them.

"It does. Even the room cleaners aren't out and about," he answered.

Turning to their left along the covered walkway beside the main building, they soaked up the last images while leaving. The tall palms gently moving overhead, the broad leaves of the banana trees rustling as the green fruit hung in bunches, slowly ripening, and the small birds flitting about the bushes. Passing the gift store on their right, they turned into the open air foyer where the front desk stood. Both were surprised to find it full of people.

The hotel manager was there with what appeared to be every employee in the place. The Police Commissioner was there as well, backed up by several of his officers. Others were in the group, unknown to LJ and Edith, but all stood quietly facing them, waiting. The two departing guests were unable to figure out what was going on.

Commissioner Frank stepped forward and smiled. His uniform was especially perfect this morning, indicating the great care he had taken in making it the very best this day. The polish of his shoes was blinding, the crispness of his white shirt startling and the smile on his face dazzling. He looked simply spectacular.

"Good morning Mr. and Mrs. Livingston. How nice to see you," he said with great formality as he stopped before them two paces in front of the rest of the group.

"Good morning Commissioner. What is all this?" said a surprised LJ, indicating all those standing quietly in a semi-circle around them.

"These people, sir, are here to say goodbye and thank you."

"Thank you?" wondered LJ. "I don't understand. It is I who should be saying thank you for all the help we received while here."

"You're right, maybe you don't understand, so I'll try to explain," he said loud enough for the whole group to hear.

"I don't know if you're aware that every year we have a Thanksgiving Day here in Grenada much as you do in America. We don't have turkeys or pumpkin-pie, like you, and our Thanksgiving does not celebrate the end of a growing season. Our Thanksgiving celebrates the beginning of a new life for our country.

"The Thanksgiving Day celebration is a tradition here in Grenada that started spontaneously in October of 1984 and has become deeply entrenched in the lore of this land.

"In Grenada we celebrate Thanksgiving on October the twenty-fifth each year. It's a special day because it's the anniversary of the day your country, and you, came to help us end our time of troubles. It is the day a new life began here in Grenada.

"The new life is the one you have seen around you while you and your group were here. The prosperity you have seen, the happiness you have seen, the freedom you have seen, are all parts of what we are thankful for. The importance of that day long ago will never be forgotten by the people of this island."

The police officer stopped his carefully prepared speech and turned to a gentleman standing on his right. He unfolded the paper-covered package he held and passed the contents to the Commissioner.

"We seldom have visitors to our country who came here on that October twenty-fifth so long ago, to save us from ourselves. Your President Reagan did come and visit, and he helped dedicate the monument at the airport, but he did not come in the dark days in October and risk his life. You did.

"Now you have come back and it gives us an opportunity to show you how much we appreciate what you, your President, and your fellow countrymen, did for us." And using both hands, he passed the small bundle over to LJ.

"As a small token of our esteem and appreciation, we give you this flag, our flag, which has flown proudly over our government building here in St. George's while our freely elected government has been in session. Please take it with our thanks and good wishes." Everyone surrounding LJ and Edith burst into applause.

The grizzled old soldier stood very quiet for several minutes, his head bowed, gently turning the carefully folded flag over and over in his tough old hands. At last, he stopped his examination. Clasping the brightly colored bundle with both arms to his chest, he looked up, sweeping the group with rapidly blinking eyes, finally stopping at the commissioner.

"This is a very special gift and I thank you for it. Please be assured it is one I will treasure the rest of my life. It is special and deserves to be treated in a special way.

"When I get back to the United States, I will contact the National Marine Museum in Quantico, Virginia, and discuss with them an appropriate display of this flag, and the information surrounding the history of it, and all the details about this special moment. You have done me a great honor; one that will remain with me all my life."

Edith had never been more proud of her husband. The faces in the semi-circle around them beamed and she knew this little ceremony had been carefully planned.

As she looked at the faces before her, she remembered LJ saying many times over the years, '**if you stop people from telling a population how they should live, and let that population find out on it's own how it wants to live, things usually work out alright.**'

Well, her husband helped stop the bad guys from telling in 1983, and the people of Grenada had started finding out what they wanted themselves. As they drove to the airport Edith reached over and gently patted her husband's hand, now very sure he had been correct all along, things had worked out alright.

The End – For Now....

Murder Unedited

Detective Will Deas, a canny old Scot with tired eyes accustomed to seeing many strange things, was surprised to find he had little trouble locating suspects in his new case. The victim, a publisher known for his aversion to ethics, was universally hated. In fact, there were so many people overjoyed with Peter Jefferson's death, Will had difficulty knowing which one to look at first.

After sorting through the long list of suspects, Will saw this could be the most challenging case of his long career. Sifting facts in the gritty backstreets and alleys of Hamilton's industrial sector as well as the posh Mountain Brow Boulevard area, Will Deas failed to find anyone who thought well of the deceased. He knows he'll need all his thirty-five years of experience to solve this murder.

Who, amongst the hundreds that hated Peter Jefferson, finally snapped and dispatched the publisher to the great editor in the sky for the blue penciling everyone thought he richly deserved.

Join Hamilton's wily old Homicide Detective Will Deas in his search for the killer.

Watch for "Murder Unedited"

In the Spring of 2012

Another Story by Ian Stout

Necessary Larceny

Chapter One

"How the hell could you lose a *hundred thousand dollars*?" Nick Archer demanded, banging out the last three words like a hammer hitting a nail.

The silence from the phone in Florida lasted quite some time before Harry Stanton answered, his voice sounding older than Nick had ever heard before.

"It was a business investment that went south and now the money's gone. Don't get your knickers in a knot about it." A long pause followed; then Nick spoke.

"How's Kitty taking it?" Nick asked of Harry's wife.

"Oh hell, you know Kitty. She was in from the start and took the loss like a trooper. I'm sorry though. It'll change things a lot." Harry sounded sad, old, and tired.

"I'm sorry too," Nick sighed and he meant it. He and Harry Stanton went back over thirty years and though he was at least twenty years younger than Harry and his wife, the bonds of their friendship grew closer and stronger each year. Now, they were more like relatives.

Nick thought for a moment then said "Listen, I'll be in Miami later this week. I've found some old ambulances in Hartford that are perfect for the Chaves operation; you know, the guy I mean, the Cuban. How 'bout when I finish with him I drive over and we have one of our long lunches. I can arrange to fly home from Tampa."

"OK, let me know when and I'll make reservations," Harry offered. A moment later they exchanged goodbyes and ended the call.